# Rich and Mad

# Rich and Mad

## WILLIAM NICHOLSON

**EGMONT**
USA
**New York**

# EGMONT

*We bring stories to life*

First published in the United Kingdom by Egmont UK Limited, 2009
First published in the United States of America by Egmont USA, 2010
443 Park Avenue South, Suite 806
New York, NY 10016

1 3 5 7 9 8 6 4 2

www.egmontusa.com

Library of Congress Cataloging-in-Publication Data

Nicholson, William.
Rich and Mad / William Nicholson. — 1st ed.
p. cm.
"First published in the United Kingdom by Egmont UK Limited, 2009."
Summary: Seventeen-year-olds Maddy Fisher and Rich Ross yearn
for love, and after their first attempts at relationships go awry, they
find one another and form a deep bond that can only be expressed
one way.
ISBN 978-1-60684-120-4 9(hardcover) — ISBN 978-1-60684-183-9 (eBook)
[1. Love—Fiction. 2. Dating (Social customs)—Fiction. 3. Friendship—
Fiction. 4. Family life—England—Fiction. 5. Abused women—Fiction.
6. Sex—Fiction. 7. England—Fiction.] I. Title.
PZ7.N5548Ric 2010
[Fic]—dc22
2010011317

Book design by Alison Klapthor

Printed in the United States of America

CPSIA tracking label information:
Random House Production · 1745 Broadway · New York, NY 10019

# Permissions

# Rich and Mad

# CONTENTS

# CONTENTS

# 1

## A meeting in the camel shop

"I've decided to fall in love," said Maddy Fisher.

Cath nodded to show she was listening, but did not look up from her magazine.

"I'm seriously serious. I'm too young to get married but I'm too old to be single. I need love."

"And sex," said Cath.

"Well, yes. But I'm not talking about a quick grope at a party. I'm talking about can't-eat can't-sleep crazy in love."

"Any idea who?" said Cath.

"Not a single clue."

Outside the old coaching inn, on the broad grass verge beside the main road, there stood a large wooden camel. The camel was painted gold and wore a curious smirk on its face. The inn was now a shop; more than a shop, an emporium, crammed with furniture imported from India and the Far East. It was called Caravanserai. But all those who stopped to explore its warren of exotic rooms knew it as the camel shop.

Late one Wednesday afternoon in September, on the last day of the summer holidays, only three browsers remained as closing time approached: an elegant middle-aged woman and two very good-looking young men, her sons. The woman was intent on a display case of silver and coral necklaces. The older and more handsome of her two sons was sprawled in a teak planter's chair, his long legs stretched out and his eyes closed. The younger son wandered off to explore on his own.

Up a flight of broad stairs hung with winking mirrors framed in fruitwood, through the high-windowed front room crammed with lacquered Ming Dynasty wedding cabinets, he made his aimless way at last to a back room that was given over to a display of cushions, textiles, and rugs. He stood in the doorway and gazed into the cave of colors. A central skylight made of stained glass streamed crimsons and purples and golds onto bolts of glittering fabric. Beds of Indonesian bangsat wood draped in rainbow weaves crowded against chaise lounges inlaid with patterns of rosewood acacia, on which plump cushions were piled in bright profusion. The room was a nest for an oriental princess.

It was also Maddy Fisher's special place.

Unseen at first by the visitor, Maddy was curled up on

the bed, screened by a curtain of mirror-fabric. She heard the approaching footsteps and frowned in irritation, quietly closing the laptop that lay on the bed beside her. She remained still, breathing softly. Few browsing shoppers went beyond the doorway.

But now she heard the footsteps advance into the room. Round the edge of the curtain a face appeared, saw her, and smiled a quizzical smile. With the smile went a twist of the mouth, a drawing together of the eyebrows, and a look of such amused surprise that it was as if he'd spoken aloud. *Here's a bit of fun.*

What he actually said was, "Maddy Fisher!"

Maddy blushed, and at once hoped that the colored light from the lantern covered her shame. She knew him. The surprise was that he remembered her name.

He was Joe Finnigan, one year her senior, at the top of the school. Long and lanky, with his humorous face and wild hair, he somehow managed to combine all the most attractive qualities in a boy without being male-model pretty. He wasn't the cleverest in his year, or the most athletic, but he was the most desired. You only had to look at Joe to feel that it would be an honor to attract his attention.

Maddy was honored.

"What are you doing here?" he said.

"I live here," replied Maddy.

"What, in this room?"

"In the house, at the back. This is my parents' business."

"Oh, I see. What a great business."

He never asked what she was doing hiding in a curtained bed with a laptop. Instead he fixed her with his eyes, allowing the lingering remains of his smile to tell her that he liked what he saw.

His elder brother now entered the room.

"Here you are," he said with a yawn.

"Look at this, Leo." Joe Finnigan waved one hand round the multicolored space. "Isn't it fabulous?"

Leo Finnigan was a few years older than Joe and looked like a more perfect version of him. He was strikingly good-looking, his dark eyes set in pale, perfect skin. He did not gaze round the room. He looked at Maddy.

"Hello!" he said. "Is that for sale?"

"Behave yourself," said Joe.

"I'd pay top dollar."

Joe Finnigan grinned at Maddy.

"My bad brother Leo. Just ignore him."

"Hi," said Maddy.

Leo sat down on the bed close enough to brush against her feet.

"I suppose you're jailbait," he said. "I don't mind if you don't."

"Leo," said Joe. "Control yourself."

4

"I'm seventeen," said Maddy. As soon as she said it she regretted it. She hated being treated like a child, but only children felt it necessary to announce their age.

"Maddy's family owns the place," said Joe. "It's a real Aladdin's cave, isn't it?"

"Everyone says that," said Maddy.

"Have to do better than that, Joe," said Leo.

Joe laughed an easy laugh and met Maddy's eyes with a smile.

"Oh, I don't claim to be more original than everyone else. Come along, Leo. Mum'll be waiting for us."

"I'll catch you up."

"No way am I leaving you alone here."

Leo groaned and rose to his feet. "Spoilsport."

He turned and shambled towards the stairs.

"Don't mind him," Joe said to Maddy. "He's still drunk from last night. You have a great place here."

"Have you bought anything?"

"Not me. My mother's downstairs ordering wagon-loads of junk for Leo's flat. Sorry, not junk. Ethnic furniture."

"Call it what you like so long as you buy it."

"Leo's not remotely interested. He'd just as soon live in empty rooms."

He turned to go. In the doorway he paused and looked back.

"So what's the camel called?"

"Cyril."

"Why?"

"It just is."

He left her alone.

As soon as he was gone Maddy began to chastise herself for the things she had said and not said. Joe Finnigan had never spoken to her before in her life. Now he would go away with the impression that she was eccentric, rude, and immature. The truth was she had been taken entirely by surprise. Joe had formed no part of her mental world before. He existed on another plane, altogether out of her reach.

In her mind she explored the picture he had left behind, still fresh and sharp: his quirky smile, his bright eyes. What had he been wearing? Some kind of greenish jacket, black T-shirt, jeans.

The way he laughed. It made everything feel easy.

The shop was closing. Maddy could hear the clicking of light switches as Ellen, the assistant manager, made her way from room to room. Maddy jumped off the bed, smoothed the cloths and cushions she had been lying on, and headed out with her laptop in her arms.

As she descended the stairs she tracked her reflection in the mirrors that lined the walls. The light on the stairs came from a single narrow window before her, which had the effect of making her reflection look flatteringly moody. She flicked back her long brownish hair, trying to catch a glimpse of herself as others saw her. Big brown eyes, oval face, a mouth that seemed to her to be too small. A few stubborn spots, mostly on her forehead where her hair hid them. Tall figure, nothing much in the way of breasts. Good legs. Pretty enough, was the verdict she usually accorded herself. Not as pretty as her older sister, Imo, of course. Imo was the beauty of the family. But boys noticed Maddy. Joe Finnigan's brother Leo had virtually made a pass at her. What had Joe thought about that?

There was something scary about Leo, but on the whole Maddy was pleased by his attention. It helped her to believe something that she found hard to believe about herself: that she was sexy.

# 2

## Just another loser bitch whore

Behind the coaching inn, across a yard, stood a deep-roofed building that had once been the inn's stables. The old brick walls were almost completely covered by Virginia creeper, its leaves just beginning to turn the burned red of autumn. This was Maddy's family home. The front door opened directly into a long low-ceilinged kitchen, which filled most of the ground floor. At one end, steep stairs rose to attic bedrooms. At the other end, several sagging armchairs stood round a small television.

Maddy found the kitchen empty. This was good news and bad news. She had taken a vow not to eat between meals, but when there was no one to see, it was as if she wasn't doing it.

She put a slice of bread in to toast and got out the butter and the lemon curd. To distract herself from what she was doing she turned on the TV. It was the six o'clock news. Someone was forecasting that the economy was heading into recession. A businessman had shot his wife and daughter dead and burned his own house down. Scientists were warning that pre-packed salads give you food poisoning. A man had been murdered for asking some other men to stop smoking.

*Why are they telling me this? What am I supposed to do about it? Feel bad?*

The toast popped. Maddy laid on the butter and the lemon curd with generous knife strokes.

*Am I allowed to be happy in this sick world of ours? Or here's a tougher one: am I allowed to be unhappy? I may not be starving to death in a brothel but I don't have a boyfriend. I've had my times crying in bed at night. Can't I be one of the world's suffering victims too?*

The news rolled relentlessly on. Houses being repossessed. Families standing by stacks of sad old furniture in the street. Wagon-loads of junk.

The toast and lemon curd seemed to have gone. She had no memory of having eaten it. She put a second slice in the toaster. *No point in breaking a vow if you don't enjoy it.*

*Actually when you come right down to it what does it matter if I'm happy or unhappy? It's not as if my life has any meaning. I mean, I want it to go on. You can't help that, you just do. But from the point of view of the rest of the world I might as well not exist. I'm just one more pointless creature taking up space and resources on an overcrowded planet.*

*Just another loser bitch whore, as Cath would say.*

The toast popped.

Her sister, Imo, came into the kitchen as Maddy was once more lathering on the lemon curd.

"Jesus, Maddy. How can you eat that stuff?"

"I like it," said Maddy.

"Have you any idea how many calories there are in every bite?"

"I don't care."

All Maddy's life Imo had been thin as a pole. She looked stunning in whatever she wore. Imo was three years older, and ever since Maddy could remember she had wanted to be like her, but she had given up long ago trying to be that thin. Her body simply refused to go there.

"Imo," said Maddy, "doesn't it ever strike you that your life has no useful purpose and you're pretty much a waste of space in the universe?"

"No." Imo picked up Maddy's knife and ran one finger along the blade. Then she licked the lemon curd off her finger. "Oh my God!" she said. "That is so disgusting."

"Not just you," said Maddy. "Everyone. I mean, maybe the things we do just don't matter. Maybe our life is just pointless."

"Not to me it isn't." She licked more lemon curd off the knife. "Really, Maddy, it's not fair of you. You know I've got no powers of resistance."

"Pointless to everyone else, then."

"My life isn't pointless to everyone else. Alex minds about what I do. I wish he wouldn't mind quite so much, actually."

Alex was Imo's boyfriend.

"Is that enough to give your life a point? Alex minding?"

"Not really. Not Alex. But the right guy'll come along one day. You know what, Mad?" Imo pointed one finger glistening with lick. "You need a boyfriend."

"So you keep saying."

Imo pulled her phone out of her jeans pocket and tilted her head towards it as if into a private space.

"Hi," she said. "Talking about you."

She moved slowly backwards, retreating to her own room, no longer fully present in her body. Phones did that to you. Maddy didn't mind. She was no different.

Of course she needed a boyfriend. But it wasn't that simple. Maddy wasn't gorgeous like Imo, or like her friend Grace; but nor was she desperate. In her own way she was quite proud. She didn't want just any boyfriend, for the sake of appearances, the way you might want a designer top. She wanted a boy to love.

The difficulty was the boys she had grown up with, the boys in her year at school, were simply not up to the job. Undersized, badly dressed, noisy, and stupid, there wasn't a single one about whom she could summon up the smallest tremor of excitement. And falling in love, if nothing else, had to be exciting.

Maddy and Cath and Grace often puzzled over this

conundrum. How was it that at sixteen and seventeen some of the girls were truly stylish, while the boys still thought it was funny to make fart noises?

"Girls grow up faster than boys," said Grace. "It's well known."

"But why?"

"Because girls have to get ready to be mothers."

"So? Boys have to get ready to be fathers."

"Being a father isn't such a big deal as being a mother."

"Says who?"

"Well, you may or may not have noticed, Maddy, but in all the one-parent families, the one parent is the mother."

Grace had always had this way of making pronouncements as though what she said was divine law. She'd been the same since they first met, at the age of five: Grace so perfectly formed that Maddy had idolized her from the start. It wasn't just her adorable appearance—it was her precocious composure. Grace was never flustered, never in a hurry, never had a hair out of place. In more recent years Maddy had grown apart from Grace in many ways, but neither of them had ever admitted it to the other. They had a history together. They were best friends by default.

"I don't really know Grace anymore," Maddy said to Cath. "She's so secretive."

"Maybe it's all a front," said Cath. "Maybe her life's just empty and sad."

Maddy didn't believe this. She saw the way boys acted round Grace. But if Grace did have a boyfriend, no one knew his name.

The change had begun when they all moved up to their senior school at the age of eleven. Grace's family had taken her away for two years. When she came back she was older, more sophisticated, more remote.

"What you need," said Grace to Maddy as they talked about the curious immaturity of boys, "is an older boyfriend."

"How much older?"

"Five years minimum."

"Five years! I don't know anyone that old."

"They exist," said Grace. "And they like us young."

"You, maybe," said Cath.

Cath was the opposite of Grace in every way. Cath wasn't at all pretty. Quite why she wasn't pretty was hard to say. There was nothing obviously wrong with her face.

"I've got eyes in the same place as you," Cath would say, "and my nose is the same length, and my mouth's the same." They had actually measured each other's features with a ruler. "I don't see where I've gone wrong. It doesn't seem fair. Just a few millimeters here and there and you end up looking like a witch."

"You do not look like a witch."

"And no one loves you and you die alone."

"The man who loves you will love you for your true qualities."

"Like I'll love him for his dog and his white stick."

"Come on, Cath."

"What true qualities? Deep down I'm bitter and twisted."

"Okay," said Maddy. "You'll just have to be amazing in bed."

"Now you're talking. Once the lights are out they won't know the difference."

They returned to Grace's theory of natural selection.

"Since when have you been out with anyone five years older?"

"I didn't say I had," replied Grace.

"So you're just making it all up as you go along."

"Sure," said Grace. "I've no experience at all. I don't know anything. I just say the first thing that comes into my pretty little head."

After that they believed her, of course. They'd never seen Grace with an older man. But then, they'd never seen Grace with any kind of boyfriend. Her love life happened somewhere else.

The low grade of available boys wasn't Maddy's only problem when it came to love. She was dissatisfied with her own character. It seemed to her that she was essentially passive. Her natural instinct was always to please others. She rarely made demands of her own and hated taking risks.

Cath agreed.

"You're just too nice, Maddy. You should hate more people."

"I don't want to hate people. I just want to do things for myself."

"It comes to the same thing. The minute you put yourself first, they stop liking you. Then you either cave in and go back to being nice, or you say fuck 'em all."

"I want to be somewhere in the middle. Friendly but decisive."

"There's no middle, sweetie. It's rule or be ruled out there. You have to come out fighting."

She punched imaginary enemies with her fists.

"I've never hit anyone in my life."

"There's your problem. You need more aggression."

Maddy half agreed with this diagnosis. She lacked aggression. But it wasn't the power to biff people she sought: she wanted to take control of her life.

She wanted to fall in love.


So as the new school year was about to begin, she told Cath, "I've decided to fall in love."

Announcing her decision to Cath didn't amount to an action in itself, but it was a start. It shifted her expectations. Instead of sitting round waiting for something to happen, she would make things happen herself.

If she was to fall in love it would have to be with someone

she admired; someone older and more experienced. Grace was partly right. Older, but not five years older. Maybe one year older.

Someone like Joe Finnigan.

As soon as she formed the idea in her head she knew it was a no-hoper. Joe already had a girlfriend, Gemma Page, one of the prettiest girls in the school. But Gemma was dull and stupid, and school relationships never lasted long; and Joe had smiled at Maddy and looked at her in a way that implied he was interested in her. Or was she just imagining that?

Joe was attractive in just the kind of way that Maddy liked. He was clever enough, and sophisticated without being showy. If she was attracted to him maybe that meant that he was attracted to her.

Or maybe she was away in fantasy land.

She could hear Cath's voice in her head, the voice of reality. Yes, of course it was a fantasy. But Maddy hadn't had a real fantasy for a long time. And no one need ever know. It was like a secret game she could play with herself: *adoring Joe Finnigan*. It could be quite exciting in its way.

This is the first boy I've ever felt excited about.

That thought alone was exciting. Maddy wanted to be loved, just like everyone else, but there was something else she wanted almost as much. She wanted to love. She wanted to yearn and pine and feel a prickly feeling all over her skin when her loved one was near. She was tired of laughing at the boys, even though they were ridiculous. She wanted a boy to treasure.

*It can be practice,* she thought. *Practice in falling in love. It's just a matter of taking control of my life.*

That night, alone in her room, she opened her laptop and logged on to MSN. Cath was online.

*Guess what?* she tapped out to Cath. *I decided who to fall in love with.*

Cath messaged back: *So who's the lucky boy?*

*No names. I'm superstitious.*

*So why tell me, bitch?*

*Can't help it.*

*Call yourself a friend. I'll never have a love life of my own. You owe me yours.*

*If anything happens I swear I'll tell you.*

*Go get him, girl.*

# 3

# A deep meaningful conversation

On the first day of term it was raining. The rain fell all through the day. Maddy's English teacher, Paul Pico, announced to his class that there was to be a drama production—a comedy—for the end of term. It was to be *Hay Fever*, by Noël Coward. Any sixth-formers could audition. There were nine parts: four male and five female. The established actors in the Upper Sixth would have the best chance of getting parts, but not all would apply.

"They have entered the valley of the shadow of death," Mr. Pico said. "The eclipse of sunshine and freedom and joy, otherwise known as A-levels."

Mr. Pico talked like that. He was a small, neat man of no known age or nationality, with thick-lensed spectacles and a bow tie. Because his name sounded Spanish he was known throughout the school as "Pablo." Maddy liked his classes, and as far as she could tell, Mr. Pico approved of her in return.

Maddy thought perhaps she should audition for the play. She asked her teacher's advice.

"I've not acted before," she said. "Would I have a chance?"

"Certainly," said Mr. Pico. "Take a look at the part of Jackie."

Grace noticed Maddy talking to the teacher and guessed the reason.

"You going to try for this play, Mad?"

"I might," said Maddy. "Just for fun."

"I didn't know you liked acting."

"I don't know if I do yet. Anyway, I don't expect I'll get a part."

"School plays are crap."

Typical Grace. She spoke her damning verdict without energy, as if she was merely repeating a well-known fact.

"They're supposed to be a hoot if you're in them," said Maddy.

"A hoot?"

"Fuck you too, Grace."

Grace smiled her mischievous smile that said, "Yes, I know, I can be a bitch."

"Okay, why not? Maybe you'll be a star."

Maddy did not expect to become a star. Her hopes lay altogether in another direction. Joe Finnigan liked acting and had

had parts in many of the school plays. This was his big exam year and he might not audition, which would normally have been enough to make Maddy give up and do nothing. But this was the new Maddy, the Maddy who took decisions, the Maddy who had determined to put herself out there.

She found a copy of the play in the school library and took it home to read. Jackie turned out to be one of the smallest parts, for a girl who was described as "small and shingled, with an ingenuous manner." Maddy looked up "ingenuous." It meant "innocent, artless." In the play Jackie emerged as timid, naïve, and not at all attractive. The main female parts called for beautiful and spirited performers. For a few moments Maddy was annoyed that Mr. Pico saw her as mousy little Jackie, but then she reflected that at least it would mean no one else would want the part.

She retreated to the cushion room in the shop to learn a page of Jackie's lines off by heart. She meant to impress Mr. Pico with her commitment, if nothing else.

Here her sister tracked her down.

"I've been looking all over for you. Why don't you answer your phone?"

"I've got work to do."

Imo took the book from Maddy's hands.

"*Hay Fever*? What on earth are you reading that for?"

"It's being done at school. I thought I'd audition."

"But you can't act."

"How do you know?"

"Well," said Imo, "I've never seen you act."

She settled down beside Maddy on the bed.

"I've come for a DMC."

This meant a Deep Meaningful Conversation, which for Imo could only be a conversation about her love life. Maddy didn't mind. She regarded Imo as a kind of crash-test dummy for her own future adventures.

"It's Alex," Imo said. "I've decided we'd get on better if we saw less of each other."

"You mean you want to dump him."

"No. I just want to cool things down a bit."

"Have you told him?"

"I've dropped great big hints. But he doesn't get it."

"Then I suppose you're going to have to actually tell him, Imo. You know, using words. Aloud."

Imo didn't hear this. She was working her way towards making some kind of demand on her sister, as Maddy well knew. This was not a dialogue. It was a preamble.

"Don't you think Alex is quite a needy person?" she said.

"I like Alex."

"Yes, but he's needy, isn't he? He's always hanging around."

"Well, he is your boyfriend, Imo. Or he thinks he is."

"Yes, but we don't have to be together all the time. I mean, you run out of things to say. And anyway, he should be more—oh, I don't know—more forceful."

"What's he supposed to do? Hit you?"

"No. Just know what he wants more. All he ever wants to do is what I want."

"But you really like getting what you want, Imo."

"Yes, I know. But it's different with a boyfriend. You'll find out one day. You want them to . . . to . . ."

"To be mean."

"No. Just not to want you *too* much."

"I wouldn't. I'd want mine to want me as much as anyone can want anyone. I'd want mine to worship me."

"Oh, Mad." Imo smiled at her younger sister. "I keep forgetting you're so young."

This was code for lack of sexual experience. Once you started having sex, apparently, everything looked quite different.

"So anyway. You've decided to dump him."

"I don't *dump* people. That sounds horrible. People aren't garbarge bags. I really like Alex. I just want to give us both a bit more space."

"He won't like that."

"It all depends on how it's done. If he decides it for himself he'll be fine about it."

"Why would he decide it for himself?"

"I thought maybe you could put the idea into his head."

So there it was. Imo wanted Maddy to do her dirty work.

"You could find a moment to talk to him alone. You could say how you know me well, and how I like to be given space. You could tell him how if I feel too crowded I react badly. You could—"

"No. I couldn't."

"Why not?"

"Tell him yourself, Imo."

"But I don't want to hurt him."

"You want to dump him but have him go on liking you."

Imo wrinkled her pretty brow and considered this, with an air of giving the notion a fair hearing.

"I don't see there's anything wrong with that."

"It's cheating."

"Cheating? How's it cheating?"

"I don't know, but it is."

"All you have to do is give him a hint. I'd do it for you."

Maddy sighed. She knew in the end she'd agree. She always did.

"Must I?"

"You said you liked him. And boys are so much happier if they think they're the ones making the decisions."

"I suppose there's someone new, then."

"No."

"Poor old Alex."

"Not yet."

"Do I know him?"

"I'm not telling. So you'll talk to Alex?"

"You owe me."

"Love you."

Imo kissed her and left.

When Maddy got back to the house her mother looked up from her paperwork with a sigh. She was always sighing these days.

"You're soaked, darling."

"Well, it is raining."

"Have you turned out the lights and reset the alarm?"

"Yes, Mum. I always do."

"I don't know why you can't do your reading here."

"I was reading aloud. I'm learning lines. It's for a school play."

"That's a new one. Acting."

"I thought it might be fun. I probably won't get a part. At least I'll have a better chance if I'm prepared."

"Surely the others will prepare too?"

"Haven't you noticed, Mum? Most people don't do things. And anyway, why always expect the worst?"

Mrs. Fisher sighed again.

"You're quite right. I really don't know why I worry so much about everything. It's not as if it helps."

"Oh, Mum."

Maddy leant over her as she sat at the table, putting her arms round her and kissing the side of her face.

"What are you worrying about now?"

"Oh, just stupid things. Money as usual. And cell phones."

"Cell phones!"

"What if they send out waves that damage your brain? You really mustn't talk too long on your phone, Mad."

The house phone rang.

"That'll be Dad."

Maddy's father was in Shanghai. Mrs. Fisher checked the time as she picked up the phone.

"Hello, darling. Up early. Quick word with Maddy."

Maddy took the phone.

"Hi, Dad."

From far away came his tired voice. He spent weeks on these trips, haggling with manufacturers in languages he didn't understand.

"Hello, sweetheart. Shouldn't you be in bed?"

"Just going now. When are you coming home?"

"A couple of weeks or so. Maybe more. I'm changing suppliers. It's all an endless hassle. How are you? Back at school?"

"Just started today."

"What's the news in Maddyland?"

"No news. I'm going to try and get a part in a school play, but I probably won't. All the teachers are telling us this year it gets serious and we have to work twice as hard."

She chattered on about nothing much for a while, knowing he liked to feel in touch, and then handed the phone back to her mother. It would never have occurred to Maddy to talk to either of them about what was really filling her waking hours. Her decision to fall in love was too private, and as yet too fragile.

# 4

# The boy with the sex manual

By Monday morning the rain of the last few days had blown away and the sun shone out of a clear autumn sky. The vapor trails of high-flying jets were slowly disintegrating, forming long streamers of transparent cloud against the blue. It was a day of cool, bright air. A day of new beginnings.

Maddy made her way to the Upper Library where the auditions were to be held for the play. She was one of the first to arrive. She settled down to wait, her copy of the play in her hand, glancing up from time to time to see if Joe Finnigan had entered the room.

To her surprise the next person to show up was Grace.

"Grace! What are you doing here?"

"Same as you, sugar."

"But you think school plays are crap."

"You talked me into it. Here I am."

Maddy frowned. She felt invaded. Why should Grace take over here as well?

"You want me to go away?" said Grace.

"No, of course not. I just didn't think acting was your thing."

"I expect it isn't. We'll find out, won't we?"

"Have you read the play?"

"I tried. I thought it was pretty stupid, to be honest."

The boys waiting in the group threw covert glances at Grace. She seemed not to notice. As for Joe Finnigan, it began to look as if he wasn't going to show up. Then at exactly the appointed time he came sauntering in, followed by Gemma Page.

Maddy watched them together, keen to learn from Joe's behavior how close he was to Gemma. The answer seemed to be, not close at all. He paid her no attention whatsoever. His easy, roving gaze lit upon Maddy and he gave her a smile of recognition. He mouthed to her across the room, "How's Cyril?" She grinned and nodded back like a total fool, but she was pleased.

Mr. Pico arrived. He looked round them all, his birdlike eyes magnified by the thick lenses of his spectacles, and tapped one neat finger on the table.

"Ladies and gentlemen, we are going to perform a play from a bygone age. You will find in this play that a certain stage direction appears ten times. That direction is: *Lights cigarette*. Which gives you some idea how long ago this play was written. Naturally none of you here has ever even seen a cigarette."

This was his usual style: dry, sardonic, collusive. Because his manner was eccentric and he had no known wife, he was widely presumed to be gay. No one ever laughed at his jokes in case it showed they understood gay code, and so were gay too.

"The cigarette smoking will be cut in our production." He gave a thin smile. He was himself a smoker. "*Hay Fever*, by Noël Coward. Who would like to tell me what this strange play is actually about?"

There followed the usual silence. Maddy hated these teacher-induced silences. They embarrassed her, and the embarrassment made her feel compelled to speak. This time some of the others spoke first.

"It's about a family weekend with guests."

"It's a sort of farce."

"It's about mixed-up love affairs."

Mr. Pico nodded at each offering and made no comment.

Maddy said, "The mother's an actress. It's about acting."

"Aha!" Mr. Pico snapped to attention. "Thank you, that girl! This is a play about acting. This is a play that replaces the truth of emotions with the acting of emotions. So when we act it we must know that we are *acting acting*. I trust I make myself clear."

For the audition he asked each student to pick a section of a part to read aloud with him. This led to a flurry of page-turning. Maddy, alone among them, had her lines by heart.

"Have you traveled a lot?" she trilled, playing Jackie.

"A good deal," said Mr. Pico, playing Richard.

"How lovely!"

"Spain is very beautiful."

"Yes. I've always heard Spain was awfully nice."

"Except for the bullfights. No one who ever really loved horses could enjoy a bullfight."

"Nor anyone who loved bulls either."

It went well, she thought.

Joe Finnigan made no effort at all, but it was at once obvious that he should play Simon. Grace was surprisingly effective. She got a big laugh when she read out in a kittenish voice Sorel's line, "I'm devastating, entirely lacking in restraint." She looked straight at Mr. Pico as she said it, and he raised his eyebrows right above the rims of his glasses.

As they were all leaving Maddy felt a tap on her shoulder. There was Joe, and there was Joe's smile.

"You're good," he said.

"Thanks. So are you."

"Oh, I've got no talent. But I can do a decent enough job."

"I'd say you're a natural."

"Well, let's see who Pablo picks. Should be fun."

Off he went, with Gemma following him half a pace behind.

"It's like having a dog on a lead."

This was Grace, watching them go.

"You were good, Grace."

"It's not as hard as I thought. I think it could be a hoot, as you say."

They headed across the Oval towards the dining hall for lunch, along with the rest of the school. Maddy's attention was caught by Rich Ross, a boy in her year, who was staring at Grace. He too was crossing the Oval, tipped sideways by the weight of a huge bag slung over one shoulder. Maddy could see that he was heading for the lamppost. Before she could shout out to warn him she saw him give a heave to his load of books, swing to one side, and walk straight into the post.

Maddy burst out laughing. She couldn't help herself. So did everyone else who saw it happen. It was just so comical, the way he hit the post and reeled back and fell to the ground. His bag burst open and all his books came out. Then someone saw that there was blood on his face and everyone stopped laughing. A couple of boys helped him up. Maddy, a little ashamed of herself, helped gather up his books and put them back in his bag. They were all schoolbooks except for an old yellow paperback called *The Art of Loving*.

Rich was saying, "I'm fine now. Honestly, I'm fine."

"But you're bleeding."

"Am I?"

He touched his face and looked genuinely surprised to see the blood on his fingers. Maddy gave him back his books. The boys who helped him up went with him to the Med Center.

As soon as he was out of hearing Grace started to laugh, and that set Maddy off too.

"We shouldn't laugh," said Maddy, laughing. "You know why he did it? He was gawking at you."

"Was he?" said Grace. "Serve him right."

"You know those books he's carrying? He's got one called *The Art of Loving*."

Grace's blue eyes opened wide in shocked amusement.

"Rich! With a sex manual!"

There was something ridiculous about it. Rich was the quiet, studious type and had never been known to have a girlfriend. Maddy found herself wishing she'd kept quiet about the sex book. It was Rich's private affair, and now Grace would spread it round the whole school. Rich had done nothing to deserve such mockery. He was harmless.

Suddenly she caught a memory of how he had looked just after banging his head: straw-colored hair flopped over his brow, blood streaming down one cheek, a bewildered look in his eyes. His expression seemed to be saying, "Why do you want to hurt me? What have I ever done to you?"

# 5

## Rich's impossible dream

"But how on earth did you do it, darling?"

"I don't know. I just wasn't looking."

Mrs. Ross gazed up at her son across a kitchen table covered in papier-mâché masks.

"You're such a dreamer."

"No, I'm not, actually."

Rich had no desire to explain that he'd walked into a lamppost while looking at Grace Carey. When she wore her hair pulled back in a ponytail, revealing the curve of her high cheekbones and the line of her slender neck, he could hardly take his eyes off her. His appreciation of her beauty went unnoticed, of course. But it was not a dream. Grace Carey was real. One day she would know all about him.

He retreated from the chaos of the kitchen, which was given over these days to Tiny Footsteps, the kindergarten his mother ran from the big front room. He found his sister Kitty reading on the stair-lift.

"What happened to your head?"

"I fell over."

"Oh."

"Why are you reading on the stairs?"

"I like it."

"But there's no light and you're in the way."

"Maybe I like no light and being in the way."

No one ever won an argument with Kitty. Only ten years old but fiercely assertive of her rights, she rejected all criticism on principle.

"You should be nicer to me. When you were a baby I held you in my arms."

"Shut up."

He climbed past her up the stairs to his room and picked through his collection of vinyl records. He pulled out Pink Floyd's *Dark Side of the Moon* and set it up on the deck. As the opening heartbeat drum notes shivered through the air, he lay down on his bed and mouthed with the voice that followed.

"I've been mad for fucking years . . ."

He waited for the guitars to enter, and as the great wave of sound began to roll he picked up the book he was currently reading, *The Art of Loving*.

"The deepest need of man," he read, "is the need to overcome his separateness, to leave the prison of his aloneness."

He should be doing schoolwork. Instead he was listening to Pink Floyd and reading Erich Fromm and savoring the sharp alien taste of his life. His mother called him a dreamer. For Rich it was the world round him that was a dream, school most of all. In the dream of school everyone was wearing masks and no one could hear anyone speak. Each one in the prison of their aloneness.

*Holy crap*, he thought, *I'm channeling early Simon and Garfunkel.*

*A rock feels no pain.*
*An island never cries.*

Time to move on. "The Boxer," now, that was Paul Simon in his more mature phase.

*A man hears what he wants to hear and disregards the rest.*

Rich was developing a liking for irony. On the fly-leaf of his copy of *The Romantic Poets* he had written: *I am a genius with no talent.* If challenged he could pretend it had been written by Coleridge, but he wrote it about himself.

He lay on his bed pondering the possibility that he was a freak. Alone among his peers he had no mobile phone, no iPod, no laptop. It had started with an impulse of pride. Knowing that money was tight in the family, he had taken over his father's old hi-fi system together with his collection of LPs, and turned this eccentric preference into a boast. Vinyl delivered a fuller acoustic range than digital, he told his disbelieving friends. Modern technology had taken several steps backwards. The present was not better than the past.

Max Heilbron called him a retro-geek. He refused to share Rich's interest in sound recordings that crackled. Grace Carey was another matter. There was nothing eccentric about obsessing over Grace Carey. It was merely hopeless.

"Your trouble, Rich," said Max, "is that everything happens inside your head. You're neglecting the outside of your head."

"What's the outside of my head?"

"Your face."

"What's my face got to do with anything?"

"It's the bit you need if you're ever going to kiss Grace Carey."

"Oh, that." Rich sighed. "I can't imagine any circumstances in which Grace Carey would let me kiss her."

"You could always pay her."

"Oh, sure. And what would I use for money?"

"True. You're not just a loser, you're poor."

"And short."

"You're not short. I'm short. I have the patent on that particular inadequacy."

Max *was* short. It was his most visible characteristic; so much so that he was widely known as Mini-Max.

"Well, I'm shorter than Grace Carey," said Rich. "What do they feed these girls on? Fertilizer?"

"How about you kidnap her and keep her chained in a cellar until she falls in love with you?"

"Yeah. Why don't I? Excellent plan, Max. Except we don't have a cellar."

Rich heard the *shuffle-clunk shuffle-clunk* of his grandmother's Zimmer frame heading across the landing outside his room. He pictured her frail form negotiating the transition from Zimmer to stair-lift. A second Zimmer frame waited at the foot of the stairs. Gran had lived in the house for her entire married life. It was in fact her house. Now widowed and made wobbly by two minor strokes, she persisted with her familiar routines as best as she could.

Rich read more from his book.

"People think that to love is simple, but that to find the right object to love or be loved by is difficult."

*Well, yes. You find the right object easily enough. But how do you get the right object to love you back?*

Mr. Pico had lent him the book.

"I think you're ready for this," he had said. "I wish someone had given it to me to read when I was your age."

Rich liked Mr. Pico and wanted to like the book, but it was not proving to be an easy read. Also it didn't always get things right. For example: "Infantile love follows the principle, I love because I am loved. Mature love follows the principle, I am loved because I love." This second principle seemed to Rich to be plain nonsense. He could love Grace Carey till he popped, but it wouldn't make her love him back.

As Max Heilbron pointed out to him on a daily basis, he should not have picked on Grace Carey for his love obsession.

"She's way out of your league. You have no chance whatsoever."

"She hasn't got a boyfriend."

"You don't know that."

"And anyway, I can't help myself. I'm addicted. There's nothing I can do about it. Maybe it's an impossible dream, but at least I have a dream."

"Christ! Next you'll be saying you're going to climb every mountain."

"If necessary."

"But you don't, do you? What you do is walk into lampposts."

"Yes. Well."

"You're a tit, Rich."

"Even a tit can reach for the stars."

At supper that evening Rich's father gazed at him with a thoughtful, puzzled look.

"You seem different."

"I've got a bandage on my head."

"So you have."

Harry Ross's mind reverted to ancient Sparta, the subject of the book he was currently writing.

"I want a fig," said Gran.

"Try again, Gran," said Rich's mother. All morning she fielded the babbling of toddlers. Then for the rest of the day she interpreted the fractured speech of her crippled mother-in-law.

"Fig," said Gran. "String."

"You want some water?"

"Yes, dear."

Rich's father called Gran "the Oracle."

"You've become Delphic, Mummy. We have to interpret you."

It was hard to believe that the Gran they had known for so long was still in there, just the same as ever, understanding everything they said. Her mind was unimpaired. Only her spoken words came out scrambled.

*Maybe we're all like that,* thought Rich. *Maybe we all find when we speak that the words don't match our ideas. We talk to each other, but never know each other.*

*Loneliness is the default mode.*

Rich found the idea consoling. All those crowds of happy, laughing people just faking it. Noise against the void.

*I'm not so different after all.*

No, that didn't feel right. He wanted to be different. Different enough for Grace to love him.

He remembered the moment when he'd walked into the lamppost and everyone had laughed. He'd been looking at Grace and so knew for a fact that she wasn't looking at him. She never saw the actual idiot moment. But she heard the laughter.

A wave of frustration washed over him. Why did it have to be so hard?

*My problem is I should be more spontaneous. I should be swept by passion. Instead I have this burdensome longing.*

He pulled his diary towards him, feeling a deep thought coming on. He wrote:

*Unrequited love—like carrying a jug of pure cool water. I must take care not to spill it because this is what I have to give. I will give it to the one I will love forever. The jug of water gets heavier every day. My greatest fear is that I'll let it fall and all my love will drain away before I find her.*

He reread what he'd written and sighed. Was it tragic or merely ridiculous? Seventeen years old, zero experience of love, dreaming of the most beautiful girl in the school.

*Face it, I'm screwed.*

As ever, writing down the words made him feel better. He might be a fool but he wasn't fooling himself. There was something to respect in that.

# 6

# Flirting with Joe

Maddy loved her phone. It was a silver Nokia, with a two mega-pixel camera and a funky ringtone—although it was mostly set to silent or vibrate. Its background was customized with a photograph of her favorite spotty heels from Topshop. Every time she saw its little blue message-light flashing, or heard the perky double chirp that told her she had received a text, she felt a stab of love. Someone was thinking of her, and her phone was the bearer of the news. Someone wanted her, and her phone was their go-between.

She lost her phone once, for a whole day, and during that time she felt as if she had fallen to the bottom of the sea. A great silence surrounded her: she was overwhelmed by a panic fear of isolation. Using Imo's phone as an audio sniffer dog she retraced her steps, calling its number, like a mother calling for a lost child. Her phone answered at last, in the quiet of the evening, jiggling away in the outbuilding that housed the customers' toilets. There it lay, vibrating on the cistern, forgotten but still faithful. She took it up and cradled it in her palm and kissed it. There were forty missed calls listed. Over half of them were from Imo's phone, but all the time she'd been at the bottom of the sea her friends had been calling to her too, and her loyal phone had displayed every name with every call. Only she hadn't been there to see.

"I'll never lose you again," she told her phone. But already in her secret heart she was plotting to upgrade.

Was this fickleness? Without ever quite putting it into words, Maddy believed that the soul of the phone was independent of its body. She had changed phones many times in her life, but each time the phone's soul, its own unique number and its bank of remembered numbers, migrated into the new body. Her fidelity was to this invisible essence of phone, which was also a part of the invisible essence of herself, much like her name. Maddy, often reduced to Mad, was so exactly and rightly her name that to utter it was to bring her to life, complete with her curtain of brown hair and her loopy grin.

It was therefore a shock to learn that Rich Ross did not own a phone.

She had come into school early to finish her English homework. Rich was already in the classroom, deep in a book. He had a bandage on his forehead. Remembering how she had laughed at him, Maddy felt a stab of guilt.

"Are you okay?" she said.

"Yes, I'm fine," said Rich. "It's only a cut."

"Your books went everywhere. I put them back in your bag."

He looked up at her, surprised to hear this. "Thanks."

"You could have lost your phone or anything."

"I don't have a phone," said Rich.

"You don't have a phone?"

"No."

"Why not?"

"I just don't."

"How do people reach you?"

"They speak to me. Like you, now."

Maddy was stupefied.

"What if someone wants you and you're somewhere else?"

"They come and find me."

"What if they don't have the time?"

"If they want me they find the time."

"Do they?"

"Sometimes."

"You really should get a phone. It would—"

She stopped. She wanted to say, "It would get you more friends." But that sounded mean.

Now others were drifting in, and she had work to do, so the moment passed. But for the rest of the day the puzzle tugged at her. Rich had no phone and seemed not to mind.

Mr. Pico arrived. Maddy saw him go over to Grace Carey and murmur a few words. Grace went pink and looked pleased. That could only mean she had a part in the play. Maddy just had time to feel resentful when she saw Mr. Pico looming over her.

"I want you to be Jackie," he said. "You're the only one who knows what's going on, so I have to have you. Cast meeting right after lunch in the dance studio."

Maddy exulted in silence. It was a small moment of triumph. But she also knew as soon as Mr. Pico spoke the words that she had expected it. She had wanted a part in the play, she had prepared herself thoroughly, and now she had got it. This was what happened when you took *action*. She had got what she deserved.

*Do I deserve Joe Finnigan?*

She would now be thrown into his company twice a week for five weeks.

*At least I'm in with a chance.*

Mr. Pico was saying something to the class. They were to open their books to a poem by Matthew Arnold called "Longing." He read out the last verse in his uninflected voice, making long pauses between the lines.

"Come to me in my dreams, and then
By day I shall be well again!
For then the night will more than pay
The hopeless longing of the day."

It was oddly effective, the way he made no attempt to put expression into the words. He left a long silence at the end.

"Every poem," he said at last, "is a dialogue between the poet's sensibility and your own. A dialogue requires a response. I invite your response. You don't have to tell me your dreams. Just write about how you understand these four lines. And if you don't understand them, write about that. There are no wrong answers."

Max Heilbron put up his hand.

"Sir, if there are no wrong answers, does that mean I'm guaranteed an A?"

The class laughed.

"I neither know nor care," said Mr. Pico. "Damnation to examinations."

The class did not laugh at that.

Later in break, feelings ran high.

"All very well for Pablo not to care, he's not doing university entrance."

"He never tells us what we're supposed to put. How are we to know?"

"If you ask me he's a weirdo."

"He's not weird. He's gay."

"So who's coming to Pablo in his dreams?"

Grace came over to join Maddy on the bald lawn known as the Paddock. She was wearing heels, which was against the rules, but being Grace she got away with it.

"You got a part in the play, didn't you?" Maddy said as Grace curled up on the ground beside her.

"Yes. I'm Sorel."

"I'm Jackie," said Maddy. "The silly one."

She said this to show Grace that she didn't take herself seriously as an actress. She felt a need to apologies to Grace for being cast, as if her presence lessened Grace's glory. Then she felt annoyed with Grace for making her feel inadequate.

"At least I'll have to do some acting. She's not at all like me."

"Sorel's tremendously like me," said Grace, impervious to the hint of criticism. "I shan't have to act at all."

"Joe Finnigan's going to be Simon. That makes you his sister."

Maddy had found out the details of the entire cast. Grace gave an odd little smile.

"That should be fun."

"And I get engaged to him."

"Do you?"

She looked surprised. Clearly she still hadn't read the play.

"For about five minutes," Maddy said. "But I don't want to be engaged to him at all."

"Don't you?"

"Jackie doesn't. In the play."

"Do you get to get off with Joe?"

"No. I don't think so."

"Well, what a lot you know, Maddy."

"It's not exactly hard. All you have to do is read the play."

"I expect I'll just read my own part. I find reading quite tiring. All those words."

Maddy laughed out loud.

"You posy slag!"

Grace shot her a knowing look.

"I'm devastating," she said, reciting the line from the play. "Entirely lacking in restraint."


After lunch the nine who had been given parts, plus Gemma Page, assembled in the dance studio behind the sports center. It seemed to be accepted that Gemma had to be wherever Joe Finnigan was. She sat alone at the back, looking decorative and expressionless.

On that first afternoon they formed a circle and read through the play.

"No acting," said Mr. Pico. "That comes later."

Joe was directly opposite Maddy. He read his part lightly,

easily, as if not trying at all, and as a result he was perfect. Maddy couldn't help herself from flashing a smile of approval from time to time, and once he caught her smile and smiled back.

Grace noticed. During the break Grace took Maddy into a corner and got serious with her.

"What's going on, Mad?"

"What do you mean?"

"You're flirting with Joe."

"No, I'm not. Honestly I'm not."

But the very vehemence of her denial gave her away.

"Christ, I don't care," said Grace. "I don't even care about Gemma."

"What about Gemma? I'm not doing anything."

"Oh, come on, Maddy. You go pink every time Joe looks at you."

"I do not!"

"Are you telling me you don't fancy him?"

"No, I'm just . . ." But she couldn't complete the sentence.

"So there. You do. It's okay. No one's blaming you. It's a free country."

"I'm not doing anything," Maddy repeated. "Joe's with Gemma, everyone knows that. Why would he even look at me?"

Grace gazed silently at Maddy for a long moment. Then, seeming to reach a decision, she said, "If you ask me, Joe's been ready to dump Gemma for a long time. Maybe all he needs is a reason."

"But they've been together forever! It would kill Gemma!"

"You don't know that. Look at her." They both looked at Gemma, sitting by herself at the back of the dance studio. "Don't tell me she's having a good time."

"She could be. You can't tell."

"I can ask her."

Maddy laughed.

"Bet you don't."

After the rehearsal Joe left at a run, already late for training. Grace moved in on Gemma, beckoning Maddy to join her.

"You must have been bored to death," she said, "having to sit through all that."

"No," replied Gemma. "I thought you were all really good."

As soon as she spoke Maddy knew she was one of those gentle slow-witted creatures like rabbits who are doomed to be run over by the faster-moving traffic.

"Do you always go everywhere with Joe?" said Grace.

"I do when I can."

"And you don't ever get bored with each other?"

"No, not much."

"Don't you run out of things to say? I always worry that if I was in a long-term relationship I'd run out of things to say."

"I don't know." Gemma wrinkled her smooth brow as

she pondered this novel question. "We don't say that much, really."

"So what do you do?"

"Oh, you know. Just hang out."

"Like you know each other so well you don't have to speak anymore?"

"Something like that."

"And you don't ever get jealous?"

"Not really. Sometimes, maybe."

"And what do you do when you do?"

"Do what?"

"Get jealous."

"Nothing much."

"You don't have some way of making sure he still loves you?"

"Like what?"

"I don't know. Like kissing, maybe."

"How would that tell me if he still loves me?"

"The way he kisses. I don't know, Gemma. It must be different, mustn't it? If a guy really means it."

"I don't know."

Gemma seemed genuinely puzzled by Grace's stream of questions, as if they were taking her into regions she'd never thought to enter before.

"If I'd been going out with someone as long as you have,"

said Grace, forcing the pace, "I'd want some way of knowing I was still special to him. Wouldn't you, Maddy?"

"Yes," said Maddy. "Definitely."

"Oh, I know I'm special to him," said Gemma. A faint blush spread over her baby-doll features. "I'm the only one he does it with."

Grace was satisfied.

"Lucky you," she said.

She switched off the tractor beam of her attention, and they parted.

"Jesus!" exclaimed Grace. "She's so stupid!"

Maddy laughed.

"You should be a lawyer. You were amazing."

"So now we know. He only stays for the sex."

"She's so nothing. It's like she has no feelings at all."

"There you go. If he dumps her she'll hardly even notice. Go for it, girl."

Maddy glanced round at Grace's mischievous face, grinning back at her.

"Me?"

"Hey, hey! This is Grace. The not-dozy one. I've got eyes, Maddy. You've got a thing for Joe Finnigan."

Again, Maddy blushed.

"What's the problem?" said Grace. "Take a shot. You never know till you try."

"Why would Joe Finnigan be interested in me?"

"Because you're not Gemma Page."

Secretly Maddy agreed. Gemma Page was far prettier than she was, but by now she must be driving Joe crazy. Maddy was confident she would be more fun to hang out with. But it looked like Joe's requirements extended beyond just hanging out.

"What about the sex thing?"

"What about it?" said Grace.

"Well . . ."

"Oh, you've never done it. Okay. Sorry, I didn't realize."

Maddy hadn't meant Grace to know, not for sure. They just weren't close in that way anymore. But Grace had caught her in a trap. She could lie and say that she had experience, but Grace would demand details. And it wasn't as if being a virgin was such a shameful secret. It was just that Maddy liked it better when no one knew for sure.

"Is it a problem?" said Grace.

"No," said Maddy. "I just want it to be the right guy."

"Sure. Don't we all?"

"And I want to . . . well . . . do it right."

"Why wouldn't you? You know how it works."

"Yes, I know. I know how it *works*. But I don't know . . . oh, what and when and how much. I mean, people talk as though it just happens, but you still have to actually *do* things."

"And you're not sure what?"

"Not in detail."

Grace pondered in silence. Maddy found herself wondering if she was going to launch into a detailed description of her first time. Instead Grace took her arm and drew her close and said, "All you have to do is watch some porn."

"Porn?"

"On the Internet."

"Is that what you did?"

"I have done, yes."

"Does it help?"

"Well, yes. Of course. I mean, porn is people doing it."

"Yes. I suppose it is."

Maddy found the prospect scary for a whole lot of reasons.

"Don't you have to pay?"

"No. There's lots that's free."

"Isn't it kind of gross?"

"Some of it. And some of it's kind of fun."

"Did you look at it by yourself?"

"No. With someone else."

"Who?"

"A sort of boyfriend."

Maddy was hugely impressed. She had assumed Grace had a secret love life, but had never guessed it could be so sophisticated.

"Who?"

"Just someone."

"You watched porn with him?"

"Yes."

"And then?"

"What do you think?"

That evening Maddy had a long phone conversation with Cath. She told Cath what Grace had said and they speculated wildly about Grace's mystery lover and made plans to look at porn on the Internet.

"We'll do it on my laptop in the cushion room."

"What if your mum finds us?"

"She won't."

"She might."

"We'll say we're downloading tracks from iTunes using the shop credit card."

"Why do we have to say we're using the shop credit card? That'll seriously piss her off. It's almost stealing."

"Because she'll be so shocked we're stealing she won't ever think to ask herself if we're doing something worse."

"Mad! You are awesome!"

"Tomorrow after supper, then. Cath and Maddy's porn night."

"Ciao, baby."

# 7

# Fear of rejection

Harry Ross steadied Gran's arms as she made the tricky move from zimmer frame to wheelchair.

"There you go, Mummy," he said.

Rich found it both touching and embarrassing that his father called Gran "Mummy."

"Thank you, Tom," said Gran. Tom was the name of her dead husband. Rich's father didn't correct her.

"You can come again," said Gran. "You're a crumpet."

"A gentleman," translated Harry Ross. "And I accept the compliment."

"How do you know she means that?" said Rich.

"Oh, we used to have a savory spread that went with crumpets called Gentleman's Relish. Gran always said my father was a real gentleman. In their courting days."

"Was Gran courted by other men too?"

"Ask her."

"Were you, Gran? Did you have lots of men chasing after you when you were young?"

"Six."

"Six boyfriends?"

"Six paper . . . six paperback . . . No, no. Oh, these words."

"Six proposals?" offered Rich's father.

"There you are. Six."

Kitty came bounding down the stairs, her plaits flying.

"I'm coming too!"

Rich told her about Gran's six proposals. Kitty was thrilled.

"Did they go down on one knee, Gran? How did you say no? Did you break their hearts?"

Gran, now safely stowed in the wheelchair, smiled and shook her head, but finding the right words would not come she said no more.

Rich wheeled her out and into the park, with Kitty dancing along by their side. The sky above was rippled pink and gray, like the surface of the sea.

"Imagine Gran with boyfriends!" said Kitty.

"Imagine proposing and being rejected."

This was what struck Rich's imagination. He found himself wondering how much encouragement the young men had received before daring to propose. It wasn't the sort of thing you'd do on a whim. You pluck up the courage at last and you get the brush-off. What did that feel like?

"I'm glad I'm a girl," said Kitty.

"So you can have six proposals?"

"Doesn't have to be six. Maybe two. Or three."

A band of boys on skateboards hurtled by, only just missing the wheelchair.

"Hey! Watch where you're going!" Rich shouted after them.

"Fuck off!" they shouted back.

Apart from that the park was peaceful. A pale sun began to break through the clouds and all over the park the wet grass glittered. They wheeled Gran round to the pond, where the mad lady was feeding the ducks. She had a pushchair full of plastic carrier bags.

Kitty whispered to Rich, "Do you think the mad lady ever had proposals?"

"I doubt it."

"That's so sad. I bet that's why she went bonkers."

Then following a generous impulse of her young heart, Kitty said to Rich, "You must propose to people. You don't have to marry them. Just let them be able to say they've had a proposal."

"What if they say, 'Yes thank you, I'd like that very much?'"

"You say you've changed your mind."

"I have to give a reason."

"No, you don't."

"Well, anyway," said Rich, "you'll get masses of proposals when you're bigger."

"I don't want masses. Just two. Or three."

They wheeled the wheelchair on into the rose garden. The roses were long over.

"Have you got a girlfriend, Rich?" said Kitty.

"No," he replied.

"Why not?"

"I just haven't."

"But don't you want one?"

"Yes."

"So why don't you get one?"

"They don't sell them at Tesco, you know. You can't just go out and take a girlfriend off the shelf."

"But think of all the girls who haven't got boyfriends. All you have to do is pick one of them."

"What if I don't want any of them?"

"You can't not want *all* of them. There must be some girls you like."

"What if the ones I like already have boyfriends?"

"Well, that's just silly. Wanting ones you can't have and not wanting ones you can have. That's just silly."

"Or maybe they don't want me."

"Why wouldn't they want you? You're lovely."

"Not everyone thinks so."

"Who doesn't think so?"

"I don't know, Kitty. I'm just talking in theory. I'm not talking about anyone in particular."

"So there isn't anyone in particular?"

"Not really."

"That means there is."

"No, it doesn't."

"Who is she? Have I seen her? I bet it's Grace Carey."

"Grace Carey!" Rich concealed his amazement at Kitty's insight. "Why Grace Carey?"

"Because she's so pretty. It is, isn't it?"

"I'm not saying."

"So it is."

"I'm not going on talking about it."

"It is, it is, it is!"

Rich scowled and didn't respond.

"Purples," murmured Gran, watching a flurry of pigeons. They were purple, too, or at least a blue-gray on their breasts.

"So have you told her?" persisted Kitty.

"No, of course not."

"You have talked to her, though."

"Not exactly."

"You've not talked to her?"

"Not much. No."

"Oh, Rich!"

"Now you shut up about all this, Kitty. It's none of your business."

"Oo! Oo!" She danced about, pressing her hand to her mouth. "None of my business!"

Rich didn't need Kitty to tell him how stupid he was being. His waking dreams were filled with thoughts of Grace. But still he made no move.

Alone in his room he wrote in his diary.

*Why am I so afraid of rejection? One rejection doesn't mean everyone will reject me for the rest of my life. Only Grace. Only the beautiful girls. Only the ones I want. So what happens if all the girls I want turn out not to want me? Then that's it for the rest of my life. Second best. Always wondering what it would have been like to have first best. Fuck it. It's too soon to give up on my life.*

He sat and stared at the diary page. The obvious and only conclusion stared back at him. He had to try. He had to give it a shot, if only for his self-respect. He couldn't go on in this fantasy love, walking into lampposts, having everyone laugh at him.

Piss or get off the pot.

But still he quailed at the thought of a direct approach. If only he could test her response from a distance. If only he could draw himself to her attention without any need for her to respond, so that any subsequent move he might make wouldn't come as a complete surprise. He wrote again in his diary:

*Bring back dragons. You put on your armor, name the lady you love, and go out and slay a dragon. When you come back with the dead dragon she has to love you. It's understood. You know where you are. But where are the dragons when you need them?*

Or I could find a friend to talk about me to Grace. That way, if there's just no point at all, I don't have to take the risk of talking to her myself. Plus it would start Grace off thinking about me.

*For example, Maddy Fisher. Maddy and Grace are close.*

The prospect of talking to Maddy Fisher didn't frighten Rich at all. She was one of the few people in Mr. Pico's English class who actually read the books they were studying. There, right away, was something they had in common.

So there was a plan.

He closed his diary and picked up his English homework. Time to respond to Matthew Arnold's poem.

# 8

# Maddy the go-between

Mr. Pico read out loud to the class from a single sheet of paper.

"The poet knows his love is hopeless but that does not stop him dreaming about her. His dreams make him happy. Waking hurts. But he would rather dream and be hurt than not love at all."

The teacher folded up the sheet of paper, closed his eyes behind his thick lenses, and repeated:

"He would rather dream and be hurt."

Everyone in the class was looking round at Rich Ross. He alone had his head bowed over his desk.

"That is a personal response to a poem, and a very insightful one. This writer is musing aloud about what the poet's lines mean to him. That is all you have to do. Please, my friends, remember this. A poet is a person like you, living a life more like yours than you imagine, trying to put into words the feelings and ideas that come to him. A famous poet is someone who has done this so well that readers have responded, *Yes, that's how it is for me too*."

Maddy was impressed by what Rich had written. She had paid only passing attention to the poem herself. As a result she associated the feelings more with Rich than with the poet.

She and Cath were talking about it during break when Grace joined them. As Cath said, Grace seemed to be honoring them with her presence more often these days.

"I think it's a bit sad," said Cath about what Rich had written.

"I think it's sick," said Grace.

"Why's it sick?" said Maddy. "Don't you ever feel that way? Like you'd rather dream and be hurt than not love at all?"

"Are you saying I want to be hurt?"

"Chill out, Grace. I'm not saying anything, okay? We're only talking."

"It is all a bit creepy," said Cath. "He's got a sex manual that Pablo gave him."

"Pablo gave it to him? How do you know?"

"Max told me. Rich is Pablo's pet."

"He must be gay," said Grace.

"He doesn't have to be," said Maddy. "Though it's true he doesn't have a phone."

"Maybe he can't afford a phone."

"He says he doesn't want one."

"He's gay," said Grace.

Maddy looked round. Rich was over by the Paddock with his friend Max. Because the others were being so hard on Rich she felt the urge to be nice to him.

"Well, I liked what he wrote," she said. "I'm going to tell him so."

She crossed the bald grass to Rich. He looked up as she approached, openly surprised that she was coming to speak to him.

"Hi," she said. "How's the bang on the head?"

"Fine now." The bandage was gone.

"Was that your thing Pablo read out?"

"I wish he hadn't."

"It was good. I liked it."

"I wish he hadn't done that."

He seemed about to say something more, but nothing came. She found herself taking in the detail of his face, and realized she had never looked at him properly before. His skin was very pale, his eyes a light hazel, and unexpectedly open, undefended. *It would be easy to hurt him*, she thought. Then came another thought: *He doesn't deserve to be hurt.*

"So anyway," she said. "Good for you."

There seemed to be nothing more to say, but as she turned to go he called her back.

"Maddy?"

"Yes, Rich?"

"You're friends with Grace, right?"

Maddy's heart sank. Something in her had wanted to believe that Rich was different to the other boys. He was different, in some ways; but not this way, it seemed.

"Does she have a boyfriend?"

"I don't really know," said Maddy. "Why?"

"I was just wondering. She's always going about by herself. I never see her with a boyfriend." His eyes told her what he dared not put into words. "So I thought I'd ask you."

"I think you have to ask her yourself, Rich."

"Yes, I know." He looked down. "Only, I'd rather not make a complete idiot of myself. If there's no point."

Maddy was quite sure there was no point at all. But she didn't know how to say this to Rich without hurting his feelings.

"I'm not sure she's ever thought of you that way," she said.

"I'm sure she hasn't."

"She's always saying the boys in our year are useless. Not you 'specially. Just all of them. I think she likes older boys."

"The thing is," said Rich, "I'm not really like the others."

"No, I expect you aren't."

"Sometimes I feel like I've landed from some other planet. I know that makes me a bit strange. But maybe Grace would go for strange."

*Maybe she would*, Maddy thought. It struck her for the first time that she had no idea at all who Grace would go for. Maybe she needed someone odd like Rich, but didn't yet know it.

"If only she'd give me a chance," said Rich wistfully. "Get to know me."

"That's the thing," said Maddy. "She might not."

"You could say something to her, maybe."

*Here we go again*, thought Maddy. *What is it about me that makes everyone pick me as their go-between?*

"What would I say?"

"Anything, really. Just to get her past the first surprise. If you know someone's thinking about you, you can't help thinking a bit more about them."

"You want me to tell her you're thinking about her?"

"No. Not like that."

"What then?"

"You could tell her I'm a genius."

"Are you?"

"Well, I might be. A whole lot of unusual stuff goes on in my head. It might just be random clutter, of course."

Suddenly he grinned, and Maddy grinned back.

"Don't tell her that."

"All right," said Maddy. "I'll tell her you're a genius. But I wouldn't get your hopes up."

"I expect nothing and everything," Rich said.

"That sounds like something you read in a book."

"It is, in a way. It's from my diary. But I wrote it."

"Okay. Maybe you are a genius."

"My diary's full of stuff like that."

"But only you get to read it."

"Not even me. Once I've written it I never look back."

"So what's the point of writing it?"

"I don't know, really."

He gave a shrug that said, "What can you do?" Maddy found herself liking him.

"If you do talk to her about me, will you tell me what she says? Really truthfully?"

"What's in it for me?"

"You get to watch me blundering about and you feel superior."

Again that wry grin.

"Okay," said Maddy.

She returned to Cath and Grace, smiling to herself.

"What was that all about?" said Grace.

"It was about you."

"Me?"

"He wants you to know he's a genius."

"Genius?" Grace almost snorted in her contempt. "He's not a genius. He's just gay."

"I don't think he is gay. He fancies you, for a start."

"Yuk!" Grace shivered.

"So don't you feel like getting to know him better?"

"Like I want a hole drilled in my head."

Maddy felt this was unreasonable.

"You don't know anything about him."

"Except that he's Pablo's pet and reads sex books and doesn't have a phone and hangs about looking sad. Give me a break, Maddy. I'm not that desperate."

"Okay. Forget it."

When Maddy got home after school she was annoyed to find Imo's boyfriend, Alex, in the kitchen. He was sitting at the kitchen table half-heartedly doing the quick crossword.

"Hi, Maddy."

"Hi, Alex."

"So you heard the good news?"

"What good news?"

"The world isn't going to be sucked into a giant black hole."

"Oh, that." Maddy had some dim notion that some nuclear experiment had been due to take place that morning, some-where in Switzerland.

"They're looking for the God particle," said Alex.

"God's a particle? That's a bit of a let-down."

Alex grinned.

"If you want Imo, she's washing her hair."

"Washing her hair? What, literally?"

"So it seems."

Usually at this time of day Maddy had the kitchen to herself.

She always came home starving. Furtively, not watching herself, she would fill a bowl with porridge oats, add a large lump of butter and three tablespoonfuls of golden syrup, and put it in the microwave. Then all she had to do was stir and eat. It was a treat she looked forward to all afternoon.

There was no way she could spoon the sweet sticky mixture into her mouth under Alex's lugubrious gaze. It looked too much like baby food.

"Want a cup of coffee or something, Alex?"

"No, thanks. We're supposed to be going out."

Maddy helped herself to two digestive biscuits as a temporary substitute. Imo appeared with a towel round her hair, turban-style, wearing a kimono bathrobe.

"I'll be at least fifteen minutes," she said. "You and Maddy can have a nice little chat."

She shot Maddy a meaningful look and retreated back to her bedroom. Maddy resigned herself to her fate.

"So how's things, Alex?" she said.

"Oh," he said. "You know."

"Haven't you got fed up with Imo yet?"

"No. Why would I?"

"Oh, most of her boyfriends do. There's something about Imo, I don't know what it is, they get a certain way with her and then it's like there isn't any more. Like getting to the bottom of a milkshake."

"Really?"

Maddy warmed to her theme. There was a lot she could say about Imo now she thought about it.

"I'm not saying Imo's shallow. I don't know what it is. Maybe it's fear of intimacy."

"She can be quite remote sometimes."

"Almost like she wishes you weren't there."

"Almost."

"That's when her boyfriends usually dump her. Poor old Imo. It keeps on happening." This was quite untrue, but Maddy was letting herself get carried away. "She thinks there might be something wrong with her."

"Have there been many who've dumped her?"

"Well, they call it giving her space."

"Doesn't she mind?"

"Not at the time. She's usually quite grateful. She's quite weak herself. She needs people to take the hard decisions for her. She respects that a lot."

"Yes. I suppose she would."

"What she really hates are clingy people."

"Clingy people?"

"You know. Weak boyfriends who let her kick them around."

Alex said nothing to that. Maddy thought maybe she'd gone too far. But Alex seemed not to notice.

"So she's had several boyfriends dump her?"

"At least four that I know of."

Maddy told the lie with a straight face, hoping that Alex would find safety in numbers. Alex gave a deep sigh and rose from the kitchen table.

"Oh, well. That's life, I suppose."

Imo came back downstairs, now dressed and ready to go out.

"Let's go if we're going. This place is miles away."

"Where are you going?" said Maddy.

"Some kind of do somewhere," said Imo.

"It's supposed to be very beautiful," said Alex sadly. "Holkham. On the Norfolk coast."

Left alone at last Maddy felt her spirits slump. She put this down to the lack of golden syrup oats. The shop would close soon and her mother would return to the house. She took another two digestive biscuits out of the packet and retreated to her room. Digestive biscuits were basically dull but if you ate them slowly they turned out to have some taste. Then she had an idea. She could spread them with lemon curd.

Alone in her room, trying to concentrate on the origins of the Cold War, she found her thoughts drifting back to the enigma of Joe Finnigan and Gemma Page. Joe was so acute and unusual, Gemma so blank and ordinary. How could he bear to have her trail round after him? Boys were supposed to be obsessed by sex, but it seemed to Maddy that it would be as uninteresting having sex with Gemma as it was having a conversation with her. But maybe sex was different. Maybe some people had a natural talent for it that you couldn't spot in their everyday lives. For something that was everywhere, in all the papers, on billboards, in every movie, sex somehow managed to remain hard to fathom. It couldn't be as simple as big tits and short skirts. Could it?

Maddy struggled on with the Cold War for another half hour, then gave in and opened her laptop. There was no one on MSN she wanted to talk to. After a little while she felt cold, so she got into bed. In bed, she closed her eyes and curled up into a ball. Something deep inside her began to ache, but not like a hurt. Like an emptiness.

*I don't want to live in that world,* she said to herself. She meant the world where the interesting boys chose the sexy girls, where Joe loved Gemma and Rich loved Grace. That was the victory of the obvious. If that was all there was to love, why bother with it? Love could be so much more. It could be so wonderful to be special to someone, as close as two people could be, telling each other everything, kissing because you wanted more than anything in the world to feel his lips on your lips.

Her phone rang. It was Cath to remind her they had a plan to meet later that evening and look at Internet porn.

"Let's do it some other time," said Maddy. "I've got too much reading to do."

She wasn't in the mood. You needed to be a little bit happy and a little bit drunk for porn, and she was neither.

# 9

# The sex lives of teenagers

Cafés in bookshops were a terrible temptation. Behind the glass wall on the café counter, presented enticingly on sloping glass shelves as if eager to tip themselves into your hands, lay chocolate croissants, custard crowns, maple pecan plaits. Rich had not found a single book he wanted to buy, but the pastries called to him.

Then he realized that the hunched figure at the table before him was his English teacher. Mr. Pico sat alone, sipping a black coffee, intent on the pages of a thick volume.

Rich hesitated to speak to him, not wanting to interrupt his reading. But he was so close to him that it seemed ruder still to say nothing.

"Hello, sir."

"What? Oh, hello."

As always, Mr. Pico's attention swam up from the depths to

break surface in his thick-lensed glasses. He raised the book he was reading.

"I'm taking a look at the new translation of *War and Peace*. It's supposed to be the first really authentic English version. Have you read any Tolstoy?"

"No. Never."

"Oh, treats in store. Can I buy you a coffee or something?"

Rich hesitated. He wasn't really interested in Tolstoy, but he was hungry now.

"I wouldn't mind a Danish pastry."

So courtesy of his English teacher, Rich sat down at the café and ate a maple pecan plait and discussed *War and Peace*.

"Tolstoy's insight into youthful love is extraordinary. His characters all make terrible decisions, but even as they're making them you understand why, and feel for them. Pretty Natasha falls for bad, handsome Anatole, when we know she should love clumsy, sensitive Pierre. But she needs to grow up to know it for herself."

Rich began to think he might be interested after all.

"And does she?"

"Oh, yes." He tapped the cover of the fat book. "A deeply satisfying experience. Take it from me."

"Do you believe it?"

"How do you mean?"

"Well, in real life the pretty girl would marry the bad,

handsome one and have a not very happy life and never know how it might have been."

"My dear boy. Do I detect a note of bitterness?"

"I'm just saying that's usually what happens."

"You think beauty trumps character?"

"Well, yes."

"I don't agree. Beautiful women are constantly falling for odd-looking men. I knew a very ugly man who said to every attractive woman he met, 'I'd like to kiss you.' He told me he got his face slapped a lot, but that he got kissed a lot too."

Rich contemplated this picture with disbelief.

"I could never do that."

"There are other ways."

"How does clumsy, sensitive Pierre do it?"

"He loves her unwaveringly for many years. Plus he's a millionaire."

"Oh."

Rich caught sight of a boy in his year at school staring at him with openmouthed curiosity. At once, for no good reason, he felt guilty, as if talking with his teacher in a bookshop was a form of cheating.

"I'd better go," he said, rising. "Thanks for the pastry."

Walking home, Rich pondered what it would be like to ask pretty girls for kisses and not mind if they refused. It was beyond his own powers, he knew that for certain. But evidently some boys, some men, were so sure of themselves that they expected girls to welcome their advances.

*So why don't I?*

It wasn't as if Rich had had a series of bad experiences. He had had no experiences. The shaming truth was he had never yet kissed a girl, not a true romantic kiss. There had been times when he had suspected the girl was willing, but he hadn't found her attractive enough. With the girls he admired, he was paralyzed.

He could see no way out of the dilemma. Talking, yes. He could just about bring himself to talk to a pretty girl. But touching: that was another matter. He could not imagine any circumstances in which he would draw Grace Carey into his arms and kiss her, other than Grace saying to him, "Kiss me." The prospect of going on a date with Grace filled him with terror. What was he supposed to do? Should he take her hand? Were they to kiss in the back row of a cinema? As for actual nakedness, and sex—How? Where? You had to plan things like that. You didn't just melt into each other's arms.

Rich had read a newspaper report the other day on the sex lives of teenagers. According to the report the average age for first sexual intercourse was sixteen, with a third of all teenagers being sexually active before that age. Rich was seventeen. He could see no prospect of sexual intercourse in the near future;

or even the far future, for that matter. It was all very well for clumsy, sensitive Pierre. Beautiful women had always gone for millionaires. But even if you weren't a millionaire you still wanted the beautiful women. Nature just made you that way. It all seemed to Rich to be very badly arranged.

At home he found Kitty weeping in front of her doll's house.

"Look!" she said. "They've knocked everything over. They've broken the kitchen dresser and the ironing board. I found the little packets of cereal all over the stair carpet. I hate Tiny Footsteps! I want to kill them!"

"I thought they weren't allowed upstairs."

"They got out."

"Have you told Mum?"

"She said sorry, and we'd better put a lock on the doll's house. I think we should put a lock on Tiny Footsteps. They should wear tiny handcuffs and be put in a tiny prison."

"I'm really, really sorry, Kitty. It's horrible. It's like a burglary."

"Oh, Rich. You're so lovely." She huddled in his arms. "You're the only one who understands."

Together they reinstated the doll's house furniture as it had been, and even made some small improvements. It was Rich's idea to put the basket armchair in the kitchen.

"It makes a kitchen more homey if you have armchairs in it."

To make room for the armchair they put the dresser in the dining room, where the display of tiny willow-pattern plates fitted much better; and the writing desk, which had been in the dining room, moved up to the master bedroom.

"That's so the father can do his work undisturbed."

"And the mother too," said Kitty.

"What you need is lights in the rooms."

"You can get lights, but it's really hard fitting them."

"I expect I could manage," said Rich.

Gran emerged from her room, going *shuffle-clunk* behind her Zimmer frame. She stopped to admire the doll's house on the landing.

"Dear Richard," she said.

"It's mostly me, Gran," said Kitty. "Rich hardly did anything."

"Well, well," said Gran, lowering herself onto the stair-lift. She raised one withered hand in farewell as she sank silently downstairs.

Rich retreated to his room. He spent many minutes going through his LPs, unable to decide on the right sounds to accompany his mood. In the end he went for *Blonde on Blonde*. He settled down to write his diary to the plangent sounds of Dylan singing "Sad-Eyed Lady of the Lowlands."

*Sometimes when I watch her, she seems to have gone somewhere very far away. She hardly ever smiles. I want to say to her:*

*I feel the same way. I'm not like the*
*others. I could understand you.*
*Beautiful but lonely. Could be true.*
*Suppose I told her I'd guessed her*
*secret. It would shock her, but she'd*
*see me differently. I'd be the only one*
*who knows her as she really is. She'd say,*
*How did you know? I'd say, Because I'm*
*lonely too.*
*After that we'd be close.*

He stopped writing and listened to the song for a while. Max told him on a daily basis that his choice of music made him middle-aged.

"You know how long ago that stuff was recorded?"

"I don't see what difference that makes."

"You have to live now, brother."

Max had played him some hot new band on his iPod but Rich had remained unconvinced.

"The Who did it all before, and better."

"You know what you're doing? You're hiding in the past."

"So?"

"It's wrong."

"Why? What's so great about the present?"

In his heart he knew Max was right, but the truth was he'd

never liked the present very much. He wasn't interested in reality TV shows. He found the credit crunch boring and frightening at the same time. The only movies worth watching in the last ten years were *Before Sunrise*, which was actually made in 1995, and *Before Sunset*. And just maybe *The Dark Knight* because the Joker got the essential stupidity of existence.

They did things better in the past. They had real tunes and real passions and real despair. Nowadays it was all just a game.

He thought of Grace and wanted to say it to her: how life could be so much more intense than it was. How all you had to do was stop being afraid.

Maybe Maddy Fisher had already spoken to Grace about him. Maybe everything was about to change.

# 10

# Amy the bunny

The first proper rehearsal for the play was not a success. Neither Joe Finnigan nor Grace had learned their lines, and so they played their long opening scene together reading from the book, without looking at each other. Mr. Pico watched in dismay.

"I know this is the first time, but do at least make a faint attempt at expression."

"Why does she say all this?" complained Grace. "Does she like her brother or not?"

"It's really very simple, Grace. All Sorel is interested in is herself. Do you think you can manage to convey that?"

"Okay."

"Just imagine everything rather bores you."

After that Grace improved noticeably. Joe Finnigan felt it, and his reading became both more energized and more languid. He seemed to enjoy striking poses and stretching out his vowels.

"How *lovely* for them," he cooed, and "Do-oo-oo, darling." Then to Mr. Pico, "I suppose I don't go to the piano and light a cigarette."

"You do not."

Grace had a line that got a laugh from the rest of the cast.

"Abnormal, Simon—that's what we are. Abnormal."

She said it with slow-burn surprise, as if she had just that moment discovered it.

The rehearsal never got as far as Maddy's entrance. A great deal of time was taken up by the pages where the Bliss family perform lines from an old play, "acting acting," as Mr. Pico had said.

"I've dreamed of love like this," proclaimed Emily Lucas playing Judith Bliss playing a ham actress. "But I never realized, I never knew, how beautiful it could be in reality!"

"Bigger!" cried Mr. Pico. "Grander! More shameless!"

Maddy sat and watched the proceedings from a position where she could see Gemma Page and Joe Finnigan at the same time. Joe's gaze never once sought Gemma out. Mostly his attention was on Grace, with whom he was acting. Twice he glanced over and caught Maddy's eyes and smiled.

As the rehearsal broke up he said to her, "How's Cyril?"

"He's not been sleeping at all well lately," said Maddy.

"Whisky before bed," said Joe. "It always works."

"What on earth was all that about?" said Grace, watching Joe and Gemma depart.

"Oh, nothing," said Maddy. "You're good, Grace."

"It's a stupid part, but it's quite fun. Who's Cyril?"

"The camel outside our shop."

"If you ask me, Joe's got his eye on you."

"He's just being friendly."

"Boys don't do friendly with girls."

Secretly Maddy thought Grace might be right, mostly because of the way Joe had said, "How's Cyril?" It was like a private code between them. Then he had picked up her silly answer and said, "Whisky before bed." That was suggestive, surely?

Maddy repeated the short exchange to Cath.

"He came up to you, right? He started it."

"Well, we were sort of standing around."

"But you didn't speak first?"

"No. He did."

"There you are, then. He's definitely interested."

"But you don't think every boy who speaks to you is trying to get off with you."

"No boy ever speaks to me, Mad."

"Of course they do."

"Not like that."

"It wasn't like anything. Maybe he was just being friendly."

But it was gratifying that Cath shared Grace's view. Something was going on.

Later that evening Maddy and Cath snuggled up side by side on the bed in the cushion room with the door closed and a wedding chest pushed against it. Maddy had her laptop on her knees. This was their night for looking at porn.

"It's not made for girls," said Cath. "It's made for boys. We may not like it at all."

"We can always stop watching."

"What if it puts us off sex for ever?"

"Would you rather not do this, Cath?"

"No, come on. I'm quite curious, really."

It was just curiosity in the end. Neither of them expected any kind of thrill.

Maddy typed the address Grace had given her into Google. Up came a warning saying they must be eighteen or over. One button said ENTER, the other said LEAVE.

"Who do you think ever clicks LEAVE?" said Cath.

Maddy clicked ENTER.

Up came a page of little pictures, each with a title underneath. *Pinky booty ass shake. Deep throat and swallow. Hot Asian bathroom show.*

Twenty-five images on the page. Hundreds more pages waiting.

"Wow!" said Cath.

"Which one shall we click on?" said Maddy.

"How about that one?"

The picture showed a dark-haired girl smiling at the camera. It was titled: *Amy in hot Playboy bunny outfit.* It looked less frightening than the others.

Maddy clicked.

The picture jumped and filled the screen. There was Amy, her eyes heavily made up, her breasts hanging out of her skimpy bikini top, leaning forward and down, grinning at the camera. Fuzzy rock music squeaked out of the laptop's speakers.

"She's not all that pretty," said Maddy.

"Look at her mascara! She's a mess!"

"If I had boobs like that I'd keep them out of sight."

"Oh my God! Bunny ears! That is so tacky!"

Maddy and Cath giggled, and then fell silent. The camera had followed Amy's descending head to discover a big erect cock.

"Okay," said Maddy.

"Is that normal size?" said Cath.

"How would I know?"

They both started to laugh. On the screen Amy was looking up at the camera as her tongue reached out to lick the tip of the cock.

"She's looking at me!"

Cath covered her eyes. Maddy smacked her.

"She can't see you, you stupid cow."

They rocked with laughter. On screen Amy's head was

now bobbing up and down, the cock in her mouth.

"I want to see the man," said Maddy. "I want to see his face."

"Maybe he doesn't want to be recognized."

"She doesn't mind being recognized. Imagine meeting her in the supermarket. Hi, Amy. Loved your movie."

Once more they dissolved in laughter.

"For God's sake! How long does it go on?"

"You want to look at a different one?"

"Not really. Now we've started we might as well see it to the end."

It lasted just over three minutes but somehow seemed much longer. As the first shock passed their giggles faded away. Maddy found that she didn't really like it, but she hadn't yet worked out why.

"I wonder why they do it," she said.

"They get paid," said Cath.

"I don't think so. I think they're just ordinary people. That's how the site is free."

"So why video yourself for everyone to see?"

"I suppose it turns them on."

They fell silent. They had expected it to be personal and intimate, but somehow it had been neither.

"It was all for him, wasn't it?" said Cath.

"Definitely," said Maddy. "She was wearing the outfit he

wanted and doing the things he wanted and videoing it for him to look at afterwards. It was all for him, all right."

Another silence.

"So did you like it?"

"Well, it didn't disgust me," said Cath. "And I guess I kind of liked seeing the big cock."

"I liked it for about a minute. After that it annoyed me. It was like a little god wanting to be worshipped. On and on with the worshipping, bowing before it, kissing it, on and on. I wanted to hit it with a spoon."

"I wonder what it's like, doing that."

"She didn't look to me like she was having any fun."

"I suppose she liked it that she was keeping him happy."

"Who?" said Maddy. "He didn't even have a face. And I'll tell you what." Maddy was discovering her reactions only as she spoke. "I wasn't turned on. How could anyone be turned on by that?"

"People are."

"Boys are."

"Okay, boys are."

"Yes, but not all of them, Cath. I can't believe it. There must be some boys who want more than that."

"Tell you the truth, Mads, I haven't a clue. But you know what? It didn't look hard. If I had a boyfriend and doing all that made him happy, I could handle it."

"But what about love?"

"Yes, that'd be nice too."

Back in her bedroom after Cath had gone, Maddy lay on her bed with the lights out and the curtains open, looking through her window at the night sky. A rising moon cast a pale glow over the few clouds, and between the clouds the brighter stars were showing. The clouds were moving slowly. She fixed her gaze on the stars, and it felt as if it was she who was moving, and the house and all her world, sailing gravely through the night.

Maddy's thoughts were a strange mixture of Joe smiling at her, and the big cock on the laptop screen, and a nameless excitement that streamed out of her to touch everything she saw. She liked looking out of the window: the sky had no boundaries, it went on forever, anything was possible. She felt as if she was on the brink of an enormous adventure.

Before going to sleep, she checked her phone for messages. There was nothing. On a whim she checked her Hotmail account.

The most recent message had been sent at 6:14 p.m.

*Hey Maddy,* she read. *I'm worrying about Cyril. Maybe he's pining for Mrs. Cyril. Camels have feelings too. Joe.*

Maddy stared at the screen. It was from Joe Finnigan. How had he got her Hotmail address? Was it really Joe? She checked the sender's address: Joefinn41@hotmail.com.

Her heart started to pound.

Camels have feelings too.

She checked the time. Past ten o'clock. But emails didn't wake people up.

She answered:

*Hi, Joe. Cyril touched by your concern but says he's just fine. How did you get my email address? Maddy.*

She clicked SEND and climbed back into bed. There was no question of going to sleep. She lay and felt her chest and diaphragm shivering. She ran over in her mind all the various ways she might meet Joe tomorrow, and where it might lead.

A faint ping alerted her to a new email. She leapt out of bed. Joe had replied.

*Do me a favor, Maddy. Go on the same as ever at school. I don't want anyone to get hurt. Love to Cyril. Joe.*

# 11

## Love is a decision

Maddy dressed the next morning with extra care, but the truth was that whatever she did with the range of clothing permitted under the school's uniform rules, she looked drab. How was it that Grace could wear a dark gray skirt and plain white shirt and manage to look glamorous? It was something to do with her slim, boyish figure, and something to do with her attitude. Grace dressed as if she expected clothes to flatter her, and they did. In school uniform she looked like a model going to a party dressed as a school girl. Maddy just looked like a school girl.

There was nothing to be done about it. Whatever had caught Joe Finnigan's attention in her so far must have overcome the dead weight of her uniform.

*It must be my merry eyes,* thought Maddy.

Her father had once said on coming back from a buying trip

abroad, "Oh, I've missed those merry eyes." That was many years ago. The merriness might have faded since then.

*Actually,* she thought, *if anyone's got merry eyes it's Joe.* She longed to see him even though they were to go on the same as ever, if only to catch that laughing look when they met. But it turned out that Joe was not in school that day. He was away for a college open day. Tomorrow was Saturday. She wouldn't see him till Monday. The one boy she saw everywhere she went was Rich Ross.

She had been avoiding Rich. She knew he wanted to talk to her about Grace. She didn't feel able to lie to him and give him false hope, but she liked him, and dreaded hurting him.

"He's in fairyland," said Cath. "He has to wake up."

"I know," said Maddy. "But why does it have to be me?"

After lunch there was Rich once more, hovering by the dining hall exit. He wasn't staring at her in any obvious way, but she knew he was waiting for her.

Best to get it over with.

They walked together down the beech path.

"So I talked to Grace," she said.

He had his eyes fixed on hers with a pitiful intensity.

"What did you say?"

"Nothing very direct. I thought you didn't want me to come on too strong."

"No, no."

Now that the moment had come, Maddy found herself unable to tell the hard truth.

"She didn't really react," she said. "I don't think she's ever thought much about you one way or the other, to be honest."

"No, I'm sure she hasn't."

"Grace is quite . . ."

Maddy hesitated, aware that Rich saw Grace in a different light. No need to shatter all his illusions.

"A bit of a loner, maybe?" he said.

"Yes. I suppose she is."

It hadn't struck Maddy before that Grace could be called a loner.

"I think something's hurt her," said Rich.

Maddy thought nothing of the sort, but she understood Rich's thinking. He wanted Grace to be a wounded creature, so that he could be the one who brought her comfort and healing. She'd played the same game herself.

"Maybe," she said.

"I know she's not remotely interested in me," Rich went on. "I expect I'm just a joke to her."

"Well . . . ," said Maddy.

"It's okay. She doesn't know anything about me. She's never even spoken to me. But whoever she thinks I am, that's not who I am. I just have to get to the next stage."

Maddy was surprised. Rich wasn't fooling himself after all. Also, he was showing impressive determination.

"Can you do that without any encouragement?"

"I have to, don't I?"

"You could just give up."

"I could. But I'm not going to."

He pulled a book out of his bag and flipped its pages. Maddy saw that it was the old yellow paperback called *The Art of Loving*. Many passages were marked in the margin with pencil.

"Listen to this." Rich read from the book: "'To love somebody is not just a strong feeling—it is a decision, it is a judgment, it is a promise. If love were only a feeling, there would be no basis for the promise to love each other forever. A feeling comes and it may go. How can I judge that it will stay forever, when my act does not involve judgment and decision?'"

"Wow!"

"Exactly. Wow. Love is a decision."

"And you've made this decision?"

"Yes."

"Do you really believe it? I mean, can you just *decide* to love someone? What if they don't love you back?"

"Okay. Listen." Rich was flipping more pages. He read aloud again. "'Love is a power which produces love.'"

"Who is this guy?"

"He's called Erich Fromm. He's a psychologist. Mr. Pico gave it to me to read."

"Why?"

"We were talking about things he wished he'd known when he was my age."

Maddy took the slender paperback from him and opened it to the first page. There was a quotation from Paracelsus facing the table of contents.

"Who's Paracelsus?"

"No idea."

"He who knows nothing," she read, "loves nothing . . ."

Not a sex manual after all.

"When you've finished with it, do you think I could borrow it?"

"Take it. I've copied the best bits into my diary. Just don't lose it. I have to give it back to Mr. Pico."

"Your diary that no one reads."

"I thought about that after we talked before. I think the point is I do read it, but only as I'm writing it. It's my way of finding out what I'm really thinking."

"Don't you know anyway?"

"Well, I think I tell myself a lot of stories. Somehow when you start writing it down you get more honest."

"Isn't that kind of depressing?"

"Yes. It is a bit."

"I couldn't do that."

"So, anyway. You haven't actually told me what Grace said."

Maddy simply couldn't make herself pass on Grace's true level of contempt.

"She said you weren't her type."

"What is her type?"

"I've no idea. Grace is very secretive."

"She's lost," said Rich.

He fell silent, following his own thoughts.

"This decision you've made," said Maddy. "I suppose if it doesn't work out you can always cancel it and make another decision."

"I don't know. Maybe." He looked away. "The thing is, I think about her all the time."

Maddy felt a stab of pity. He was going to get so hurt.

Then it struck her that she was in much the same position with Joe. She hardly knew him, but she could truthfully say she thought about him all the time. The big difference was that Joe was sending her emails.

"I know how it is," she said.

"You've got someone too?"

"Sort of."

"I'm glad." He gave her such a sweet, warm smile that she was touched. He meant it. He wanted her to be happy too. "It's the only way to live, isn't it?"

They turned back.

"So what will you do now?" said Maddy.

"Talk to her."

"Do you think that's a good idea?"

"Not really. But it's the next thing. I have to do it."

Like a soldier going into battle. Death or victory.

Rich found Grace almost at once. Maddy watched from a distance, thinking that when the point came he'd lose his nerve. Grace was alone, moving fast, head down, making for the playing fields. Rich started to follow her, then hesitated, then went on. Maddy found she couldn't bear to look anymore. She went in search of Cath.

"It's horrible," she said. "Rich is about to have his bubble burst."

Just before the playing fields began there was a large timber hut, used for storing the groundsman's tractor-mower. Grace headed straight for it and disappeared round the back.

Rich, following her, approached more slowly, and then came to a stop. He thought maybe she had gone there to smoke or take drugs, and he didn't want to be the one to discover her. That would only annoy her. He had just decided to walk quietly back to the main buildings when he heard a sound from behind the shed. It was the sound of choking.

He hurried forward, thinking Grace must be ill. As he came round the corner of the shed he saw her, standing with her hands on her knees, bent over a pile of grass cuttings, throwing up. She choked out the last of the sick, then straightened up and wiped her mouth with a tissue.

She turned and saw Rich.

"Have you been following me?" she said.

"Yes."

"Serves you right, then."

She didn't seem angry with him; just tired.

"Are you okay?" he said.

"What does it look like?"

Rich wanted to ask why she hadn't gone to the toilet block to be sick. Why come all the way to the playing fields? He wanted to say to her, "Something's wrong, isn't it? Tell me about it." But he said nothing.

"Do me a favor, Rich. Don't tell anyone. It's a bit gross."

"I won't tell anyone."

"Not even Maddy Fisher."

"Okay."

He hesitated for a moment, trying to find the words to say that he understood what she was going through, even though he didn't.

"That's it," said Grace. "I'm fine now."

She wanted to be left alone.

"Okay," said Rich.

He left her alone.

That night Rich wrote in his diary:

No one else knows what I know about her, even though I don't know what it is I know. Only that she isn't the way everyone thinks she is. And now she knows I know. It's like I've found my way into her secret place. Now it's just a matter of time. She'll tell me more, she'll learn she can rely on me. All I ask is the chance to show her how I can love her. Love is a power which produces love. I believe it. I'm living it.

# 12

# Looking forward to everything else

Maddy caught Joe Finnigan's eye as he entered the dance studio for the play rehearsal. It was four days since she had last seen him and only a few hours less since they had been in contact by email, but it felt to her like the blink of an eye.

He gave her a wave of one hand, little more than the opening and closing of his fingers. She was careful to say and do nothing to give them away. But all through the rehearsal she felt as if she was tied to Joe by fine invisible threads. His every smallest movement tugged at her.

The rehearsal moved far more rapidly than before, and they got well into Act Two. At this stage in the play the Bliss family and their guests attempt a game called In the Manner of the Word. Maddy played her few lines with many a coy glance at Joe, in order to make sense of what happens later in the play.

"Simon's the one who takes me out into the garden," she

explained to Mr. Pico. "So there has to be something happening between them."

Joe was very amused, and played up to her fluttery little looks as if he was progressively smitten. When the others try to make Jackie perform a dance "in the manner of the word" and Jackie is too shy to do it, Joe took Maddy by one arm and patted her hand. For one brief moment Maddy met his eyes and let him see the happiness that was overflowing within her.

When the rehearsal was over Joe said to Maddy, "You're really good, you know."

"I wonder why," said Maddy.

But there was Gemma, pale and lovely and mute, so Maddy gave Joe an airy wave and went off with Grace.

"What got into you?" said Grace as soon as they were outside. "You were all over Joe."

"No, I wasn't. I thought I was very restrained."

"No, Maddy. Wrong. That was not restrained. That was come-and-get-me-lover-boy."

"You're the one who told me to give it a go."

"Yes, I know." Grace was studying her curiously. "Something's happened, hasn't it?"

"Might have."

The truth was, Maddy was bursting to tell someone, and since it was Grace who had first encouraged her to have hopes of Joe, it seemed unfair to leave her in the dark.

"It's a total secret, okay?"

"Of course it's a total secret. What do you take me for?"

"Joe's been emailing me."

"What!"

"I'm not to let on at school, because of Gemma."

"What does he say in his emails?"

"Just jokey stuff so far."

"What sort of jokes?"

"Oh, about Cyril the camel who lives outside our shop. It's all about nothing, really. But the thing is, it's a secret, and he started it. So you see, you were right."

"Well, well. Well done, Maddy. A secret romance." Grace went on looking at her intently, as if there was more to know that Maddy wasn't telling. "So why exactly does it have to be a secret?"

"Because he doesn't want to hurt Gemma."

"You mean he doesn't want to lose Gemma."

"No. He's just being sensitive."

"Maddy, being sensitive would be finishing with Gemma before starting with you."

"Well, he hasn't started with me. Not really. All it is is a couple of friendly emails."

"Maybe he doesn't want to finish with Gemma."

"What do you mean?"

"Maybe he wants Gemma for the sex and you for the jokes."

"That's horrible, Grace! Joe's not like that."

"He might be."

"Well, I don't believe it."

"I hope you're right," said Grace. "But my advice is, don't get in too deep until you know what's really going on. Boys aren't like us. Take it from me."

Having let Grace into the secret, Maddy knew she must tell Cath too. Cath's response was far more gratifying.

"Mad! Omigod! That is so fucking romantic! You must be wetting yourself! Omigod! I told you so. Didn't I tell you? Admit I told you. I have to get something out of this. You get to be love's young dream. I'll settle for being right."

"Yes. You were right."

"Secret emails! It's like a movie. You'll have to have secret meetings in lonely churchyards. So how much do you like him out of ten?"

"We haven't even started yet."

"So what? Give me a score."

"Six."

"Liar. That's just bullshit."

"Maybe seven."

"Look me in the eyes."

"Okay. Nine."

"There you go."

"Grace thinks he's not serious and I shouldn't get too excited."

"Ha! Jealous!"

"I did wonder."

"She's always been the one the boys want. She can't take it that Joe's after you and not her."

"Except she did encourage me to start with."

"She never thought Joe would bite."

"You don't think it's possible Joe wants me for company and Gemma for sex?"

"No. I don't. And anyway, all he has to do is have a go at sex with you. I bet a million pounds you'd be more fun in bed than Gemma Page."

Maddy laughed out loud. Cath couldn't have said a nicer thing.

"We're nowhere near that," she said.

"Even so, you'd better get yourself fixed up."

"Oh, God. Do you think so?"

"Suppose Joe came round one evening and you started fooling around, can you absolutely guarantee you wouldn't let him go all the way?"

"Yes. No. Oh, God, I don't know."

"You can't leave it to him. Boys never even think about it for one moment."

"How do you know?"

"Where do you think all the teen pregnancies come from?"

"Are you fixed up?"

"Give me a break, Maddy. This is my contraception." She pointed to her face.

"Oh, shut up, Cath. As if. I do love you though."

There was another email from Joe waiting for Maddy at home.

*I shouldn't have looked at you so much. Gemma got suspicious. I hate that it all has to be a secret. I'll sort things out very soon, I promise. Then we'll be able to meet properly. And everything else.*

Maddy read the email over and over again. She wanted to phone Grace and say: "I told you so." But she was afraid Grace would find some new way to cast doubts on her happiness; and anyway, it was too early to share with others. She wanted to keep it for herself for a while.

It was the last three words that intoxicated her: three words that managed to say nothing and everything all at once; three words that were both discreet and passionate. Maddy lay on her bed recalling Joe's every move as they had rehearsed that afternoon: the way his quirky, smiling face had sought her out; the way he had spoken to her without words. She had felt his presence reaching into every corner of the long room. He made her tremble.

She replied to his email.

*Today was fun. It's like we're playing a game where we're*

*the only ones who know the rules. Which is what happens in the*
*play, if you think about it. So we're playing a game while playing*
*a game. Pablo would like that. Even so, I'm looking forward to*
*everything else . . .*

Her fingers were shaking as she typed the words. They seemed to her to be an unambiguous declaration of love, as transparent as if she had written: *I'm yours, do what you want with me.* But he had offered the words first, so she felt safe.

She heard the door slam downstairs, and Imo's bright, high voice. Maddy jumped up at once, eager to see Imo again. There were matters on which she needed her advice.

"You should have seen the beach!" Imo was saying to their mother as Maddy came rattling down the stairs.

"I have seen it, darling. It's a famous beach."

"No, you should have seen it! Miles and miles of empty sand. Miles and miles of sky. Thousands and thousands of birds settling on the marshes at sunset. It was like being in a movie."

"It was in a movie," said Mrs. Fisher. "That one with Gwyneth Paltrow."

As soon as Maddy had Imo on her own she said, "Let's walk down by the river."

"Oh, it's like that, is it?"

The river walk was their favorite place for the exchange of secrets. A cinder track led from the side of their house and followed the bends of the river into open countryside. There were always a few walkers out with their dogs, rarely more than two or three, so the path felt both safe and private.

The river was full, its dull brown water flowing fast after recent rains. Two swans stood disapprovingly on the far bank, watching them go by. The evening light lit the underside of the low cloud on the horizon. The fields were turning the color of straw.

Maddy wanted to tell Imo how happy she was, how even with the day ending and the year fading she felt as if a new world was being born. Nothing had happened between her and Joe, just a few looks, a few words, but he was there, in the very near future, waiting for her.

But Imo had her own secrets to tell.

"Alex and me have decided it would be best if we gave each other some space. The truth is I knew it was never going to be serious with him."

"No, you didn't. You've just forgotten."

"What have I forgotten?"

"You said Alex wasn't like the others, he was more quiet and real. You said you were tired of all the clubbing and Alex was like a grown-up."

"Did I?" Imo seemed genuinely surprised. "Well, anyway, maybe I'm not quite ready to grow up yet. I'm only twenty. And I've met someone else."

"I knew it! So who is he?"

"He's no one you know, and it's early days still. But he's amazingly gorgeous and a bit on the wild side and unpredictable and—oh, so sexy. He's just so sexy."

"And single? And into you?"

"How do I know? He's not married, that's for sure, but I doubt if he's alone any more than he wants to be."

"What's his name?"

"Leo."

Maddy knew as soon as she heard the name.

"He's not Leo Finnigan, is he?"

"Yes. How do you know?"

"I've met him. His brother Joe's in the year above me."

"You've met him?"

"He and Joe were in the shop. He asked if I was for sale."

"That's Leo. He's so bad."

"How far have you got with him?"

"He was at this party in Norfolk. He flirted with me outrageously all weekend. But of course I had Alex dangling around. Now that's all sorted out I can stop being Miss Virtuous. Though I think it did rather turn him on."

"Listen, Imo. If I tell you something—"

But Imo wasn't done with her own story yet.

"I've got two weeks before I go back to college. So however bad he is, he can't break my heart too much, can he? You know he's got his own flat, on the High Street?"

"That's right." Joe had said. "He's got his own flat."

"Up above Caffè Nero. So convenient, darling."

"But why doesn't he live at home?"

"He's twenty-two, Mad. He's busy applying for jobs and stuff. He was going crazy living at home. So Mummy darling, who dotes on him, decided to rent him his own flat so he doesn't go and live in big bad London and never see her again."

"That's why they were buying furniture."

"Leo says all he needs is a fridge for the booze and a bed for the babes. He's tremendously un-PC. Just as well. I've only got two weeks."

"Can I tell you my secret now?"

"I thought we were talking about me and Leo."

"This is about Leo's brother, Joe."

"What about him?"

"I'm having a sort of a thing with him."

"You're not!"

"All we've done so far is email each other. He has a female Alex he has to dump before we can come out into the open."

"This is unreal! You and Joe Finnigan! Is he as gorgeous as Leo?"

"He's different. Kind of sweeter. Leo scared me. Joe's not scary at all. He's very sure of himself, like Leo. But he's all open and smiley."

"My God, Mad, this is getting practically incestuous."

"You're not to tell anyone, right? Not even Leo. Joe's being very proper about this. He's not two-timing anyone."

"Just like me. I've been very proper with Alex. But it doesn't take long. When's he going to do it?"

"I don't know. I don't really care. I'm loving this in-between time. I'm just so happy."

"Look at you." Imo smiled at Maddy fondly and took her arm in a sisterly embrace. "I've never seen you like this before."

"I've never been like this before."

"So you think this could be it?"

"Could be."

"Are you ready for it, Mad? You don't want to go getting pregnant."

"No way."

"You can't trust the boy. You know that?"

"I don't think Joe would do anything stupid."

"He's a boy, isn't he?"

"All boys aren't the same."

"Yes, they are. All boys don't get pregnant. It's different for them."

"So what do you do? Carry condoms in your handbag?"

"I can't stand condoms. Real passion-killers. I've been on the pill since I was fifteen."

"Oh."

"Go and see Dr. Ransom. She'll sort you out. And don't leave it too late. It takes a few days before it starts working. And it'll clear up your spots."

With this forthright advice Imo felt she had covered her little sister's sex life and could return to talking about Leo and the Norfolk house party. In the old days Maddy would have been hungry for every detail, but now she hardly heard a word. She was struck by Imo's casual assumption that she should be "sorted out." It was easy enough to make an appointment with their family doctor, but around this simple decision danced a crowd of confused emotions: excitement, pride, fear, all stirred up by the prospect of her very own sex life. Even the term "sex life" sounded different to her now, because it had taken on a face, a body, a name. It meant "sex with Joe."

What would it be like to make love with Joe? She tried to imagine it, without too sharp a focus on the physical detail. No Amy-the-bunny sex for her. Instead, she let herself think of it as an extension of touching, as a closer form of closeness, in which their bodies merged and she no longer knew where she ended and he began. Yes, she liked that. She hugged herself as she walked, pretending her arms were Joe's arms round her. She felt a shudder of gratitude and tenderness. She felt her body ache for the real thing.

This was all entirely new for Maddy. She had shared in the giggly talk with her friends over pictures of boy bands in magazines. She had daydreamed about what it would be like to be in bed, naked, with some unknown boy. But it was all a game. In her fantasies the exquisite thrill lay in being chosen by her dream boy, rather than in the delights that might follow. Even with Joe, until now the biggest rush had come from his response to her, not hers to him. He wants me, he wants me, was the song of her secret heart.

But now there was something else. All through rehearsals she had watched Joe, lingering over every detail of his physical being: his gangly legs, his long-fingered hands, his bare forearms dusted with tiny black hairs, his strong shoulders, the place where his bare neck met that tangle of black hair—not quite black, very dark brown, you could see that in his eyebrows—and his eyes of course, blue-green and limpid, intent as they caught hers, brimming with soundless laughter, and his mouth, a strong mouth, a beautiful mouth, a mouth she wanted to be kissed by, a mouth she wanted to kiss . . .

"Mad?"

"What?"

"Do you think I should or I shouldn't?"

They were almost home. Maddy had no idea what Imo had been talking about.

"You won't pay any attention to anything I say," she said. "You're only talking out loud to find out what you think yourself."

"Actually that's quite true," said Imo. "I'm going to say yes.

Actually I've said yes already. I just don't want to rush things."

"Things go the way they're going to go, whether you rush them or not."

"You've got very wise all of a sudden. It must be love."

Maddy called the Health Center and asked for an appointment with Dr. Ransom. She was offered five o'clock on Thursday. This was sooner than she had expected. She found she had said yes before she had time to think about it. For some time after the call ended she sat quite still in her bedroom staring ahead at nothing. When she came out of her trance she found she'd been staring at Bunby, the cloth rabbit who had been her closest companion for as long as she could remember. Bunby's little brown bead eyes seemed to be fixed on her reproachfully. One of his well-worn ears was folded back behind his head, making him look drunk.

"It's all right, Bunby," she said, picking him up and hugging him tightly in her arms. "I'll never love anyone as much as I love you."

In bed that night she opened *The Art of Loving* and read some passages that Rich had marked with a line of pencil. One in particular held her attention.

"Love," wrote the author, "is active penetration of the other person, in which my desire to know is stilled by union . . . In the act of loving, of giving myself, in the act of penetrating the other person, I find myself, I discover myself, I discover us both, I discover man."

For all that it seemed to be written by a man for men, these lines had a strong effect on Maddy. She understood them to say that through the act of physical love she would find peace. The endless unanswerable questions would cease: Who am I? Why am I alive? What right have I to happiness? In their place would come the one simple but immense certainty: I am to love and to be loved.

She phoned Cath.

"You still awake?"

"No. I'm asleep."

"It's really true, Cath."

"What's really true?"

"I'm in love."

"I had noticed, actually."

"I just had to tell somebody."

"Okay, sweetie. You can say it again if you like."

"I'm in love."

# 13

# Rich writes Grace a letter

"When are you going to put lights in my doll's house?" said Kitty to Rich. "Because you did say you could do it, even though I don't believe you can."

This was typical Kitty—a plea linked to a criticism.

"Soon," said Rich.

"In time for Gran's birthday?"

Gran's eightieth birthday was less than two weeks away and was turning into a watershed event, like Christmas, or the summer holidays. Whatever was discussed in the family was now defined as before or after Gran's birthday: specifically, anything required to be done by Rich's mother was postponed to after Gran's birthday. Mrs. Ross was organizing the party. She was also training her Tiny Footsteps to sing a special birthday song for Gran as a surprise. It was unlikely to be a very great surprise, since every morning for days now the house had been filled with their reluctant trilling, lagging behind Mrs. Ross's brisk piano.

> "I love you
> A bushel and a peck
> A bushel and a peck
> And a hug around the neck . . ."

The song from *Guys and Dolls* was one of Gran's favorites. Gran's celebration was to be big on the singing of old songs.

"Where are they all going to sit?" worried Mrs. Ross. "Who's going to hand everything round?"

There were to be almost twenty guests in the big front room, the room that housed the nursery school on weekday mornings.

"Couldn't you bring a friend, Rich? I could do with more pairs of hands. I'll be at the piano so much of the time."

Rich asked his friend Max if he wanted to help out. Max declined.

"I won't know anyone and I'm no good at pouring and anyway I'm not a pretty girl. My dad says you can tell it's going to be a good party if there are pretty waitresses."

"I don't know any pretty girls."

"You know Grace."

"Oh, sure." He almost said, "Better than ever," but he had not told Max about the scene behind the playing field shed. It was too private, and too unfinished. "I can just see Grace handing round sausage rolls to my uncles and aunts."

"Maybe she'd pop out of a cake in a bikini."

"Have you ever seen Grace in a bikini?"

"No. You?"

Rich shook his head. But he enjoyed the imaginary scene. It was sufficiently unreal to be harmless. He and Max operated an unspoken rule that the subject of girls and sex was to be treated either as a joke or as a species of higher theory.

It was in this spirit that Rich introduced Max to *The Art of Loving*.

They were sitting in the curtained gloom of Rich's bedroom playing *Blood on the Tracks* on Rich's turntable.

"Love is not the result of adequate sexual satisfaction," Rich read from the extract copied into his diary, "but sexual happiness, even the knowledge of the so-called sexual technique, is the result of love."

"Pass that by me one more time," said Max.

Rich repeated the passage.

"Okay, I've got it now," said Max. "It's bollocks."

"It might not be."

"Listen, bozo." Max began to bounce up and down on Rich's bed with the earnestness of conviction. "Any girl who gives me sexual satisfaction gets my love. Hundred percent guaranteed, no questions asked."

"You don't know that."

"Okay, I don't *know* it. I *feel* it. My body feels it. Love is passion. Passion is sex. People only talk about love because they're desperate for sex and haven't had it yet."

"If you're that desperate you can always have a wank."

"Not the same thing. Not the same thing at all."

"I don't see why not. If you don't want to be bothered with love, why bother with another person at all? Cut out the middle man. The middle girl. Go straight for the orgasm."

Rich thought this rather witty.

"All I can say," said Max, speaking with slow emphasis, "is that if a fuck is no better than a wank I shall be bitterly disappointed. Centuries of propaganda will be shown to be a lie. It would be enough to make me lose my faith in the human race."

"Of course it's better," said Rich. "It has to be better. Like going to a movie with a friend is better than going alone. Like talking with you now is better than talking to myself."

"Oh, bollocks to all that," said Max. "Sex isn't about conversation. It's about bodies, and nakedness, and feeling the excitement, and—oh, oh—"

Little elfin Max with his scrunched-up face and sticky-out ears hugged his knees to his chest and rocked back and forth on the bed. He should have been comical in his helplessness, but Rich saw nothing to laugh about. He shared Max's hunger, and would have moaned as loudly alongside him on the bed had he been a little less inhibited.

Later, after Max was gone and supper was over, Rich found he couldn't concentrate on his schoolwork. He suddenly felt that he had to get out of the house.

"Going up to the wood," he called to his mother.

He cycled the short distance out of town and left his bike chained to a fence at the bottom of the farm track. The track, deeply rutted by farm vehicles, climbed to a dense beech wood that covered the north flank of the hill. At this time of evening the wood was shadowy and full of rich leafy smells. The ground was squelchy under foot after the rain, and the low branches on either side of the path slapped wet against him as he passed.

Rich knew this woodland path well. He had walked alone here in springtime, as the leaves were unfurling; and in the high glory of summer, when bright shafts of sunlight speckled the beech mast underfoot. Now in mid-September the evenings were closing in, and the wood had grown older and less brash. The muted colors in the fading light suited his mood.

Entirely alone at last, he allowed himself to think about love and sex and Grace, but mostly about Grace. Max was totally wrong, that much Rich knew. Love was not just sex. When Rich thought about Grace, his greatest happiness came in the imagined moment when her eyes met his and she didn't look away; when she let him take her hand in his; when she leaned in close to him so that he could put his arms round her slender body.

His fantasies had no need to venture further. His heart beat too much simply at the dream of her touch.

Then there was the dream of words. He neither offered nor expected grand talk of love. What did it mean anyway? In his fantasy, it was enough to have her say to him, "I'd like to see you in the lunch break." If he went any further than this, it was only to have her tell him what it was that made her so unhappy, so that he could console her. Rich wanted Grace to see him as the one person who truly understood her. He had no confidence in himself as a seducer, but he knew he could be a comforter; hoping through kindness to arrive at closeness.

This, Rich realized, treading his way through the wood, was what Max didn't understand. It's closeness we all want. Sex too, in time, but only because it's the closest kind of closeness. He was far more afraid of being alone than of being a virgin. Also—it struck him suddenly and he blushed—closeness is safe. Closeness is manageable. Sex is scary. Do it wrong and there's nowhere to hide. Everyone makes out it's as natural as breathing, but you can breathe with your clothes on. For sex you have to take your clothes off *while she's watching*. As for the next stage, the passage from nakedness to sex, where was the instruction book for that? The situation seemed to lend itself to moments of ridicule. And if he became ridiculous, his dick, so insistently pushy at inappropriate times, would shrivel to nothing, and the long-awaited sex act would not take place after all. Then what?

*So I'm nervous about sex,* he told himself. *Nothing unusual there. So I want the safety of closeness. So I want the no-fail-zone of love. It's a start.*

At the top of the sloping wooded hill, just where the path emerged through a broken gate onto the bare sheep-grazed summit, there stood a ruined barn. The barn had been built into the hillside, its back wall made of flints hammered into the chalky soil. Its other walls, once lapped boards, had rotted away, leaving the oak frame standing like a scaffold. The roof was entirely gone. At one end of this abandoned structure grew an ash tree, within the walls, its upcurved branches and gray-green leaves forming a second roof. Beneath this canopy the leaves of many autumns had blown in from the beech wood and heaped up against the one remaining wall, forming a soft and sheltered bed. Rich came here sometimes with his books and lay in the speckled light and read and dreamed.

Dusk was deepening to night as he reached the tree barn, and he could barely make out the burrow beneath the ash branches. Rich liked the sheltered darkness. He stayed for a while in the quietness, looking up at the rafters black against the fading sky. One day, he thought to himself, I'll come here with Grace.

Later he wrote in his diary:

*If being in love means thinking about*

*someone all the time. If being in love means wanting their happiness more than you want your own. If being in love means wanting someone to know you as you truly are. Then I am in love with Grace. So here's the big question. Could Grace ever be in love with me? Honest answer: unlikely. Even more honest answer: I only tell myself it won't happen to protect myself from rejection. Final truth-drug answer: if Grace never loves me the rest of my life will be joyless, lonely, and futile.*

Rich's mother said to him at breakfast, "Don't you know any nice girls who could help out at Gran's party?"

"He knows Grace Carey," said Kitty. "She's a nice girl."

Rich gave Kitty a death stare.

"Do you think she'd help us out? I suppose we could offer to pay."

"Don't be silly, Mum."

Money was tight enough without paying friends what they should do out of friendship. Except Grace wasn't exactly a friend.

"She could sing 'Bushel and a Peck' with Tiny Footsteps," said Kitty.

"Oh, does she sing?"

"No, Mum. Kitty's just being moronic as usual."

However, the notion took root in Rich's mind. He had to take a next step of some kind with Grace; something more than talking in break time, but less than an actual date. Why not ask her if she would help out at Gran's eightieth birthday party? It would be public and unthreatening, not a date at all, but at the same time it was personal. She might think it would be fun.

Then again she might laugh in his face.

Here was the difficulty he faced in making any move that required an answer from Grace. The prospect of open rejection appalled him. He could picture so vividly the expression on her face as she tried to find a way to tell him he was living in dreamland. The thought of those moments before she spoke the words made his face flush and sweat break out on his brow. What he needed was a way to make his offer and receive her response indirectly.

He couldn't ask Maddy Fisher to act as go-between again. He couldn't text because he didn't have a phone. But he could write Grace a letter.

The more he considered this idea, the more he liked it. No one wrote letters anymore. The very act of committing words to paper had an eccentric novelty. Grace would find it unusual but not incomprehensible. Then having read his letter she could reply to it by the same means, and if it was a rejection he could take the blow in the privacy of his own room.

So he sat down and wrote Grace a letter. It was a simple request for help, not an invitation.

*My mother asked me if I knew any girls who'd be willing to help and I thought of you. It'll be quite a strange party, with lots of tiny tots and lots of oldies, but I think it'll be fun. I expect you're busy that day—*

this was to allow her a get-out—

*but if not, maybe you'd like to come and lend a hand. It's 1 p.m. next Saturday. Write me a note to say if you can do it or not.*

Then he had a further idea. He drew out a second sheet of paper and headed it "Vatican City, Rome."

*Dear Miss Carey,*
*A big hello from the pope. I expect you're wondering whether to go to Rich's gran's party. You've never met Rich's gran. You hardly know Rich. So what? The earth may be destroyed by a meteorite tomorrow.*

*Live now! Say yes to life! That's how I got to be pope.*
*Yours infallibly,*
*Benedict XVI*

Rich went to school the next day with both letters in a single envelope, and the envelope in his book bag. He saw Grace twice before lunch, both times at a distance, but his courage failed him. Then he came upon Maddy Fisher and her friend Cath Freeman, and tried out his idea on them, without saying who the letters were for.

"A letter from the pope?"

Maddy burst into laughter.

"You think the pope's a mistake?" said Rich. "You think it would be better coming from the Archbishop of Canterbury? Or Bob Geldof?"

Cath now realized Rich was mocking himself. She started laughing along with Maddy.

Maddy said, "You are seriously strange."

Cath said, "I'd love to get a letter like that."

"You would?"

"God, yes. Mind you, I get excited when I get junk mail."

"You get junk mail?" said Maddy.

"Well, no, actually. But my parents do. They bin it, but I take it out and open it. Is that sad or what?"

"It's sad, Cath."

Rich felt encouraged.

"So we vote I deliver the letters?"

Maddy hesitated. She knew who the letters were for.

"She might not get it quite the way we do."

"If whoever it's for doesn't get it," said Cath, "she doesn't deserve it."

"She might just think you're crackers."

"I don't mind being crackers," said Rich. "I just don't want to be pathetic."

"No, it's not pathetic. Sending someone a letter from the pope isn't pathetic at all."

Maddy started laughing again, and that set Cath off. Rich was gratified.

All at once he realized that Grace herself was approaching them.

"What's the big joke?" Grace said.

Maddy and Cath fell silent and looked at Rich. Rich went pink in the face. A ringing sound filled his ears. He took the envelope from his bag, pushed it into Grace's surprised hands, and turned and walked away. He didn't run, but only by a supreme effort of will.

He went to the English classroom, expecting to find it empty, wanting to be alone. He was shivering all over.

Mr. Pico was sitting at the teacher's desk.

He looked up as Rich entered. For a fraction of a second Rich caught on his face a look of blank desolation. Then he removed his glasses and wiped them. When he put them back on his usual ironic manner had returned.

"Can you be hungry for more learning, Rich?"

"No, sir. Sorry, sir. I thought the classroom would be empty."

"And so it is." He rose and packed up his books. "I'm on my way. As no doubt you know, it's a school rule that a member of staff must never be alone in a room with a student."

"No," said Rich. "I didn't know that."

"Adults can no longer be trusted with children. The modern child has no concept of self-restraint."

So speaking, he left.

Rich sat down at his desk, opened his copy of *The Tempest*, and pretended to study. He tried not to think of Grace reading his letter, and thought of nothing else. He felt the shivering deep in his stomach and a dryness in his mouth.

*Stupid, stupid, stupid,* he told himself.

But the others had laughed. If Grace laughed it would be all right. She might laugh.

*Please laugh, Grace.*

# 14

# Maddy sees the doctor

"Hey, guess what, Joe?" Maddy said to Joe Finnigan, adopting a light and casual tone of voice. "Your brother's going out with my sister."

"Since when?"

"Well, maybe not quite going out. But they talked on the phone for ages last night."

"Tell her not to trust him one inch," said Joe. "Leo's a bad boy."

Maddy and Joe and Grace were gathered in the dance studio waiting to begin the rehearsal. Mr. Pico was late. All the cast were present, but for once there was no sign of Gemma.

"What happened to Gemma?" said Grace.

"Hospital," said Joe. "She'll be off for a couple of days."

"Poor Gemma," said Maddy. "Nothing serious, I hope?"

Joe met Maddy's eyes.

"Very minor," he said. "She'll be fine."

To Maddy it was as if he was saying: We'll be fine.

"That's all right then," she said.

A small boy appeared at the door, out of breath. He'd been sent with a message from the staff room. Mr. Pico couldn't come. The rehearsal was cancelled.

Maddy moved slowly as the group dispersed, half expecting that Joe would hang back too. But he called out, "Gotta go!" and went loping off.

Maddy walked back to the Sixth Form Center with Grace.

"So what do you think's up with Gemma?" said Grace.

"I've no idea," said Maddy.

"Joe dodged telling. Did you notice?"

"I suppose he did."

"So what's this about Leo and your sister?"

"It's true. They met at some thing in Norfolk."

"Well, there you are, then." A spiteful edge entered Grace's voice. "Imo and Leo. You and Joe. You could have a double wedding."

At the end of the school day Maddy parted from her friends as usual outside the station and set off home along the river path. Once out of sight she moved more slowly, and finally sat down on a riverside bench. She had time to kill. In just under an hour she had an appointment at the health center.

Now that the appointment was near she found herself looking back wistfully over the last few days. She realized she had loved the secrecy, the wordlessness, the exchanged looks, the emails waiting when she got home. Now, although nothing had changed with Joe, she sensed that the first innocent phase was coming to an end. Gemma was away. Joe would be free now to speak openly. And after the appointment with the doctor a whole new world of possibility would open up.

Maddy was not looking forward to her appointment. She felt shy of talking about personal matters, and squeamish about the physical details. Also she couldn't help feeling superstitious about it. Up to now she had had no need for contraception. It had seemed to her that going on the pill would be like dressing up for a party to which she hadn't been invited. She didn't like the way it made sex into a premeditated act. She wanted it to be sudden and close, so close that you felt it but never quite saw it. She wanted it to sweep over her like a summer storm, leaving her giddy and breathless: an act without self-awareness, without distance. It had to be wild and liberating or it would be ridiculous.

She watched the swans circling on the river. Swans were supposed to mate for life. Animals didn't need contraception, they just multiplied. There'd been a woman on TV recently who'd had fourteen children. Such a long way from Amy-the-bunny. Sex wasn't one thing at all, it came at you in so many forms. It was pornography, and it was childbirth, and it was love.

*Maybe taking the pill will clear up my spots.*

She rose at last from the bench and walked slowly down the river path back into town. What if she met someone she knew in the health center? Better have a cover story. A rash on her back, nothing too serious, only sensible to have it looked at. Very minor.

That's what Joe had said about Gemma's visit to the hospital: very minor.

The shabby red-brick-and-glass facade of the health center was now before her. Odd how the new buildings always ended up looking more worn out than the old buildings. A plaque on the wall said it had been opened by Princess Michael of Kent in 1977. Over thirty years ago. The parade of shops beside it was Victorian, and ageing with pride.

A friend of her mother's came up the pavement towards her, carrying a bulging Tesco bag.

"Hello, Maddy. Out shopping?"

"Just waiting for a friend," said Maddy, blushing.

"How's school?"

"Not so bad."

"Tell your mum I'll give her a call. I haven't seen her for ages."

She went on her way. Maddy looked up and down the street, checking for any other witnesses. Then she dived through the glass doors.

She was early. The receptionist took her name and told her

to take a seat. She sat down alongside half a dozen others, none of whom she knew. She picked up a magazine and turned the pages inattentively. Then she started reading the notices on the facing wall. "We welcome breastfeeding on the premises," said one. Another showed a baby in sunglasses with a speech bubble saying, "Keep it real, Mum! Real nappies are cool." There were advertisements for baby massage and for Tiny Tiddlers Swim School. She heard a soft wail, and looking round she saw a young mother behind her with a baby on her lap. The young mother smiled, evidently believing that she and Maddy were sisters-in-arms, women braving the medical establishment together.

Maddy felt like a fraud. Everyone else was here to sustain life. She alone was here to thwart life, to trick her body into an unnatural infertility.

The baby started to cry. The mother's smile faded, to be replaced with a look of weariness.

*Not yet, thought Maddy. I'm only seventeen. Plenty of time for babies.*

The thought of having a baby terrified her. It seemed to Maddy to be some kind of cosmic joke, the way that sex, the ultimate party game, was booby-trapped with babies, the ultimate killer of all social life. Not that she was much of a party girl. She just felt that she deserved a few more years with herself at the center of her own attention before she turned into a mother.

"Madeleine Fisher, Room Three, please."

Her name sounded alien in its full form. She felt her heart start to pound. She went down the passage to Room Three. When had she last been here? It must have been spring half term when she had that cough she couldn't shake.

"Come on in, Maddy. Take a chair."

The door closed behind her, pulled by a strong spring. Dr. Hilary Ransom beamed across her desk, her mass of white curls bouncing about her plump red face. She must have been well over fifty, but she sported the jovial manner of a schoolgirl.

"How's Maddy today?"

Maddy found herself quite unable to say why she had come. Somehow in this white-walled room, under the motherly gaze of this large-bosomed woman, it seemed indecent to speak of contraception.

"You're looking well enough, I must say. Is it a personal matter?"

"Yes," said Maddy. She could feel herself digging her fingernails into her palms.

"Well, let's see. What could it be? Whatever it is, it's all in confidence. Nobody else needs to know. But we must get on, you know."

She laughed cheerily to make up for speaking of time pressures.

Maddy looked down at her hands.

"It's about the pill," she said to her hands. "I thought maybe I should be thinking about it."

Dr. Ransom seemed quite unsurprised.

"The pill. Right-ho. I'd begun to think you'd come to tell me you were pregnant."

She started tapping at her computer.

"Let's run through a few quick questions."

She asked Maddy if she smoked or had any serious illnesses or any history of family illnesses. She asked about her periods. Then in the same breezy tone she asked Maddy what she knew of her partner's sexual history.

"It's more that I'm thinking ahead, really," said Maddy, feeling like a fraud. "I don't exactly have a partner. Not yet."

"Thinking ahead. Smart girl. So I suppose you know all about STIs."

"Yes."

Maddy thought back to school talks on sexually trans-mitted infections. There were so many of them. Yes, she knew all about STIs, but what were you supposed to do? Ask a boy in mid-embrace if he was a source of infection? Some people had diseases without even knowing it, apparently. The statistics were scary: a huge percentage of teenagers had chlamydia and herpes and genital warts. They would all end up infertile. And yet somehow life went on. It was like smoking. Smoking killed you, but no one you ever knew actually died.

"Safer to use a condom if you're not sure."

"Yes."

"The pill's no use against STIs."

Again Dr. Ransom laughed, making her bosom heave up and down.

"Coat off. Let's check your blood pressure."

Maddy felt the rubber sleeve squeeze her arm.

"No problems there." The doctor returned to her desk. "Right. Let's see, shall we? What's likely to be the best one for you?" She studied her screen, scanning data. "Different pills suit different people. It's all very personal. We'll start you out on one and see how you go. Sound good?"

"Yes," said Maddy.

"Side effects. I should bring you up to speed on side effects. Here we are. Mood swings, weight gain, breast tenderness, nausea, headaches."

"Oh."

"Doesn't mean you'll get them all at once, of course." Another jolly laugh. "Or any of them ever, for that matter. But if you do, we can try something else."

"Are there any with no side effects?"

Dr. Ransom gazed at her with a look of maternal affection.

"No, my love. But it's usually nothing to worry about."

She printed out a prescription and signed it and laid it on her desk surface between them, keeping her hand on it.

"You take one pill every day. Every day, mind. Stop taking the pills, you're not protected anymore. There are twenty-one pills in each packet. You start on the first day of your period. You take the pills for twenty-one days, at the same time every day. Then you have seven days off. That's when your period will come."

She lifted her hand to release the prescription.

"There's three months' worth. Come back and see me before you run out."

Maddy took the sheet of paper.

"You'll find the instructions say to allow seven days for the pills to become effective."

"Seven days!"

"To be honest you're protected after the first day. But I'd say don't be in too much of a hurry. If a boy tells you he can't wait, you tell him, phooey!" She laughed at that. "Phooey! you tell him. If you're worth it, you're worth waiting for. And you know what? That's a good contraception all by itself. Just say phooey!"

Maddy did her best to smile. It seemed impolite not to share Dr. Ransom's generous flow of good humor. But the truth was Maddy felt as if none of this had anything to do with her. Some other person of the same name was asking for pills and was being warned of syphilis and gonorrhea, of mood swings, nausea, and headaches. Some other person would have to remember to take twenty-one pills followed by seven days of no pills. The real Maddy, the one who was in love with Joe Finnigan, remained untouched. Let the other person make plans and fear consequences. Maddy herself was embarking on an adventure called love, a journey of the body and heart that would take her to unknown lands.

Love filled her waking thoughts and her sleeping dreams. Love was new, love was a revelation, love was magic. It had the power to transform her life. The transformation had already begun.

The other person, the practical, calculating person, went from the health center to the pharmacy and received, after an agonizing wait, a paper bag containing a small box. The pharmacist presumably knew what the pills were for, but she seemed not to be interested. Maddy stuffed the package into her bag and left without a word.

The box was white with a band of green. Inside was an instruction leaflet and three green strips of pills, with a day printed beneath each pill, and a line of thick black arrows running from one to the next in a clockwise direction. That was in case you didn't know that Tuesday came after Monday. The pills inside their clear plastic bubbles were small and dull yellow.

She opened out the leaflet.

"Try taking Microgynon 30 while doing a daily chore," she read. "Take it after brushing your teeth, for example."

She was to take the first pill on the first day of her period. When would that be? She tried to work out how long ago her last period had been. As best as she could tell she was due in a week or so.

She put the white and green box away in her Indian jewel case, hidden underneath the little cushion on which her best earrings and necklaces lay. Her father had given her the jewel case for her twelfth birthday. It stood on top of her chest of drawers, its inlaid red and blue glass beads glowing in the light from her window.

After all the tension of going to the doctor she suffered a sense of anticlimax. Nothing would change for at least a week. Gemma's two days away would not be such a golden opportunity after all. Once Gemma returned they would have to wait until Joe found the right moment to end it with her. In the meantime, they had their emails.

She opened her laptop. There was an email from Joe.

*Is your sister really going out with Leo? If she is, warn her to be careful. Leo is unstable and can get really mean.*

Maddy was puzzled by this message. She wasn't surprised to learn that Leo was dangerous. That was part of his attraction. But she was surprised that Joe should choose to get himself involved in Leo's affairs. She wanted to believe it was a sign of his feelings for her, but if so why didn't he say? Even as she was framing this thought there came a ping from her laptop, and there was Joe again.

*I know I shouldn't interfere but Imo's your sister. Leo is bad bad news. He hurts girls. I'm only thinking of you really. Don't blame me for what Leo does to Imo. I'm not like Leo at all. Sorry I'm just rambling and it's late and I have this stupid feeling you understand me.*

Maddy emailed back at once.

*I have that feeling too. It's strange because we don't really know each other at all. I'll try to find a way to warn Imo. Is it safe for you and me to talk yet?*

Joe replied:

*Not yet. I'm worried about Gemma. I want her to be better before I say anything. I'm not like Leo, I don't enjoy hurting girls.*

Maddy was disappointed but she knew he was right. It made her love him all the more. He was behaving with honor. A very small voice did whisper to her that if he was truly honorable he wouldn't even email her until he had made the break with Gemma; but he was only human. That too was part of what she loved in him.

So it was all going to proceed more slowly than she had at first supposed. No harm in that. Gemma would be out of hospital tomorrow or the day after. Allow, say, three weeks for her to get back to full health. Then Joe could tell her it was over. Another week for the sake of decency. That was four, maybe five weeks. By then she would be almost on to the second card of pills. That felt good and safe. So maybe it was all for the best.

She cuddled up that night with Bunby in her arms, whispering into his floppy ear.

"You'll like Joe, Bunby. I know you will. You're not to be jealous of him. Even if I do get to love him an awful lot, I'll never stop loving you."

# 15

## Gay loser freak

"Take a seat, Richard," said Mr. Jury. "Wonderful that you're here."

Rich was here because he'd been told to be here. He took a seat and clasping his hands between his knees he fixed his gaze on the rug before him. It was a modern pattern of bright reds and oranges, and exactly represented the Head's chosen style of energetic good cheer. "We're on the way!" the Head would declare at assemblies. "We're motoring!" Once, famously, "The Beacon rocks!"

"What happens in Vegas stays in Vegas," Mr. Jury said.

"Yes, sir."

"This is just between you and me."

Rich had no idea why he had been summoned. He looked up to find the Head nodding his handsome mop of hair and smiling. With soft disconcerting *pat-pat-pat* sounds he paddled the surface of his desk with his palms. He was proud of his nickname, the Fury, and had once been referred to in the local newspaper as a "firecracker": always fizzing, always in motion, always on the point of an eruption of enthusiasm. Like every student in the school, Rich found him acutely embarrassing.

"So how's it going, Rich? Looking good for the exams?"

"I hope so, sir."

"We're expecting great things. English best of all. Paul Pico has high hopes of you."

"I'll do my best, sir."

"You get along with Paul's teaching style?"

"Yes, sir."

"I only ask because not everyone does. Some students find him—what's the word—eccentric? Not always entirely focused? I gather there are some students who don't quite get the hang of what he wants of them."

Rich said nothing. He realized he was being invited to criticize Mr. Pico, and he didn't like it.

"I take it that's not your experience."

"He's the best teacher in the school," said Rich.

"The best? High praise. Tell me more."

Reluctantly, Rich elaborated.

"He's interested in us. He's interested in how we develop our ideas. How we make sense of our lives. What it's like being alive." He stopped, frowning, feeling that his words were too thin and insubstantial to express his thoughts. "The ones who don't like him, all they want is for him to get them through the stupid exams."

"Ah, yes. The stupid exams." Mr. Jury smacked the desk. "If only we could banish those stupid exams forever. But we can't. Fact of life, Richard. Obstinate reality."

"Yes, sir."

"You say Paul Pico is 'interested in us.' Those were your words, I think. How does he manifest that interest?"

He spoke with careful neutrality, but Rich saw the trap. He recalled how Mr. Pico had left the empty classroom as soon as he had entered it.

"It's how he teaches us," he said. "He gets us to talk about poems."

"What sort of talk?"

"About what poems mean to us." His irritation was deepening into anger. "It's what you do with poems. It's why poets write them."

The Head silently noted his aggression, and Rich silently regretted it.

"I'm told you wrote about a poem recently." He glanced down at some notes. "Something about love and wanting to be hurt?"

"No," said Rich, feeling his face flush. "I wrote about dreams and waking. About how it's better to love in dreams than not to love at all."

"So nothing about hurting?"

"The waking hurts."

"Well, Paul Pico certainly seems to agree. He singled your work out."

"Yes."

Rich saw where this was all going but he felt powerless to stop it.

"Don't get me wrong, Rich. I have the highest opinion of Paul as a teacher. I have no problem with eccentricity. Whatever floats your boat, as they say. But I also have duties of pastoral care."

Rich said nothing.

"Is there anything you feel I should know?"

Many possible answers raced through Rich's agitated mind. *You should know this whole school teaches nothing of any use to anyone, with the single exception of Mr. Pico. You should know that most people are stupid, vindictive, and dirty-minded. You should know that everyone imitates the way you swing your arms and laughs at your hairstyle.*

"No, sir," he said.

"Would you say Paul Pico is a friend of yours?"

"He's my teacher."

"But you meet him out of school."

"No, sir."

"In a café? In a bookshop?"

*Jesus,* Rich thought. *What kind of police state do I live in? Everyone reports everything.*

"That was just chance. That only happened once."

"And Mr. Pico lent you a book."

"Yes. He's my teacher."

"A book relating to your syllabus?"

"Mr. Pico doesn't only teach the syllabus."

"So what sort of books does he lend you?"

"One book."

"Okay. One book. What book?"

"A psychology book."

"Could it also be described as a sex manual?"

"No. It could not. Who told you that?"

The Head raised placating palms and made I'm-backing-off gestures in the face of Rich's furious response.

"Okay, okay. I have to ask."

"Read it yourself. It's called *The Art of Loving*. It's by Erich Fromm. He's a psychologist."

"I will. I will read it. I'm sorry, Rich. I don't mean to upset you."

"It's stupid," said Rich. "People make up stupid stuff about Mr. Pico. It's all just made up. They don't understand him so they laugh at him. It's so stupid."

"But you understand him?"

"No. He's my teacher. I learn from him."

"And so you should."

The Head got up from his chair and walked over to the

144

window. He stood there, rising and falling on his toes, his back to Rich, swinging his arms.

"However, things have been said. Accusations have been made."

*Now he's going to tell me Mr. Pico's gay,* thought Rich. He had expended so much energy in recent months resisting the playground slur, the cheap insult, the automatic label for anyone who didn't conform, that he had never actually considered what it would mean if it were true.

"I don't make any accusations myself." The Head pulled back his elbows and squeezed his shoulder blades together, as if limbering up for some form of contact sport. "Paul's private life is his own affair. But it must remain private. Don't you agree?"

"Yes, sir."

"Suppose your teacher had been taking advantage of his position." He turned round, the exercises over, ready for action. "Taking advantage of his students' need for approval. I would have to act, wouldn't I?"

"Yes, sir. But he hasn't. Who says he has?"

"What I've been told, I've been told in confidence. I have to respect confidences, Rich. You understand that. Just as I respect yours."

"But you're asking all these questions."

"What am I to do? Ignore the rumors?"

"People will say anything. They don't care."

"But I do. I'm paid to care. I care for my staff. I care for my students. I care for the whole Beacon family."

Sometimes they were a family, sometimes a team, sometimes a community. Rich had never realized before how much he resented the casual and arrogant manner in which he was presumed to belong to the Beacon. It was a school. That's all.

"The buck stops here, Rich. I will not duck the—" For one glorious moment he was about to say, "I will not duck the buck." But he caught himself in time. "My head is over the parapet, Rich. Let them shoot at me if they must. I took this job to make a difference. Sometimes there are hard choices. If I'm wrong I'll be the first to put my hand up. I say to every one of you, if you believe in me, I'll believe in you. The Beacon's on the way, Rich. There's no stopping us now."

Inadvertently the Head had fallen into one of his assembly speeches. Rich saw no need for a response. A short silence followed.

Mr. Jury returned to his desk.

"Good, good. Thank you for your openness. Thank you for your trust. Come back any time. My door is always open."

This was Rich's permission to go.


As soon as he was out of the Head's office Rich felt an almost physical sense of revulsion. The stupidity and cruelty of it all sickened him. As he emerged from the Admin Block onto the

Oval he found it was crowded with gossiping groups of students. It was chatterers like this who were spreading rumors about Mr. Pico. Suddenly Rich found that he hated them. He hated the school. By what right did these giggling imbeciles presume to stand in judgment over Mr. Pico? Were their own lives so wonderful? The sound they made reached his ears like the bleating of sheep. Just because they all flocked together they thought they were safe from contempt and failure and pain.

*You're all losers*, Rich cried out in his mind. *You're all going to suffer. No one's safe in the end. No one wins.*

He launched himself into the midst of the throng, heading for the peace and quiet of the library. And there ahead of him, crossing the Oval, on a path that meant they must meet unless he turned away, was Grace Carey.

His rage evaporated. She hadn't seen him yet. Still time to take evasive action. But then she might think he was afraid of meeting her. Better to allow the casual encounter. Keep it light, exchange some meaningless words, move on.

The interview with the Head was now forgotten. The wrong done to Mr. Pico slipped into the past. What should he say to Grace? Nothing heavy. A nod, a greeting as they passed each other. He might learn something from her look, but she must feel no pressure from him. No neediness.

He kept to his path. He formed his expression into what he hoped was an easy smile. He wasn't looking at her. His thoughts were elsewhere.

Grace had stopped dead. She was staring at him.

"Hi," he said.

He too came to a stop, closer to her than he had intended.

"Everything okay?" he said.

"You fucking little freak," said Grace.

"Sorry?"

"Where do you get off, writing me letters like that? I don't even know you."

"I just thought—"

"I don't want to be part of your sick games, okay?"

"It's not a game." Rich hardly knew what he was saying. "It's not meant to be a game."

"I don't give a rat's arse what it is." She hissed at him with real venom in her voice. "Just stay away from me. And don't talk to my friends about me. You gay loser freak."

She walked off. Rich remained where he was, motionless, in shock.

Other students passed by, many in tracksuits, heading for the sports fields. He heard shouts and laughter. No one paid him any attention.

*I'm not here,* thought Rich. *I'm invisible.*

*A man hears what he wants to hear and disregards the rest.*

Someone on a faraway planet in a forgotten galaxy had called someone else a gay loser freak. Someone else was in pain. That was all happening light years away. The pain traveled slowly.

By the time it reached the here and now it would all be long ago and forgotten.

"Rich!"

Voices from the faraway planet. People calling names. People jostling people, wanting to cause distress, but nobody actually feels anything. Pressure, motion, but not pain.

"Rich!"

Maddy Fisher was standing in front of him, touching his arm. Trying to get him to respond to her.

"Rich!"

Her friendly face, smiling, worried.

"Are you okay?"

"I'm fine."

"You're not fine at all."

"Aren't I?"

Voices echoing in space. Words with no meaning. Drifting in waking sleep.

"I saw you with Grace. I was trying to find you. I wanted to tell you not to bother with her. I wanted to save you the hassle."

The hassle. Also known as the humiliation. The pain. The heartbreak. The hearing of words that you won't ever forget for the rest of your life.

Let it go. Let it all go far away. Slip into sleep.

"I wasn't looking for her," said someone. "We just bumped into each other."

"Was she horrible? She can be such a bitch. I was going to warn you."

"Oh, well."

What happens happens. Big eyes gazing with concern. Someone wants to cry. Someone wants comfort, kindness, love. But not here. Not now.

"Grace has been strange recently." Maddy Fisher trying to ease the pain. A distant act of mercy. "She's all mixed up. You said it yourself. She's a bit of a loner."

"Yes."

"At least you gave it a go."

"Yes."

A stinging sensation half woke someone from his half-sleep. A new shame.

"Does everyone know?"

"Only me and Cath. And Grace."

"She'll have fun telling everyone."

"I don't think so. I don't think she . . . I'm sure she won't talk about it."

Sensitized by pain Rich heard what Maddy did not say: that his attentions to Grace shamed her. Grace would never want to be associated with a gay loser freak.

*The deepest need of man is the need to overcome his separateness, to leave the prison of his aloneness.*

*Nice try, Erich. Easier said than done. The whole wide world is now the prison of my aloneness. I can try to leave, but where am I to go?*

"Cath thought your letter was great. So did I."

So Grace had showed it to them. They had all had a good laugh. A letter from a gay loser freak.

"It was very sweet and very funny. We both thought so."

"But not her."

"Grace is on her own planet."

*Like me: I'm on my own planet. We could have shared a galaxy. We could have been stars.*

Cath herself now came jogging up to join them. She looked different. It took Rich a moment to understand that both girls were wearing tracksuits.

"Rich spoke to Grace," said Maddy.

"Oh God!" said Cath, her eyes turning to Rich. "How was she?"

"Her usual bitchy self," said Maddy.

"Grace can bitch for England," said Cath. "You know what, Rich? You're better off without her. It's all about Grace for Grace. I don't think she's capable of loving anyone. Apart from Grace. You're better off without her."

"Maybe," said Rich.

But he didn't want to hear it. He didn't want to hear anything. Cath meant well but she had no idea. Nobody had any idea. Only him, and Grace. Of course Grace was capable of love.

She had simply chosen not to love him. Why would she? What was there to love? In rejecting him, Grace had done nothing to make herself less desirable to him. Rather the opposite. It proved to him that she had high standards. Nobody likes being called a gay loser freak, but look at it from Grace's point of view. Not a bad description. And anyway, what was he supposed to do? Stop dreaming of her love, call himself a fool, just because he was rejected? A loser, yes. His love not reciprocated, yes. But not a fool. Loving Grace was as natural as choosing light over darkness.

But now the darkness.

"Cath's right," said Maddy. "She wouldn't have made you happy."

"Or anyone else," said Cath. "Or herself."

"I'd like her to be happy," said Rich.

"Oh, Rich! You would not! You'd like her to come out in fat yellow spots!"

He shook his head. They didn't understand. No point in trying to explain.

"Look, we have to go," said Maddy. "Are you going to be okay?"

"I'm fine."

"Okay. We'll see you around."

They jogged off together, the hoods of their tracksuits bouncing on their backs. The Oval was now deserted. Rich had lost track of day and time and had no idea where he was meant to be. Possibly he was meant to be nowhere. If so, he had arrived.

Once, a long time ago, there had been a history essay to finish. He had been on his way to the library to write about the Cold War.

He went to the library and found a place in a far corner where no one would see him. No one was looking for him. No one came. He and no one looked out of the window and thought of nothing.


At home he said to Kitty, "Grace and me have had a talk and it's not going to work."

"Why not?"

"We're just too different."

"How are you different?"

"I like her but she doesn't like me."

Kitty laughed. Then she became indignant.

"How can she not like you? She'd be lucky to have you. What's the matter with her? Is she stupid?"

"Anyway, I have to fix the lights in your doll's house."

"What's that got to do with Grace not liking you?"

"Nothing."

But they both knew he wanted to help Kitty because he was so unhappy.

# 16

## Lies about Leo

Maddy felt sorry for Rich, but she had forgotten him almost as soon as he was out of sight. Her mind was filled by the coming meeting with Joe. After school there was a play rehearsal, and Joe would be there and Gemma wouldn't. For the first time they'd be able to exchange a few true words.

Maddy expected very little. Nothing major, like a kiss. Not even a touch. All that in good time. But to be able to speak a little more freely about what was happening between them, to look into Joe's eyes and say, "I think about you all the time," to feel the warmth of his answering smile: that was life to her. She longed for the moment when their eyes could meet and not have to look away.

In the changing rooms after games she and Cath whispered together about Joe. Cath was now a full partner in Maddy's secret romance.

"Now's your chance," said Cath. "Gemma's away. Now's the time to pounce."

"I'm not a pouncer."

"So smolder."

"Smolder? How do I do that?"

"You look into his eyes. You don't say anything. You don't smile. You just magnetize him. Then very slowly, you part your lips."

Maddy burst into laughter.

"I can't do that!"

"I'm not saying show your tongue or anything tarty. Just part your lips." Cath demonstrated. "While being pretty."

As it turned out, Maddy never had the opportunity to try, because the play rehearsal never happened. A notice went up on the main board in the Oval saying the production was cancelled "due to unforeseen circumstances." Maddy was bitterly disappointed. Where was she to meet Joe now? She half expected him to come looking for her in the areas of the school where he would be most likely to find her, but he didn't. So as the end of the school day approached, which was also the end of the school week, she decided to go looking for him.

His last class of the day was economics. That meant he would be in the Allen Building. From there he would either go back across the Oval, if he wanted to link up with friends, or he would cut straight across the Paddock and leave school by the

Dewsbury Road gates. Without ever admitting to herself that she was doing it, Maddy had amassed a great deal of information about Joe's school day.

Where to loiter? The only sure place was by the doors out of the Allen Building. But she had no good reason to be standing there, and it would make her intentions far too obvious. She could hang about in the Oval more or less unnoticed in the bustle of the end of the school day, but what if he went the Paddock route? Her only real option was to station herself by the gates. People often waited there for friends who were late getting out of classes or sports. The walk into town was a sociable time.

Maddy recruited Cath to wait at the gates with her. She felt less like a stalker with a friend by her side.

"What if he's already left?" said Cath. "Or goes out by the Victoria Road gates? Or stays late to do training or something?"

"Or has a heart attack and dies?"

"Jesus!" said Cath. "What a lot there is to worry about."

"If he doesn't come by half-past, we'll forget it."

He did come. They both saw him at the same time, approaching with a crowd of friends, striding along with his loose-limbed gait, not a care in the world. Cath poked Maddy and Maddy almost squealed.

They could hear the group's voices. They were arguing about going to a film.

"I'm not wasting my time on that junk," said Joe cheerfully.

"You're such a wanker, Joe."

They were now quite close. Joe saw Maddy.

"Maddy Fisher!" he cried. No awkwardness, no attempt to hide anything. Just that wide smile and her name on his lips.

"Oh, hi, Joe." Very casual, very unplanned.

"So what's up with Pablo?"

"I don't know."

"Looks like we're not going to get our moment of glory."

"And there I was, hoping a Hollywood talent scout would spot me."

Their eyes met. His sudden intense gaze reached into her.

"Your day will come," he said.

The band of boys was moving on past. Joe looked like he was about to follow them. Maddy made a quick decision.

"Joe," she said. "About my sister Imo. I'll be seeing her this evening."

"Okay," said Joe.

"You coming?" his friends called to him.

"Be right with you," he called back.

"So I'll pass on the message," said Maddy. She could think of nothing more significant to say.

"You do that," said Joe.

A smile and a wave, and he jogged away to catch up with his friends.

Maddy and Cath followed more slowly down Dewsbury Road, past the semi-detached houses with their neat front gardens.

"He looked like he was pleased to see you," said Cath.

"He was strange."

Maddy was puzzled by Joe's behavior. He could have said so much more.

"He wasn't strange," said Cath. "He was covering up."

"You think?"

"It's too public. Anyone could see."

"But Gemma's away."

"So? Hasn't it occurred to you that his friends know Gemma? You know what boys are like. All he has to do is walk with you for thirty seconds and they'll be all over him. 'Ooo! Fancy a bit of Maddy, do you, Joe? Want to give her a poke, Joe?'"

Maddy blushed.

"They don't talk like that."

"Oh yes, they do. Take it from me, Mad. They only talk about one thing. And football."

Maddy didn't argue. Cath's explanation pleased her because it seemed plausible, and because it meant everything was all right. And Joe had said, "Your day will come."

Mrs. Fisher was sitting at the kitchen table surrounded by account books and invoices, tapping away at the shop laptop.

"Dad phoned," she told Maddy as she came in. "He's coming home next week. On Friday."

"That's great!"

"I have to get the accounts up to date so he can see how things are. He keeps saying there's no need to worry."

"That's because you always worry, Mum."

"Yes, I know. But sometimes there really is something to worry about. You read the papers. You know we're in a recession."

"Actually I don't read the papers. Not those bits, anyway. They're too depressing."

"Well, it's never been this bad before."

"Really?"

"Yes, really."

Maddy sat down at the table and looked sternly into her mother's tired eyes.

"Come on, Mum. Stop frightening me. Are we going to go bust? Are we going to have to sell up?"

"I expect we'll muddle our way through somehow. Mike keeps saying we'll be okay."

Maddy was relieved. She trusted her father's business sense more than her mother's.

"Make me a cup of tea, darling."

"Sure."

Maddy jumped up and filled the electric kettle.

"Not so much water. No need to boil what we don't need."

Maddy tipped some water down the sink and started the kettle boiling.

Imo appeared.

"Dad's coming back," said Maddy.

"Yes, I know. If you're making tea, do one for me."

"There isn't enough water in the kettle."

"Why not?"

"Mum's saving money. I'm only to boil enough for one cup."

"What's the matter with you, Mum? Is it the menopause?"

"We have to reduce our costs somehow, darling. Business is very slow."

"We'll manage. We always have."

Imo was not a worrier. Maddy felt this was unfair on their mother.

"We are supposed to be in a recession," she said.

"Well, what does Dad say?"

Like Maddy, Imo had faith in their father.

"He's in China," said Mrs. Fisher.

"Yes, Mum. We do know. But presumably even though he's in China he knows what's going on here."

"I think things must look very different when you're far away. I have told him. He says it'll all work out."

"So there you are. Cheer up, Mum. It may never happen."

In the past this sort of hard comfort would have enraged

their mother. Now her mind was back on the accounts and she didn't respond. Maddy felt that Imo was being insensitive.

"It's all right for you to say don't worry. You don't do anything for the business. You just live off Mum and Dad."

"So do you."

"I'm at school."

"I'm at college."

"So maybe we should both be a bit more sympathetic if Mum's worried about money."

"She's always worried about money. Okay, if we have less, we spend less. I'm cool with that. What do you want me to do, Maddy? Live on air?"

"Just be a bit more sympathetic."

"I am sympathetic."

"You could have fooled me."

"Please, girls," said their mother. "I'm trying to work."

But Imo was annoyed now.

"You know your problem, Maddy? It really is time you got a boyfriend."

"Well, I hope I do better than you when I do."

"You'll be lucky."

"Oh, yes? What about Leo? He's unstable."

"What?"

"He's bad news. He's mean. He hurts girls."

"What are you talking about?"

Maddy hadn't meant it to come out this way, but it was done now. Imo was shocked.

"What's Leo got to do with you? You don't know anything about him."

"His brother does."

"Joe?"

"Yes, Joe."

"Joe's been telling you all this crap about Leo?"

"Yes."

"I don't believe you."

"So don't believe me. I don't care. He only told me to help you."

Imo stared at her, shaking with anger. But she wanted to know the details.

"So what did Joe say?"

"He said Leo's unstable and mean and likes hurting girls."

"That's just bollocks."

"All right. It's bollocks. You know best."

"Keep out," said Imo. "Just keep out of my affairs. Get a life of your own."

She stormed upstairs to her room. Maddy stayed in the kitchen, her heart pounding, almost as agitated as Imo. She knew she had done it in the wrong way at the wrong time, but Imo always had that effect on her.

Their mother seemed to have taken in none of it, beyond

the disturbance to her work. "I wish you wouldn't argue in the kitchen, Maddy."

"Well, why do you do the accounts in the kitchen, Mum?"

"Oh, I don't know," said her mother. "I feel nothing can really go too wrong in the kitchen."

Maddy had no answer to that because she felt it too.

"Is it okay if I have something to eat?"

"Help yourself, darling."

She made herself a bowl of golden syrup oats. She had just settled down to eat it when Imo reappeared.

"I phoned Leo," she said. "It's all lies."

"He says Joe's lying?"

"No, of course not. He says you're lying. He says Joe would never say things like that about him."

"I'm lying?" Maddy was too stupefied to protest.

"He says you're probably hormonal and need a good seeing to."

Maddy flushed red with shame and rage.

"That's enough, Imo," said Mrs. Fisher.

"Tell Maddy to stop spreading lies about my boyfriends, then."

"I was trying to *help* you."

"I don't see how making up lies helps me."

"Joe emailed me. It's all in his emails. I can show you."

"No thanks. I've got better things to do."

She departed again.

Maddy felt like bursting into tears.

"She'll have forgotten it all tomorrow," said her mother. "You know what Imo's like. She's like Dad, they only think about what's in front of them at the time. It's the source of their strength, really."

"What are you talking about, Mum?"

"Well, I do worry rather about things that haven't happened yet. Mike never does."

"If you ask me Imo's just totally self-centered."

It struck Maddy then that Leo would get on to Joe and demand to know why Joe had been telling tales about him. Joe must be warned. She hurried up to her room and sent an email.

*I told Imo what you said about Leo and she doesn't believe me. She phoned Leo. He says it's all lies. Thought you should know. Hope I haven't landed you in a mess.*

She sat by the laptop waiting for Joe to reply, but no reply came. Then she remembered he was going out to see a film with his friends. She went back to the kitchen and found the local newspaper. Most of the early evening showings ended just before eight o'clock. Afterwards Joe would most likely have a curry with his friends, or go to a pub. He wouldn't get home to check his emails till ten or later. He might not even get her message until tomorrow.

Maddy couldn't wait until tomorrow. She needed to know

that Joe was with her against Imo and Leo. She wanted him to tell her it wasn't her fault. She wanted contact.

*I could always go to the cinema.*

The thought jumped into her head. She knew where he was, and roughly when he was coming out. If she wanted to she could be there. She could take him aside. They could have a few brief words.

She wanted to.

What would his friends think? She could make up something about the play rehearsals if she had to. But the fact was Maddy no longer cared what his friends thought. She had to see Joe, just for a moment. She had to know that all was well between them.

"I'm going out, Mum. I won't be long."

"What about supper?"

"I'll get myself something later. Don't worry about me."

"I don't like you going out by yourself at night, Maddy."

"I'm only popping in on Cath. And it's still light."

Dusk was falling as Maddy walked the short distance into town. The cinema stood at the top end of the High Street: a 1930s building with a pillared front, set back from the traffic behind a broad pavement. In more recent times the town council had planted two small trees in this pavement, and provided two iron benches that faced the passing traffic. The shops were long closed now, and the only signs of life came from the pub opposite and the takeaway kebab counter further down the street.

Maddy sat on one of the benches. She felt dampness on her bottom. She stood up. There was a Coke can lying on its side, and a puddle of spilled Coke on the bench seat. She was wearing blue jeans. She went over to the dark window of a greeting card shop and twisting round, examined the damp patch. It was all too visible, a dark stain on the seat of her jeans. It looked exactly as if she had wet herself.

"Great. Just great."

A sensation of helplessness possessed her. It was all going wrong. How was she going to explain to Joe why she was waiting for him outside the cinema with wee all over her bum? There wasn't time to go home and change.

She could always give up. But the sky was getting darker. He wouldn't notice the damp patch, not if she was facing him. And if they were talking to each other, they had to be facing each other. As for why she was there: she was there to warn him that Leo might be angry with him. Nothing like the simple truth.

She positioned herself with her back to one of the benches, facing the cinema doors, and waited for Joe's film to end. It was strange to think that he was in there right now, and had no idea that she was outside. She followed the slow movement of the clock hands in the lit foyer.

Then people started coming out. Maddy did her best to look relaxed and casual. Her plan was to make eye contact and then to beckon Joe to her. That way his friends wouldn't hear what she said to him.

People were coming out in groups of two and three, laughing, talking over each other. They moved away towards the car park and more came after them. There was no sign of Joe. Then a big crowd came out all together, and she couldn't be sure if he was somewhere in the middle or not. She followed the crowd with her eyes, turning as they passed to catch sight of the ones on the far side. Most of them were boys, but they didn't look to her like Joe and his friends. It was getting darker.

"Maddy Fisher!"

She spun round. There he was, smiling at her.

"What happened to your bum?"

There by Joe's side, holding his hand, was Gemma Page.

"Oh, nothing," said Maddy.

"That movie truly sucked," he told her. "Just in case you're thinking of seeing it."

"I liked it," said Gemma.

"You like everything." He grinned at Maddy. "Gemma has no powers of critical thinking whatsoever."

"No, I haven't really," said Gemma, unoffended. "I like most things."

"You coming, Joe?" called his friends, already crossing the street.

"See you tomorrow," said Joe to Maddy. Gemma gave her a smile. He and Gemma went on their way.

Maddy stood outside the cinema as the last of the departing crowd trickled away. She felt cold.

Slowly she made her way back home. Nothing made sense.

What was Gemma doing there?

No surprise that Joe had said nothing when he saw her. What could he say with Gemma standing right beside him? But wasn't Gemma supposed to be in hospital?

She reran the brief exchange in her memory, analyzing it for clues. Joe had been quite rude about Gemma, almost as if he'd been saying to Maddy, "I'd rather be seeing a film with you." He had said, "See you tomorrow." Was that his way of telling her they'd find a moment tomorrow to talk to each other openly? She replayed the way he had said, "What happened to your bum?" He had grinned, as if he was saying, "I really like your bum."

So maybe not such a disaster after all.

That night after she had gone to bed an email came from Joe at last.

*We have to talk. Meet me at 10 a.m. tomorrow by the pond in Victoria Park.*

He must have sent it in a hurry. But it was enough. They'd be able to talk properly at last.

She could sleep now.

# 17

# Only a bit of fun

From the moment Maddy entered the park she was looking out for Joe. It was Saturday morning and there were several other people in the small park, strolling its winding paths, sitting on its many benches. She hurried past the banked masses of rhododendrons, past the disused bandstand, to the pond at the heart of the park.

Benches stood at intervals all round the pond, and on each bench there was a single person. It was comical and sad at the same time, the way each of them wanted a bench to themselves. But then Maddy thought, *I want a bench of my own too, where Joe can join me. Maybe they're all waiting for the one they love.*

Pigeons rose and fell in sudden clatters. Ducks came waddling out of the shallow water, stabbing for the torn bread and the cold chips thrown their way by the lone watchers on the benches. Occasionally a seagull came squawking out of the sky to carry off a fragment of food.

Maddy walked right round the long tree-fringed pond and did not find Joe. So she had arrived first.

A middle-aged woman who had been feeding the birds from a Waitrose bag now came to the end of her supply. The pigeons and the ducks at once abandoned her. The woman rose from the bench and shuffled away.

Maddy took her place.

*How cruel animals are,* she thought. *They make no pretence of love.* Feed them and they come to you. Offer them nothing and they go. And yet lonely people return day after day, with more bread in their plastic bags, willing the birds to remember them, hoping this time the grateful clamor will turn into love.

Her phone beeped. A text from Cath: *Where R U?* Maddy checked the time on her phone. After ten. Where was Joe?

"Maddy?"

She jumped up, looked round. It was Grace.

"Oh, hello, Grace."

"I was hoping I'd find you," said Grace.

"Actually, now's not a good time," said Maddy quickly. "I'm meeting someone here."

"Yes, I know," said Grace. "You're meeting Joe."

Maddy stared. "How did you know?"

"He told me."

"I don't understand," Maddy said.

"Joe was going to come. Really he was. But in the end he

couldn't face it. So I said, 'Someone has to go and tell her.' Joe said, 'I can't.' So I've come."

Maddy sat down on the bench. She felt faint.

"Tell her what?"

"I'm really sorry, Mad. It was never meant to be much of anything. But it's not fair to let it go on any more. Like I said to Joe, better to stop it before it goes too far. Joe says it's only a bit of fun and no harm done, but even so."

"Only a bit of fun?"

"We did it so Gemma wouldn't find out about Joe and me."

Maddy heard a rushing sound in her ears. Everything was turning fuzzy before her eyes.

Grace chattered on.

"Gemma was getting so sharp-eyed. Don't you believe that dumb blonde act. Gemma knows what's what. So we wanted to give her someone else to watch. And you were having a bit of a flirt with Joe. It wasn't anything serious, so we knew Gemma would find nothing."

Maddy dug her fingernails into her palms.

"What do you mean, Joe and you?"

"We've been seeing each other."

Joe and Grace. It wasn't possible.

"How? Where?"

"Where no one sees us. Mostly in Leo's place. He's often away."

Joe and Grace in Leo's place. In the evenings after school. A fridge for the booze, a bed for the babes.

"I just thought you had to be told before you got in too deep. It's okay so long as it's just a bit of harmless fun. Joe kept on saying to me, 'Stop worrying, Maddy's cool, she's a great girl, we're just having a laugh.' But I said, 'Maddy's my friend. We've got to stop.'"

Maddy felt sick. Not like she wanted to throw up, but like the swimmy feeling that comes before.

"How long has this been going on?"

"Oh, weeks. Since the summer."

Weeks. Grace's secret lover. Had she watched porn with him?

"So all those emails. They were just for a laugh?"

"Well, and to keep the flirtation going. So Gemma wouldn't get suspicious of me."

"Joe didn't mean them?"

"I don't know what he said. He told me there was nothing serious in them. I mean, no wild declarations of love or anything. He said he was taking care not to lead you on or anything."

Maddy said nothing.

"Is that right, Mad? It was all pretty silly stuff, wasn't it?"

"Yes. Pretty silly stuff."

She couldn't help herself. Tears started to roll down her cheeks.

"Oh, God. You really mind, don't you?"

Maddy couldn't speak.

"Oh, hell. What a stupid bitch I am. It's all my fault."

She sat down on the bench by Maddy.

"It was Joe's idea," she said, "but I never should have gone along with it. All I was thinking was how to keep our secret. I'm so sorry, Mad. I've really messed you up, haven't I?"

Maddy shrugged as she wept.

"Have you really got in deep?"

Maddy nodded. She pulled out a tissue and dabbed at her eyes.

"Oh, God. I'm so useless. Now you'll hate me forever. I don't blame you. Can I borrow a tissue?"

Maddy handed over a tissue. Grace had tears in her eyes too.

"At least I told you before it really went too far. I mean, nothing's really happened, has it?"

"No," said Maddy.

"It's not like your heart's broken or anything."

"No," said Maddy.

She watched the ducks on the pond, wanting not to think about the hurt. Wanting not to enter the waiting unhappiness. The ducks went round and round, up and down the pond. Why? All that energy, all for nothing.

"Maddy, I don't have the right to ask this. But will you keep our secret?"

"What?"

"Me and Joe."

"Yes. Of course."

"It's just that we don't want Gemma to know."

Gemma who had been by Joe's side as they came out of the cinema last night. Gemma who was supposed to be in hospital. What was all this about Gemma?

"I don't get it," said Maddy. "Why doesn't Joe just leave Gemma?"

"He wants to," said Grace.

"So why doesn't he? Do us all a favor."

"It's not as easy as that."

"Okay, so Gemma won't like it. But it's coming anyway."

"Yes," said Grace.. She spoke hesitantly, as if there was more.

"If you ask me," said Maddy, "Joe's behaving really badly. He should be straight with Gemma." Her voice rose as she found this outlet for her own anger. "What does he think he's doing, letting Gemma go on believing he loves her? Is everything just a game to him? I can't believe he can be so uncaring, and selfish, and —and—just so stupid."

"You're right," said Grace. "Of course. Only, it's more complicated than that."

"How is it more complicated?"

"Well, I'm not supposed to tell anyone."

"So don't tell me. I don't care. What difference does it make anyway? You're all right, aren't you? You've got what you want."

Tears welled up in Grace's eyes once more.

"I knew this is what would happen. I knew you'd end up hating me."

"I don't hate you," said Maddy, feeling the anger tearing at her inside. "I don't hate anyone. I just think it's all horrible and stupid and wrong."

"Sorry," said Grace. "I need another tissue."

"Get your own tissues!"

Grace gave a little gasp. Maddy stood up. It had all become unbearable. She had to get away.

She would have walked away there and then, except that Grace grabbed hold of her left wrist and wouldn't let go.

"Please, Maddy."

She started to sob.

*Who's having the bad time here?* thought Maddy. But she didn't pull her hand away from Grace's desperate grasp.

"We used to be really good friends, Maddy. Please. I need friends."

The situation was becoming ridiculous. Grace was the winner here, now and always. Grace was the one the boys wanted. But she had to have Maddy too.

"Friends don't do what you've done, Grace. Not even for a laugh. Not what you've done to me. Not what you're doing to Gemma."

"If only you knew."

"Knew what? Go on. Tell me Gemma's got terminal cancer."

"No. It's not cancer."

"So what is it?"

"Swear you won't tell a soul?"

"Yes, yes. I won't tell."

Grace let go of her hand and blew her nose with her old tissue. Then she looked up at Maddy, eyes glistening, more gorgeous than ever.

"She's pregnant."

"Oh." Maddy frowned. That changed everything. She thought, *This isn't about me anymore.* "What's she going to do?"

"Joe wants her to get rid of it. She wants to get rid of it. Mostly because she knows that's what Joe wants, and she wants to please him. But if Joe told her he was going to break up with her—you know, Gemma's not the way she comes across: she's really sly and manipulative. If she thought Joe wanted to leave her she'd go ahead and have the baby. To make him stay."

Maddy struggled to make sense of this.

"He's going on being nice to her so she'll have an abortion?"

"Yes. And like he says, that's best for Gemma too. She shouldn't be having a baby at eighteen. Not on her own."

"But she's not on her own."

"She will be."

In its crazy way it was beginning to make sense.

"You really think she'd have the baby even if she knew Joe wanted to break up with her?"

"Come on, Maddy. You know how it goes. It's the oldest trick in the book."

"So Joe has to go on pretending."

"She's almost agreed. We thought she had agreed and then she had a wobble. He's working on her."

"My God. Poor Gemma."

"Don't feel sorry for Gemma. How come you think she got pregnant in the first place? She's trying to trap Joe. Joe's trying to get out. You can't blame him for that."

"No. I suppose not."

"But you see how important it is you don't tell anyone."

"Yes."

"You see it now?"

"Yes."

"Do you still hate me?"

"A bit."

"Well, I deserve that."

She looked at Maddy with her big beautiful eyes swimming in tears, a pleading, hopeful little smile on her lips, like a lost puppy.

"You really are a bitch, Grace."

"I know."

She stood up, sensing Maddy softening, and all at once they

were in each other's arms. They hugged and sobbed and felt each other's tears on each other's cheeks until Maddy pulled out her last tissue and they shared it.

"You be good to him," Maddy said. "Even if he is a hard-hearted shit."

"And you won't give us away? Not till it's sorted?"

"I won't give you away."

They walked back through the park together.

"I promise you, Mad," said Grace, "one day we'll laugh about this together, you and me."

"And cry."

"You've been amazing. You're such a special person."

"Yeah. Tell that to Joe."

Alone once more Maddy found that she was slowly absorbing the new reality as revealed to her by Grace. Some things that had not made sense before now fell into place. Grace, who had seemed to be on her own, had a boyfriend after all. And Joe, who had seemed so eager in his emails and then not so eager when they met, Joe had just been playing a game with her.

It was hard to bear. So hard. Not just the loss of Joe. The feeling that she'd made a fool of herself.

She looked back over Joe's emails, reread through tears the phrases that had made her so happy.

*Go on the same as ever at school.*

*I hate it that it all has to be a secret.*

*I have this stupid feeling you understand me.*

Of course it all added up to nothing. She saw that now. It was the secrecy that had made it so exciting.

Just a game for Joe. He never meant to break her heart. An unkind game, perhaps. Now she would have to pretend it had all meant very little to her. Her own pride required it. No one knew she'd been in love with Joe. Only Cath and Grace. So her shame would at least not be public. That just left the heartbreak.

She decided to send Joe one last email. If he chose to think it had all been a game she didn't want to give him the satisfaction of thinking she had been fooled. She would have to go on seeing him daily right through to next summer. It was a matter of self-respect.

*I guess this is the last of our secret emails*, she wrote. *It's been fun, but all good things must come to an end. At least I've still got Cyril.*

She sent it and waited for a while for a reply, but none came. This hurt her. It would have shown generosity on his part to end their little flirtation on a friendly note. But he remained silent.

Our little flirtation.

Maddy felt the grief rising within her. She curled up on her bed and hugged Bunby close in her arms. Alone, she had no need of pride. Now came the great drowning wave of loss.

*Oh, Joe. I would have given you everything. It's taken me so long to find you. How can you be gone so quickly?*

She thought of the coming days, and it seemed to her to be impossible to live through them. *Why wake in the morning? Why open the curtains? Why eat? Why breathe?*

*I shall stay in bed in the warm and the dark until I fade into nothing. All there is left now is forgetting. There is no Joe. There is no Maddy. This girl sobbing in her bed will soon fall silent.*

*I want to die.*

Maddy felt a rush of joy at the thought. Let it all end. No more struggle. Slip away and never come back.

*Oh, Joe, I could have loved you so much.*

# 18

## Rich goes to war

On arriving at school Rich found everyone agog with the latest rumor. Mr. Pico had been sacked. Then came a counter-rumor. He had not been sacked at all, but Mr. Jury had reported him to the police. He had been caught in an indecent act. He'd been caught downloading pedophile images. The police were on their way. Mr. Pico was under arrest. He had fled the country.

No one knew exactly what was going on, but every rumor in turn was believed. All that Rich could establish for certain was that Mr. Pico had not come into school that day.

Rich flew to Mr. Pico's defense at once. He identified the smirking attackers as his own enemies. He and his teacher were allies in adversity, under assault from the same army of conformist mediocrity.

Rich needed someone to fight, to assuage his wounded pride. He decided this was his war.

"You're mad," said Max. "Everyone knows Pablo's gay."

"So why should he be sacked?"

"How do I know? Maybe he exposed himself in the library. Just keep out of it, okay? You don't want everyone saying you're gay too."

"You mean I don't want to be called a gay loser freak?"

"No way."

"What if I am a gay loser freak?"

"But you're not. Jesus, I hope you're not. Are you?"

"Might be."

Max made a theatrical jump backwards.

"You're not. You're having me on. You fancy Grace Carey. You can't be gay and fancy Grace Carey."

"I might be bisexual."

"What is this, Rich? You've gone all different."

"Thanks, Max. You noticed. Different is good."

"Yeah, okay. But not *that* different."

"Like, not gay?"

"Absolutely definitely not gay."

"You know what I think, Max? You're so shit scared of gayness, I think you must be gay."

Max went very quiet.

"Actually I was only joking," said Rich.

"How would I know if I'm gay?" said Max, looking round nervously.

"How would you know? You either like doing it with girls or you like doing it with boys. It's not rocket science."

"I just like doing it," said Max. "Or I would if I did."

They both started to laugh. This was home territory. The reluctant virgins.

After that Rich told Max how Grace had called him a gay loser freak. His fantasy was now officially over.

"Just don't tell me all the ways I'm better off without her, okay? She's still the girl of my dreams."

"Not so gay, then."

"It's a matter of pride. Have you ever seen a gay pride parade? It's fantastic. They're just so proud. You think, wow! I don't need to be the same as everyone else. I can be different and proud."

"So you want gay pride but without the gay bit?"

"Exactly."

"Even so, this backing-Pablo scheme truly sucks."

"So you're not going to join me?"

"No way, José."

"You're supposed to be my friend."

"Me? Friend? You're a gay loser freak. I don't even know you."

"I am a rock. I am an island."

Rich stole sheets of blue sugar paper and a pot of scarlet poster paint from Tiny Footsteps and made himself a sign almost a meter wide. He wrote in jagged fiery letters:

**SUPPORT MR. PICO. SIGN PETITION NOW.**

The petition was a blank new exercise book. Rich wrote at the top of the first page:

**WE THE UNDERSIGNED DEMAND THE REINSTATEMENT OF PAUL PICO TO HIS POST AT THE BEACON ACADEMY.**

He then scrawled his own slightly unconvincing signature on the line beneath.

He arrived at school carrying his rolled up sign, taking care to avoid eye contact with anyone. He calculated that word must have got round by now. Everyone would know how he had been humiliated by Grace Carey. It seemed to him from the glimpses he caught out of the corners of his eyes that people were pointing at him and exchanging amused glances. He was ready for that. He planned to give them something more to laugh about.

He unrolled his sign and pinned it to the main notice board in the Oval, obscuring the lists of teams and the announcements of forthcoming events.

## SUPPORT MR. PICO. SIGN PETITION NOW.

A small crowd gathered.

"Support Mr. Pico? What for?"

"They've sacked him."

"Why?"

"I don't know," said Rich.

"He must have done something."

"He's gay," offered one.

"Then he should be sacked," said another.

"Why?" said Rich. "What difference does it make if he's gay?"

"I don't want him groping me."

The crowd laughed.

"Why would he grope you?" said Rich. "The straight teachers don't grope the girls."

"Try standing anywhere near Mr. Bolton," said a girl.

"All right," said Rich. "Sack all the teachers."

The crowd was growing.

"Gays give you AIDS."

"He's not going to touch you, Patrick. Okay?"

"Are you gay, Rich?"

"Grow up." Rich appealed to the crowd at large. "Any of you agree with me that Mr. Pico's a great teacher, sign the petition."

He saw Maddy Fisher standing at the back of the crowd with her friend Cath Freeman. They both knew about his shame. He avoided their eyes.

"Mr. Pico's the best teacher we've got," he said to the crowd. "If we all sign the petition maybe they won't sack him."

"How many signatures have you got?"

"I've only just started."

No one came forward to sign.

"How much did Pablo pay you?"

"He doesn't even know I'm doing this," said Rich.

"So what're you doing it for, Rich? For love?"

That got a big laugh. Rich soldiered on.

"Support Mr. Pico!" he cried. "Sign the petition!"

"Rich is gay!" came a voice from the back.

Another big laugh.

"Yeah, yeah," said Rich. "Go ahead and laugh. What are you scared of?"

"I'm not scared," cried the bold voice at the back. "I don't care if Pablo gets sacked. But then, I'm not gay."

Another laugh.

Then at last there was someone pushing forward, reaching out for the exercise book. It was Cath Freeman.

"I'll sign," she said. "I think he's a good teacher."

"Great," said Rich. "Who's next?"

No one else came forward. A silence had fallen over the crowd.

Mr. Jury was approaching.

He came to a stop before the notice board and read Rich's sign in silence.

"Explain, please."

"It's to support Mr. Pico, sir," said Rich.

"Support him in what way?"

"So he doesn't get sacked, sir."

"Mr. Pico has not been sacked. Only one person can sack Mr. Pico, and that is myself. So I should know, don't you think?"

"Yes, sir."

"I have no intention of sacking Mr. Pico. So you can take down your sign and go to your classes."

"Yes, sir."

"I'm not against expressions of student opinion. There's no censorship in this school. But next time, take the trouble to get your facts right."

"Yes, sir." Rich started taking down his sign. "But sir, why isn't Mr. Pico taking classes?"

"He has requested leave of absence. For personal reasons."

That was the end of Rich's battle. The petition never got any more than the two names. The sign ended up in a school bin.


All through that day Rich brooded. Now, his cause collapsed, he found himself adrift. His reserves of courage were no longer required, his moment in the spotlight already the stuff of comic anecdotes. He realized that he had hoped in some way to share

Mr. Pico's martyrdom. Instead he was not to be persecuted at all: merely left to look foolish.

Unless Mr. Jury was lying.

Rich seized on this thought as soon as it surfaced in his mind. Perhaps the enemy was alive and well but playing a deeper game. Why would Mr. Pico request leave of absence? Surely it was more likely he had been put in an impossible position. Might it even be a euphemism for being sacked?

The only way to find out was to talk to Mr. Pico himself. But where was he? All at once Rich realized he wanted very much to find Mr. Pico. He wanted to learn why he had left the school. More than that, he wanted to talk to him. He wanted to talk about poetry and love and loss and loneliness. The things he cared about. Who else was there who had ever come anywhere near understanding?

# 19

# Eating yum-yums

On his way home after school Rich stopped at the doll's house shop. This was his sister Kitty's favorite shop in the world. It was strange being here without her. Kitty's passionate delight in the small domestic items and her dismay at their enormous prices always charged their visits with intense emotion. Rich pretended to be impatient at her endless changes of mind, her struggles to choose between a miniature bowl of fruit or a miniature shelf of books, but secretly he too entered into the dilemma. The fruit bowl should go in the kitchen, but the kitchen was already over-furnished. The books could go in the dining room, which really should be turned into a study. But the fruit was so pretty, so colorful, and would look so right on the kitchen table.

He asked about doll's house lights. The price shocked him. There followed a brief struggle, at the end of which he bought lights for three rooms, together with the kit for connecting them to the mains. The other rooms would have to wait.

Coming out onto East Street with his purchases in a paper bag, he met Maddy Fisher. She too was holding a paper bag.

"Hello, Rich," she said. "What are you doing?"

"Buying doll's house lights," said Rich.

"I've got a yum-yum," said Maddy.

Rich immediately wanted one. The bakery that sold yum-yums was close by. He took out his remaining change to see if he could afford it.

"I'm going to get one too," he said.

Maddy waited outside. When he came out they set off down East Street together.

"When are you going to eat yours?" Maddy said.

"Now."

"Where?"

"In the park, maybe."

"How about by the river?"

"Okay."

She never asked him if he wanted to eat his yum-yum with her. The river was out of his way. But he was glad of the company.

They sat down side by side on the riverbank and took out their yum-yums. For a moment, both following the same instinct, they held the sugary pastries before their eyes and did not eat.

"I've been wanting this all day," said Maddy.

"The thing about a yum-yum," said Rich, "is it's always as good as you expect it to be."

"Better."

They ate in silence, pausing only to lick the sugar crumbs off their lips and fingers. Maddy finished first.

"I can understand why people get obese," she said. "However bad things get, eating makes you feel good."

"I'm beginning to like mine less."

"The first bite's the best. Really I shouldn't have finished it."

"I shouldn't finish mine. But I'm going to."

She watched him force down the last mouthfuls.

"Do you wish you hadn't now?"

"Yes," he said.

There was something easy and companionable about sitting here with Maddy, sharing greed and remorse.

"Sorry I didn't sign your petition," she said.

"Doesn't matter. Apparently Pablo's not been sacked after all. So I end up looking stupid as usual."

"You didn't look stupid. You looked defiant. And brave."

"To be honest with you, Maddy, I don't care how I look. I've given up."

"I've had a bit of a hard time too. I've made a real fool of myself."

"I bet you haven't advertised it to the whole school."

"No."

"That's how dumb I am."

"It wasn't dumb. It was your way of saying, 'Look, I'm still standing. You've not knocked me down.'"

Rich looked at her in surprise.

"Yes," he said. "That's right."

"Me, I'm knocked down. I'm no good at fighting back."

"So what happened?"

"I don't want to talk about it. Sorry. Do you mind?"

"I don't mind. But I'll tell you what. I bet no one called you a gay loser freak."

"No. But I'm a loser all right."

"So that makes two of us. We should start a club. We could have a T-shirt."

Maddy smiled at that.

"Why were you buying doll's house lights?"

"For Kitty's doll's house. My sister."

"A doll's house with lights! Wow! Like, little bulbs hanging from the ceilings?"

Rich took out the packet and showed her.

"I wish I had a brother to do things like that for me. All I've got is a sister, and she never does anything for anybody except herself."

"I've been telling Kitty I'd do it for ages. Funny how making a total mess of your life and feeling like a total loser finally gets you to do things."

"I don't think it's funny. It makes a lot of sense to me. Being hurt makes you sensitive. You start thinking about the way other people might be hurting."

"Plus you want to feel you're not entirely useless."

"So when are you going to do the doll's house lights?"

"Soon as I get home. I have to do something or I'll start brooding."

"I brood."

"I'm going to play all my Beach Boys albums one after the other and pretend I'm surfing in California in the 1960s."

"Why?"

"I think it's called escapism."

"Oh, escapism. I want to escape. Could I come and watch? Just for a bit."

"Sure."

"I don't feel like going home quite yet. My sister and I had this argument. I don't want her starting in on me again."

Maddy phoned her mother to say she'd be back later. Then she and Rich walked through the tree-lined residential streets to Rich's house. There, as promised, Rich played the Beach Boys on the hi-fi system in his room while he lay on his stomach on the landing outside fitting the tiny lights into the doll's house.

Kitty and Mrs. Ross were out. Gran was asleep. Mr. Ross was working in his study. He appeared once to ask Rich to turn the volume down, and was introduced to Maddy, and retreated again.

"He's writing about Sparta," said Rich.

The light fitting was fiddly and difficult work and demanded Rich's total concentration. What with that and the Beach Boys there was little opportunity for conversation. Maddy was content to sit cross-legged on the floor, her back against the banisters, and drift away on the harmonies of a simpler sunnier world.

*Wouldn't it be nice to live together*
*In the kind of world where we belong . . .*

Rich found Maddy so easy to be with that he almost forgot she was there. The lighting connections were trickier than he had expected. There was a metal tape that had to be stuck to the back of the doll's house, and little sockets that had to be hammered through the tape, and tiny holes that had to be drilled for the connecting wires to pass from the room lights to the sockets.

Kitty and Mrs. Ross came back and he was still far from finished. Kitty went wild with joy.

"I love you, I love you, I love you!" she cried, kissing him as he lay on the landing. "You're the best brother I've ever had!"

"I'm Maddy," said Maddy. Rich hadn't thought to introduce her. "Rich said I could come and watch."

"I want to watch too," said Kitty. "Except I've been swimming and now I'm starving."

When the doll's house lights were working at last the whole family gathered to admire. Gran was summoned from her room where she'd fallen asleep in front of the television. Harry Ross came from Sparta. Kitty was given the honor of pressing the switch.

In the kitchen of the doll's house and in the master bedroom and in the children's bedroom the lights came on. The watching family gasped and broke into applause. The tiny lights transformed the rooms. Suddenly it seemed as if the house was inhabited by real living people, who might come back in the door at any moment and start making themselves cups of tea.

"I love it!" cried Kitty. "I love it so much I want to die!"

"Very very," said Gran.

Maddy too was enchanted.

"Now you have to do the other rooms, Rich."

"I ran out of money."

"Give him the money, Mum, give him the money," cried Kitty. "We have to do the other rooms. We have to or I'll die."

"Too much dying round here," said her father. "Moderate your desires, Kitty."

"I can't," said Kitty. "I'm too happy."

Rich caught Maddy's eye and knew she was thinking what he was thinking: how good it would be to be so easily overjoyed.

# 20

## The losers club

Maddy dreaded telling Cath but it had to be done. Cath was her partner in her love affair. Her ex-love affair.

Cath was outraged.

"You have to kill her! I'm serious. You have to smash her cute little face into a bloody pulp."

"I don't hit people, Cath."

"Now's the time to start."

"I almost wish I could."

"That is just the worst thing I've ever heard." Cath kept shaking her head. "That is so mean! I knew Grace could be mean, but that is the pits. How could they do that to you?"

"I think they thought it was all just a bit of fun."

"Fun? Love isn't fun!"

"They didn't know about that."

"You can't defend them, Mad. They're monsters. They're devils."

"I just took it all a bit too seriously," said Maddy. "It's my own fault really."

"Bollocks, Maddy Fisher. Don't be so noble."

"I'm not noble," said Maddy. "I'm unhappy."

"Oh, God! Don't cry! I'll start crying. And then my nose'll run."

They hugged each other and Maddy did her best not to cry.

"I did love him," she said. "I still do, really. I can't help it. And I don't blame him for loving Grace. She's so gorgeous."

"She's a cow," said Cath.

The more Cath took in what the two of them had done the more incensed she grew.

"You have to stop them, Maddy. What they're doing to Gemma's almost even worse than what they did to you."

"Grace says it's for Gemma's good in the end."

"She doesn't care about Gemma. She just cares about herself. I think you should tell Gemma."

"Oh, no. I can't."

"Why not?"

"Well, because of Joe."

"You owe Joe nothing, Mad."

"I know that. But even so."

It was hard to explain her feelings to Cath. Maddy felt that she was the one to blame for everything because she had allowed herself to believe Joe loved her. She had wanted it so much to be true. That alone should have warned her. The things you really want never come true. Not in the real world. But she had let herself believe in Joe's love, and now she deserved all the unhappiness she felt.

"Well, then," said Cath, "I'm going to tell her."

"No! You mustn't!"

"We can't let them carry on with their poisonous little scheme."

"Just leave them alone, Cath. Forget about it. I don't want to ever have to think about any of them ever again. Please."

"What about Grace? How am I supposed to be with her?"

"Just don't talk about it. For my sake."

"I'm through with Grace. I can tell you that right now."

"Yes, okay. But just don't make it be about me."

Cath did her best to be a loyal friend, but she found it hard.

"Don't you want to punish them, Mad? Don't you want to hurt them?"

"No. I just want to hide."

"They're the ones should be hiding. They should both be put in a bag and dropped in the river."

This conversation took place in an otherwise empty classroom, when both of them were supposed to be catching up with their course work. Maddy was quite unable to work. Since the catastrophe she had done nothing but sleep or cry, apart from eating yum-yums, and the time she had spent at Rich's house watching him work on the doll's house.

She saw Rich again at school. He told her he had tracked down where Mr. Pico had gone to hide. He had gone nowhere, and he wasn't hiding. He was at his home.

"You know the lane that goes up to the golf course? There's a fork with a track that goes left though the trees. He lives in the little house just past the fork. The one with the eyebrows."

As soon as he said that Maddy knew which house he meant. The two windows on the upper floor were topped with pointed gables that cut into the roofline just like eyebrows. It was a very pretty former farm cottage.

"I thought of an excuse to call on him. I have to give him back that book he lent me."

"Oh, yes. I've still got it."

"Could you bring it in to school tomorrow?"

"Yes, sure. Why do you want to call on him?"

"See if he's all right. See if he really did get sacked. I bet that creep Jury lied to me."

Joe Finnigan passed by. Maddy lowered her head.

"Maddy Fisher!" he called out as he passed, giving his cheery wave just as if nothing had happened.

Maddy flushed, but Rich seemed not to notice. He was following the departing figure of Joe with his eyes.

"That Joe Finnigan," he said. "He always looks like he's just woken up from this really satisfying sleep where he's been dreaming this really satisfying dream."

"Yes, he does," said Maddy, also now looking at the distant Joe. "That's a good description."

Cath came hobbling over to join them. She had a blister on the back of her right heel.

Rich thanked her for signing his petition.

"How many signatures did you get in the end?"

"Two."

"You mean I doubled the petition?"

"You did."

They all laughed.

"I just hated the way they were all making a joke out of what you were doing," said Cath. "And I don't care what they think of me anyway."

"You can join our club," said Rich. "We're going to get T-shirts saying LOSER."

"It has to be really exclusive," said Maddy. "We don't want all the riffraff in."

"Certainly not," said Rich. "Only genuine, certified losers."

Max Heilbron joined them. He was eating a packet of crisps.

"I'd offer them round," he said, "but I want them all for myself."

"Also you need feeding up," said Cath.

"Small is beautiful," retorted Max.

"Then you can't join our club. Can he, Rich?"

"No, I think Max can join."

"What club?"

"The losers club. It's seriously exclusive. We're going to have a T-shirt."

"You know what?" said Rich. "I think we should have two levels in the club. Ordinary members would have T-shirts saying LOSER. But the really top losers would have T-shirts saying GAY LOSER FREAK."

"Like a gold card."

"Or going first class."

"Now wait a minute here, guys," said Max. "I can see why me and Rich count as losers. But how's Maddy a loser?"

"I notice you don't mention me," said Cath.

"Trust me," said Maddy. "I'm a loser."

"You sure you're not just saying that to impress me?"

"Hey! Hey!" said Cath. "This is all getting out of control. Back to basics, guys. How to spot a loser." She pointed at her own face. "Ugly mug." She pointed at Max. "Little creep."

"That's nice," said Max, offended.

"The rest of you are just self-pitying phoneys."

So long as she was joking about her misery Maddy could cope. But as soon as the ordinary life of the school resumed, the misery rose up and burst its bounds and threatened to drown her. All the public places in the school were danger zones:

she did not want to meet Joe or Grace. Even when they were nowhere in sight their spirits hung over classroom and library, sports hall and dining hall. She found her copy of *Hay Fever* while rooting in her bag, and at once saw, with unbearable clarity, the Joe she had so loved, sitting in the dance studio, book in hand, speaking his lines with his easy smile. And there was Grace responding, "Abnormal, Simon—that's what we are, abnormal." And everyone was laughing.

Going home reminded her of Joe too. There outside the shop was Cyril the camel, who had always been her friend. But now he belonged to Joe, and to the memories that gave her pain. Once indoors there was Imo, who was going out with Joe's brother, and who had still not forgiven Maddy for the bad things she had said about Leo. One more week and the college term would begin and Imo at least would be gone.

"I don't know why you told all those lies," said Imo. "Leo's talked to Joe and he knows nothing about it. Nothing at all. I don't understand. What have you got against Leo?"

"Forget it, okay? It doesn't matter."

"But why did you do it?"

"I don't know. I just did. Leave me alone."

She dug out the copy of *The Art of Loving*, but didn't read any more of it. Who needed the art when there was no one to love? She took it with her to school the next day and gave it back to Rich.

"How did you get along with it?" he asked her.

"I only read a few pages. It's a bit too theoretical for me."

"I thought it was really good once, but now I can't remember why."

"When are you going to see Mr. Pico?"

"I don't know. Maybe today."

"Tell him we're all really sorry the play got cancelled."

Maddy wasn't sorry at all now. It would have been impossible for her to go on rehearsing with Joe and Grace now that everything had changed.

"You know what?" said Rich. "It's a bit tricky me calling on Pablo, what with all this gay thing going round. But if you wanted to come too, that would be different."

"Like, as your chaperone?"

"Yes, in a way."

"Well, I suppose I could."

Maddy wasn't greatly interested in seeing Mr. Pico, but she was finding she liked hanging out with Rich. Somehow, presumably because he too had been hurt by Grace, he was the only person who didn't annoy her. Even Cath could be annoying because she continued to be so angry over what had happened.

"Look at them!" she would hiss at Maddy whenever Grace or Joe passed by. "They've no shame! Let's go and spit on them!"

So Maddy agreed to go with Rich as his chaperone and visit Mr. Pico. It would be a couple more hours away from Cyril's pitying smile.

# 21

# Mr. Pico's secret

On the way to Mr. Pico's house they talked about their favorite films. In a concession to honesty Maddy admitted she still loved *The Sound of Music*. Rich said his best film ever was *Once Upon A Time in the West*. He explained the long opening sequence waiting for the train.

"What's good about that?" said Maddy.

"It's amazing. Wait till you see it. The music's great too. Everything Ennio Morricone ever wrote was great. It's lyrical and strange, both at the same time. Like Philip Larkin. Do you know Larkin's poems?"

"Not really, no."

"Larkin is one of my gods."

He quoted from memory:

"Strange to know nothing, never to be sure

Of what is true or right or real."

Maddy didn't mind that Rich knew things she didn't know. He was no threat to her, he was just this strange boy she found it easy to talk to, maybe because they'd both been wounded in the same war. Somehow he existed outside her social world, so she didn't really concern herself with what opinion he had of her, and she never asked herself what opinion she had of him. She liked it that he had all these eccentric tastes, if only because Morricone and Larkin and the Beach Boys had played no part in her life so far, and so triggered no hurtful memories.

"Do you really read poetry, Rich? I mean, other than for class?"

"Yes."

"Why?"

"It puts into words things you feel." Then, after a pause, "If I thought everyone who'd ever existed was like the idiots at school I'd kill myself."

"Why do you want to be different to everyone else?"

"Why would I want to be them? All they talk about is football and cars. All they want is tits and booze."

Maddy laughed.

"And you don't?"

"Well, I wouldn't complain. But is that it? Is that how big your dream gets?"

"Even so, Rich. You really should get yourself a phone."

"What's that got to do with anything?"

"You can't just live in your own world."

"Yes, I can. And anyway, it's not just me. I've got Philip Larkin and Bob Dylan and Janis Joplin and William Blake."

"But they're all dead."

"Dylan's not dead."

"You're strange."

"Thank you. I take that as a compliment."

They had been walking up the road to the golf course. Now they arrived at the cottage where Mr. Pico was reputed to live.

Rich approached the door, and then hesitated.

"Do you think he'll mind?"

"I don't think he's in," said Maddy.

All the window curtains were drawn.

"Maybe he's committed suicide."

"Jesus, Rich! Don't say things like that."

"I don't want to stumble over his rotting corpse. I'm squeamish about things like that."

"Honestly."

Maddy knocked on the door herself.

"You read too many books. Being different's okay. Being creepy's not okay."

"Nor is being ordinary," said Rich, nettled.

"I'm not ordinary. Are you saying I'm ordinary?"

"What's not ordinary about you?"

"Well, I'm here with you, for a start."

"True. There's hope for you yet."

There came a shuffling sound from the other side of the door. A cross voice called out, "Who is it?"

"It's me, sir," said Rich. "I've brought your book back."

"What me? What book?"

"Richard Ross, sir. The Erich Fromm book."

There was a silence, then the sound of the bolt being withdrawn. The door opened to reveal Mr. Pico wearing what looked like a nightdress. He stared at them, eyes blinking through his thick lenses.

He pointed an accusing finger at Maddy.

"There's another one."

"Maddy came with me so that . . ."

Rich couldn't think of a good reason for Maddy to be there other than the true reason, so he allowed the sentence to tail away into nothing.

"I wanted to be sure you were all right," said Maddy.

"Oh," said Mr. Pico. He frowned at Maddy. "And am I all right?"

"Yes," said Maddy. "I think."

"It's not a nightdress, you know. It's a djellaba. Men wear them in Morocco. Perfectly normal."

"Yes, sir," said Rich.

Mr. Pico gazed at them in silence for a moment.

"Well, you might as well come in," he said.

They followed him into a tiny hallway. He shut and bolted the door behind them. Rich met Maddy's eyes: had they walked in to some kind of trap?

Mr. Pico led them into what had once been a living room. Here in curtained gloom stood a single armchair with a powerful reading lamp leaning over it and a table beside it. On the table stood a bottle of wine, a glass, and two bowls. One bowl contained olives, the other held the pits from the olives. The rest of the room was completely filled with stacks of books and magazines. Some stacks were low, no more than four or five books; but some were great buttressed towers, walls of books reaching up to the ceiling, supported by heaped-up mounds of magazines, mainly copies of *The New York Review of Books*.

Mr. Pico stood frowning at the room, suddenly made aware of its limitations.

"I'm afraid there isn't really anywhere for you to sit," he said.

"Yes, there is," said Maddy. "Look. We can make stools out of the magazines."

She chose a pile of magazines of a suitable height and sat down.

"So you can. Would you think me very rude if I take my usual chair?"

"Of course not. This is your home."

Rich listened to Maddy with surprise. She was handling things so well.

Mr. Pico sat in his chair. Rich followed Maddy's example and sat on a pile of *New York Reviews*.

"I expect it will sound ridiculous to you," said Mr. Pico, "but I find one of the greatest pleasures in an otherwise unsatisfactory world is sitting in a comfortable chair."

He reached out for an olive, ate it, and discreetly transferred the pit from his mouth to the bowl.

"Would you like an olive?"

They both shook their heads.

"So you came to see if I'm all right, did you? I call that very civic of you. There was a time when one would have called it Christian. Concern for others, now seen as the function of the state. Yes, I am all right."

He smiled at them and nodded and they understood that he had decided to be pleased by their coming.

"No one's said why you left, sir," said Rich. "Are you coming back?"

"No. I am not coming back."

"Rich started a petition," said Maddy. "To support you."

"Did he? How many signatures did you get?"

"Not many," said Rich. "The Head stopped me. He said you'd requested leave of absence for personal reasons."

"This is perfectly true."

"Oh." Rich couldn't hide his disappointment. "I thought Mr. Jury was just telling me a lie to make me stop."

"You don't have a high opinion of Mr. Jury?"

"I think he's a loathsome creep," said Rich.

"A little harsh." But his eyes twinkled with amusement. "He did his best to tolerate my eccentricities. He never asked me to go. But nor did he urge me to stay."

"I wish you'd come back," said Rich. "And so does Maddy."

"Yes, I do," said Maddy.

Mr. Pico sighed.

"There are difficulties," he said. "There have been complaints. It seems my teaching methods aren't appreciated. And there have been suggestions that I'm a danger to the students." He shook his head a little sadly. "All quite hurtful in their way."

"But it's nonsense," said Rich.

"So it is. But as Socrates learned, it's not enough to be in the right. Sometimes the delusions of the crowd are too powerful to be overcome. Also, you know, one does rather want to be wanted."

"You are wanted."

"How many signatures did you get?"

"I'd have got more if I'd gone on."

"Mr. Pico's right, Rich," said Maddy. "Most of our class don't get you, sir. They think you're strange."

"Is that a euphemism, Maddy?"

"Sir?"

"You're telling me they think I'm gay."

Maddy hesitated. Then, "Yes, sir."

"Since you've taken the trouble to call on me to return my book"—he tapped the book on his lap—"the least I can do is satisfy your curiosity. Please prepare your young minds for a shock. You see before you a man with no sexual feelings of any kind whatsoever. Am I gay? I have no idea. Perhaps. I have felt strong affections in my life for young men. But sexual interest, no. I am as neuter as a spayed cat."

He smiled at them and ate another olive.

"Right," said Rich.

There was a silence.

"Yes, I know," said Mr. Pico, "it is all very embarrassing. It contravenes something fundamental in human nature. But there it is. I'm sure you feel very sorry for me. My deformity does come with a cost, of course. I live alone. I am alone. But that apart, I must ask you to believe that in my own way I live a rich, varied, and rewarding life."

"I suppose," said Maddy, "it lets you get on with other things." She looked round the book-crowded room. "Like reading."

"Like reading indeed," said Mr. Pico. "And reading, you know, is the greatest *other thing* there is. Reading is the whole world."

"But you should go on teaching, sir," said Rich.

"How many signatures, Rich?"

"That doesn't mean anything."

"I prefer to teach those that want to be taught. Why should I impose my eccentricities on those who don't find any benefit in them? I shall find a square hole somewhere for my square peg."

"I want to be taught by you, sir."

"So do I," said Maddy.

"Well, then," said Mr. Pico. "Here we are. Who needs a school?"

He picked up the wine bottle and filled his glass. He was about to raise the glass to his lips when he recalled his guests.

"What am I thinking of? There you see the force of solitary habit in action. It has made me impolite. Let me offer you both a drink. A glass of white wine?"

"Yes, thanks," said Maddy.

"All right," said Rich. "Thanks."

Mr. Pico left the room in search of glasses. Rich and Maddy spoke in whispers.

"First teacher who ever offered me a drink," said Maddy.

"We're not in school now."

"He's sweet."

"And a bit sad," said Rich.

Mr. Pico returned and filled two more glasses. He raised his own glass in a toast.

"Here's to other things," he said.

After a few sips of wine all three of them loosened up. Rich got off his pile of magazines, which had started to make his back ache, and sat down on the floor leaning against the door. Maddy rearranged herself sitting cross-legged. Mr. Pico opened the book Rich had returned to him and turned the pages looking for a particular passage.

"I hope you got a whiff of just how radical Fromm can be," he said. He read aloud: "'While one is consciously afraid of not being loved, the real though usually unconscious fear is that of loving.'"

He lowered the book and peered at them.

"Interesting, no?"

"But I'm not afraid of loving," said Maddy. "I'm just afraid of not being loved back."

"You don't find that love generates love?"

"No. Not at all."

"Nor do I," said Rich. "I'd say it's just the opposite. Loving someone makes them not want to love you."

"Oh, dear," said Mr. Pico. "So how is this love business to be managed at all?"

They talked of love and books until the bottle of wine was finished. Mr. Pico did not offer them any more.

"In the light of the rumors about me," he said, "perhaps you should not be seen to stay for too long."

They shook his offered hand and thanked him. He saw them to the front door.

"I shall probably go south," he said. "I feel the need of sunshine."

The bolt slid closed on the door behind them. They made

their way back down the road in silence. As they turned into the lower end of the High Street Maddy looked back up the hillside to the little cottage.

"I think he's amazing," she said. "I wish I'd paid more attention in his classes."

"He's the only real teacher I've ever had."

The shared experience of Mr. Pico's eccentric room and his wine and his conversation made them feel oddly intimate.

"He was funny about love," said Maddy. "About people being afraid of loving."

"I agree with you!" said Rich. "I'm more afraid of not being loved back."

"Do you still think about Grace?"

"Sometimes."

"Do you hate her?"

"No."

"Do you still love her?"

"In a way." He sounded sheepish. "I know that's pathetic."

"No. I understand. Exactly."

Maddy was thinking how in spite of everything she still thought of Joe, and he still seemed to her to be perfect.

"I had a crush on someone and it didn't work out. But I can't stop myself thinking about him."

"Who was it?"

"Joe Finnigan."

"Oh, well. I'm not surprised you went for him. He's cool but he's sunny, if you know what I mean."

"Yes. I know what you mean."

Maddy felt grateful to Rich for understanding about Joe. Of course he knew nothing about the terrible way Joe had treated her, or that his own beloved Grace was Joe's secret girlfriend. But even so, he was generous about Joe where he could have been spiteful.

"It wasn't much of anything," she said.

"I never really got beyond the wishful thinking stage."

"Me neither," said Maddy. "Oh, God. Why does it all have to be so difficult?"

They came to the parting of the ways.

"Listen, Mad," said Rich. "You remember my gran's party, that I wrote those stupid letters to Grace about?"

"I remember the pope bit."

"My mum wants me to get someone to help hand round the food and drinks. I was wondering if you'd do it."

"I don't see why not. When is it?"

"Lunchtime Saturday."

"Yes, okay."

"Great."

Then, as she was walking away, "Don't I get a letter from the pope too?"

# 22

# Maddy has monster thoughts

Maddy's father's return from China was not a success. Perhaps Maddy had expected too much. She came home from school to find him in the carver chair with the broken arm, his legs stretched out and his eyes closed. He looked thinner and paler than she had remembered. Her first thought was: *I don't know this man.* He had been away two months, not long really. But this time his return home felt incomplete.

"Dad! You're back!"

He heaved himself upright and opened his eyes.

"Maddy. How's my little Madkin?"

She kissed him and pulled a chair round so she could sit facing him.

"You must be so jet-lagged. Do you feel awful?"

"Almost as bad as I look. Can't seem to stay awake."

"It's good you're back, Dad. It doesn't feel right here without you."

He had always looked young to her before, young for a father, but now he looked old. Maybe it had never been his looks so much as his manner, his easygoing way of making light of life's troubles. His smiling shrug alone somehow made Maddy feel nothing could ever go badly wrong. But the bounce had left him now.

Imo was away with friends. Maddy did her best to make the evening into a celebration, but her father was tired and her mother out of spirits.

"Jen has passed on the joyful news," he said. "It seems that we're broke."

"I didn't say that," said Maddy's mother. "I said we're almost broke. As far as I can tell."

"In the words of the Buddha," he smiled at Maddy, his eyelids drooping with fatigue, "this too shall pass."

"All I know about the Buddha," said his wife, "is that you bought two stone Buddhas which cost over a thousand pounds in freight charges alone and they've still not sold."

"Take it easy, Mum," said Maddy. "He's only just got back."

"Things have a way of sorting themselves out," said her father.

With that he rose from the table and gave an ironic salute.

"Over and out. See everyone in the morning. Tomorrow is another day."

Maddy was left alone with her mother.

"Is it really that bad, Mum?"

"Oh, I suppose not. It's just that these things that have a way of sorting themselves out, it's me who has to sort them out. And I don't see how I'm going to do it anymore."

"Won't it be easier now Dad's home?"

Maddy's mother gazed at her in silence for a moment.

"Let's hope so," she said.

Maddy retreated to her room early. Alone in her room her thoughts strayed from her father to Joe. The trouble with men, it seemed to her, is that they were lazy. They did whatever they felt like at the time. Joe had a problem with Gemma and he thought he'd found a neat way out of it so he just went ahead. It was only a game, nothing serious, except he never took the trouble to think what it might be like from her end. No, it just suited him to assume she'd take it lightheartedly too. Not the worst crime in the world, just thoughtless, careless.

Loveless.

Boys don't do love.

The simple truth struck Maddy with the force of revelation. Boys aren't equipped to love. That's why we can never get it right with boys. We think they have the ability to love and mostly choose not to. But what if they just can't?

That would explain why they go on and on about sex. Sex is the only kind of love they know. They can touch sex. They can feel it. It's something that happens to them without them having to take the trouble to know anything about the other person.

She can be Amy-the-bunny for all they care. They don't need names or faces. Sex is love without the complication of other people. Sex is love without the love.

She phoned Cath.

"Hey, sweetie. I'm having monster thoughts. I think quite possibly I'm having a breakdown."

"Wow! That's so cool! Do you think you'll have to check in to the Priory?"

"Why have I always been so prejudiced against hard drugs?"

"Mad, this is so wild! Shall we both turn into smack heads and become addicted and die in a toilet?"

"That's *it*, Cath. That's so *it*. Self-destruction. I can relate to that."

"Or we could go shoplifting and get caught. It's a well-known cry for help."

"Or we could just cry for help."

"Oh, Mad. I'll hear your cry. What happened?"

"I don't know. Dad came home. I suppose I thought he'd be able to make everything be all right, but he can't."

"Don't go relying on men, Mads."

"But it's not because men are bad. They're not bad. They just don't really care. That's my monster thought. That's why love never works. Boys don't care."

"What, all boys?"

"All of them."

"You don't think some of them might be okay?"

"I don't know a single one who's even remotely okay."

"How about Rich?"

"Rich is different. He's a friend. Like you're a friend. Friends are basically female."

"So Rich is female."

"Sort of. You know what I mean."

"Except he's actually male."

"Yes, but you don't think of having sex with Rich."

"No. I suppose not."

"So anyway, if boys don't really care then I don't see why I should care either. So I can have sex with anyone I want and never even see their face."

"Really?" Cath sounded intrigued but incredulous. "With a total stranger?"

"The stranger the better. That way it's just for the sex. That way him not caring won't matter because I won't care either."

The ideas came as the words formed in her mouth. What was so liberating about talking with Cath was that she could say things she maybe didn't really mean just to see how it felt saying them.

"If it's just for the sex, the sex had better be worth it," said Cath. "If all you want is to get fucked it'd better be a good fuck."

Trust Cath to get down and dirty.

"Maybe all I want is to get fucked." It was fun saying the words, but even as she said them Maddy knew it wasn't true. "Damn Joe Finnigan. This is all his fault."

"And Grace's."

"I could become a nun instead."

"Or a lesbian."

"What's the point of being a lesbian? I never did get that one. Girls are friends. The whole point of friends is you don't mess things up with sex."

"You know what, Mad? All these things you're saying, these are things I think all the time."

"Are they?"

"Being me is different to being you."

"So do you spend your whole time feeling angry and miserable and like your whole life's meaningless and the world's going wronger every day?"

"My whole time."

"Jesus, Cath. I didn't know. I thought it was all, like, a joke."

"No. Not really."

"You're supposed to be my best friend and I didn't know. That's terrible. That's what Joe did to me. He thought it was just a bit of fun. I've been behaving like a boy. Maybe I'm a boy."

"So. It's complicated."

Preparing to go to bed that evening, Maddy found that her period had started. Every month it took her by surprise. Other people had cramps or mood swings or just felt it in their bodies, but Maddy never felt a thing. She was grateful for that, but she still felt somehow wrong-footed by her body, as if it had its own plans and saw no need to consult her about them.

Now she had a decision to make. If she was going to take the pill, now was the time to start.

She took the white and green box out of its hiding place and gazed at it, as if the sight of it would somehow focus her thoughts. Back then, in that long-lost age in which she had visited the health center and obtained the prescription, it had all been for the sake of Joe Finnigan. She blushed, even though she was alone in her room. Back then the white and green box had promised the ultimate closeness with Joe. But it turned out they never even had so much as a kiss.

No point in starting taking the pills, then. Leave it till there looked like some chance of action. In some unimaginable future, with some unimaginable boy.

On the other hand, should that opportunity arise, it would be awkward to have to wait for weeks before acting on it. Sometimes you just had to hold your nose and jump. Plus, taking the pill would clear up her complexion and regulate her periods. What was there to worry about other than mood swings, weight gain, breast tenderness, nausea, and headaches?

As Cath would say, it's complicated.

Maddy took out a green card of pills. Twenty-one little yellow pills in twenty-one day-named bubbles. Then seven pill-free days. In the land of contraception every month was twenty-eight days long, like living in a perpetual February. Once you start you have to keep on taking them or it doesn't work. Imagine taking a pill every night for a year and then forgetting, and next morning you're pregnant. That is so brutal. That is so unforgiving. You'd think all those pills piled up inside you, getting more and more effective; but no, forget one and all the pills you've taken in all your life are a waste of time. You'd think they'd have come up with a system that let you mess up from time to time. So now there was something else to worry about for the foreseeable future, along with boyfriends, exams, financial crises, global warming, and the meaninglessness of life.

Anyway, the whole idea made her feel like a fraud. Worse, like a joke. Look at Maddy, all ready to rock'n'roll, but no one's playing the music. Seriously, what's the point?

And yet all the time she knew deep down she was going to do it. It was her small act of faith in the future. Some unexamined superstition whispered that just taking the pill would change her. Her body would know it could go all the way without consequences and would behave differently. She might even become sexy. The boys would sense it. Like a taxi with its light on. And who knew? Maybe one day Joe would send her another email.

She popped the first pill out of its bubble and swallowed it down with water from her tooth mug.

There. She'd started.

Life would be different from now on.

# 23

# Gran's eightieth birthday party

"You're looking very well, Richard," said Great-Uncle Freddy, standing straight as a ramrod in the small living room. "I can see you're admiring my suit. I expect you're asking yourself how much it cost. Tailoring like this, £2,000 at least, eh? Guess again!"

"I don't really know how much suits cost," said Rich.

"£350! How about that? Took the wind out of your sails, eh?" He dropped his voice to a whisper. "Hong Kong. Do it all over the Internet. There, I've told you now."

Great-Uncle Freddy smoothed his white hands down over the lapels of his pale gray suit and nodded his head at Rich. He was in his late seventies, tall, slender, distinguished.

"I'm going to pass on the secret of my success, Richard. You're a young man now. You need to know these things. You may want to write it down. Three little words. Posture. Tailoring. And silence."

He raised his chin and widened his eyes, fixing Rich with a keen unblinking gaze.

"Thank you," said Rich.

"Stand tall. Wear well-cut suits. And say nothing. You'll rule the world. Look at me. I retired on a two-thirds final salary pension scheme as vice president of public affairs to the second-largest medical equipment importer in the country."

"I'd better get on and help Mum."

"You do that, my boy. And if those sausages are ready I'd be happy to test drive a couple or three."

Rich crossed the hall to the kitchen, where Sue Prior, immense and imperturbable, was grilling sausages and baking potatoes.

"Not time yet, is it?" she said.

"No. Not yet." He sneaked a sausage.

"You leave those alone."

His father's sister, Mary Harness, found him there.

"Rich," she whispered, beckoning him into the passage. "I have a very special present for Mum, but I don't think she'll be able to work it on her own. It's a Bose sound system. Between you and me it cost £650, so I want to make sure she understands what to do with it. When is she going to be opening her presents?"

"After lunch, I think," said Rich.

"Peter and I simply have to be off by four. The truth is I shouldn't be here at all. I'm missing the first day of the company retreat, which raised quite a few eyebrows, believe me. And Peter's never got a spare minute as usual."

John Staples, a cousin of sorts, a man of indeterminate age, was loitering by the back door.

"I say, Richard," he murmured, his eyes drifting from side to side without ever quite settling. "What's your parents' line on smoking in the house?"

"They don't really like it, I'm afraid."

"Very understandable. I'll pop outside. Pain relief, you know. I get these spasms of pain."

Peter Harness, Mary's husband, was sitting before the unlit fire in the front room grimly reading the newspaper. In the schoolroom Rich's mother was playing the piano and rehearsing the Tiny Footsteps in their song for one last time, watched by a smattering of parents. Kitty was at work painting a birthday card on the schoolroom table. Geoffrey and Carol Mudford, friends and contemporaries of Gran, sat side by side on the bench in the hall so as not to be in anyone's way. Gran herself had not yet come down.

The doorbell rang. Geoffrey Mudford opened the door. It was Maddy Fisher.

"I've come to help," she said.

Kitty saw her through the schoolroom door and stared with unabashed curiosity.

"Rich!" she yelled, not leaving her paints.

Rich appeared.

"Thank God you made it," he said. "It's murder here."

"What do you want me to do?"

"The party's not supposed to start for at least another half an hour. You know what would be really helpful? Talk to the ghastly old relatives. Keep them off Mum's back."

"Okay. I'll do my best."

Rich's father, Harry, came down the stairs from his first-floor study, accidentally treading on Carol Mudford's foot as he passed.

"Me and my big feet," said Carol Mudford with a tinkly laugh.

"Hello," he said to Maddy. "I expect I should know you but I don't."

"Maddy Fisher. I'm a friend of Rich's. I've come to help."

"Oh, good. I've been told to make a speech. I'm not to mention Sparta."

Geoffrey Mudford nodded at Maddy in a friendly way.

"Known Dorrie since I was your age," he said. "She was such a pretty girl."

Carol Mudford laughed her tinkling little laugh again.

"Geoff would've married her if she'd have had him," she said. "But she told him no thanks, so he had to make do with me."

The Tiny Footsteps came trooping by to be let out into the garden to run about. John Staples was stretched out on a garden chair smoking an odd-shaped cigarette.

"Pooh! Pooh!" cried the Tiny Footsteps. "There's a funny smell out here."

Rich's mother smiled inattentively at Maddy.

"I'm Maddy. A friend of Rich's?"

"Oh, yes. He said. It's so good of you to help out. Harry, we're going to have to move the piano. Maybe you and Peter could manage it between you."

Mary Harness intercepted Rich's mother.

"Joanna, about the presents. Will Mummy be opening them as she gets them or later?"

"I've really no idea."

"It's just that I've bought her something that will need some explaining, and we have to be on the road by four at the absolute latest."

Rich's mother moved on, distracted.

Mary Harness's thwarted gaze fell on Maddy.

"You can't imagine how much trouble I had persuading Peter to come today. At times like these you can't afford to take your eye off the ball for one second."

The back door opened and closed, letting in a sweet smoky smell. John Staples hovered before Maddy, one hand stroking his long graying hair.

"Don't mind if I pop outside from time to time," he said. "I get these spasms of pain. Have done for years."

"Oh. I'm sorry."

"Doctors can do nothing, of course."

"Is it very bad?"

"Like having six-inch nails hammered into your skull. Just about here." He indicated his temples.

Rich and his father passed by on their way to the schoolroom to move the piano. Rich threw Maddy a glance that said, *Can you bear it?* She smiled back.

Great-Uncle Freddy ambled into view.

"Hello, John," he said. "Hello, young lady. Don't tell me who you are, I'll only forget. I'm Fred, Dorothy's baby brother. I'm told there are sausages. Have you seen them?"

"No, not so far. Do you want me to go and look for you?"

"Maybe it's too early. One has to go by the house rules, you know. Tell me, my dear. Would you say I was overdressed?"

"No. Not at all."

"I thought I should fly the flag. But casual's the word these days. Of course, you do have to have the figure for it."

Maddy looked blank.

"For tailoring, I mean. I've been the same weight for fifty years. Nothing to boast about, just one of those things. But it does mean, whatever else I can't do, I can wear a decent whistle and flute."

Rich reappeared and squeezed his way between Uncle Fred and the Mudfords.

"Mad, come and help carry chairs. All the chairs in the schoolroom are tiny."

Maddy helped carry chairs. The Mudfords found they were

in the way and went into the schoolroom to stand unobtrusively in the place where Maddy needed to put down chairs. Then she and Rich pinned up a banner made of fuzzy felt that said: DOROTHY—80 YEARS YOUNG.

The schoolroom was bright with primary colors. The paint-spattered creations of the Tiny Footsteps pinned to the walls gave the room an air of childish chaos.

The Mudfords retreated to the corner where the larger stuffed animals were heaped.

Kitty finished her card.

"What on earth is it?" said Rich.

"It's Gran's six suitors," said Kitty. "Look. It's obvious. And that's Gran, picking the winner."

The figures were all simplified versions of fashion models, so both Gran and her six suitors were tall and slender. Gran was pointing to the winner with a long stick.

"I couldn't make her arm long enough to reach," said Kitty.

Now that her birthday card was done Kitty attached herself to Maddy.

"I'll tell you who everyone is," she said. "The one with the shiny face is my aunt Mary. We have to call her just Mary."

Mary Harness took Maddy to be the hired help.

"You see the man reading the newspaper? That's my husband Peter. Get him some sausages, will you? He gets so grumpy if he doesn't eat at one o'clock sharp."

"Right away," said Maddy.

"So, Kitty," said Mary Harness. "You must be very proud of your grandmother."

"Yes, I am."

"I expect it gets to be a bit of a nuisance sometimes, having her live with you. But then, Harry and Joanna have got the house. There's no way you could afford a house this size on Harry's salary."

"It's okay," said Kitty. "We love Gran."

Gran herself now descended in her stair-lift, wearing a maroon wool dress and a pearl necklace. The local guests were starting to arrive. It was party time.

Rich's mother unlocked the back door and let the Tiny Footsteps in from the garden. John Staples followed, feeling the walls. Rich's father was found to have gone back to his first-floor study and had to be fetched. Sue Prior declared the baked potatoes cooked. Rich and Maddy and Kitty carried the sausages and potatoes through to the schoolroom.

Gran sat in the only armchair nodding and smiling as her presents piled up on one side. The Tiny Footsteps lined up in front of the piano. Geoffrey and Carol Mudford sat down in children's armchairs so as not to get in the way. Great-Uncle Freddy gave Gran a birthday kiss.

"There, big sister. From your little brother."

Mary Harness counted the presents and looked at her watch. "Shouldn't we be starting, Joanna?"

"Have we got everyone? Where's Peter?"

"Oh, he's perfectly happy reading the paper. You know he hates parties."

Sue Prior was summoned from the kitchen. John Staples sat down and put his arms round a large white teddy bear. The Mudfords discovered they were wedged in their undersize armchairs but said nothing, not wanting to make a fuss. Rich, Maddy, and Kitty stood by the door.

Mrs. Ross called out in a clear and sprightly voice, "Ready, children?"

She struck up the introduction on the piano and the Tiny Footsteps started to sing.


"I love you, a bushel and a peck

A bushel and a peck

A hug around the neck

A hug around the neck and a barrel and a heap

A barrel and a heap and I'm talking in my sleep

About you—about you—"


As they sang they mimed the words, pointing to themselves for "I," to their hearts for "love" and to Gran for "you." The shrill voices, the flurry of gestures, and the largely unintelligible words baffled the audience.

"A what and a what?" said Mary Harness.

The chorus consisted mainly of "Doodle-oodle-oodle" and did not make matters clearer. But Gran and the Mudfords adored it, their lips moving with the familiar lines.

Maddy watched the cluster of infants gesturing "I love you" so fiercely and felt a pang of nostalgia for her own childhood. When you were little it was so easy to say "I love you." So easy to feel.

The song ended. The audience applauded. John Staples cried out, "Spiffing! Spiffing!" Great Uncle Fred offered to make a speech of thanks. "Just a few words, you know. Used to be rather one of my things, speeches."

"Rich," said Mrs. Ross, "I've got some little presents to give the children as they go."

"Boys and girls!" proclaimed Great-Uncle Fred. "Your charming young voices do honor to my dear sister. I'm sure that if she could find the words, allowing for the sad nature of her illness, and let no one deny . . ."

The Tiny Footsteps, their homage paid, were filing out of the room, taking their presents from Rich as they went.

"Best if I pop out too," said John Staples, standing up and fumbling in his pocket.

"Mummy darling," said Mary Harness, "would you like your presents now?"

"First Harry has to make his speech," said Mrs. Ross. "Then Gran has to cut her cake."

"A speech *and* a cake!" Mary Harness looked at her watch.

Maddy took round more sausages. Rich refilled empty glasses. His father made a speech.

"Happy birthday, Mummy," he began.

"Dear Tom," said Gran.

"Eighty years today," went on Harry Ross. "We're all so proud of you. I've been told not to mention Sparta, but the Spartans do come into it in a way. They were the first mature society to educate girls as well as boys. As you know, Mummy read History at Girton just after the war."

"Quite true," said Great-Uncle Fred. "Dorothy was the brains in the family."

"The brains are still there," said Harry Ross, smiling at his mother. "You may not be able to find the words anymore. But I know Mary would agree with me on this. You've been our role model. We've followed where you led. You're a very great lady, Mum. And we love you."

After a short surprised silence everyone clapped.

"First class, Harry," said Mary Furness. "Short and to the point."

"Perhaps this is the moment," began Great-Uncle Fred.

Sue Prior entered bearing the birthday cake, all aglow with eighty shimmering candles. The party cheered.

Gran blew out the candles and cut the cake. Peter Harness appeared and said to his wife in a voice of barely controlled savagery, "If you don't come now I'm going without you." Mary Harness hurriedly unwrapped her present herself and thrust it at Gran, saying, "It's a sort of a radio, Mummy. It's madly expensive so do take care of it. You'd never believe how much it cost.'

The Mudfords, who had been trying furtively for some time now to get out of their chairs, suddenly toppled over sideways, one after the other, blocking the doorway. Mary Harness stepped over them, waving her farewells as she went. In the hall, John Staples was slumped in Gran's stair-lift, fast asleep. Great-Uncle Fred found his way to the kitchen where Sue Prior was washing up and told her what he would have said in honor of his sister had the moment ever arisen.

In the quiet time that followed, Mrs. Ross sat herself down at the piano and began to play Gran's old favorites from memory.

"Come along, Harry. You know this one."

She and Harry sang together, both very well. They sang "Danny Boy," knowing how much Gran loved it, and Gran sat nodding and smiling with tears in her eyes. Then Rich and Kitty joined their parents at the piano and they all sang "My Curly-Headed Baby."

Maddy watched in wonder. There was no self-consciousness in their singing, for all the old-fashioned and sentimental words. It was obviously something they'd done many times before. They all sang well in their own way.


"Oh my baby, my curly-headed baby
I'll sing you fast asleep and love you so as I sing

Oh my baby, my curly-headed baby
Just tuck your head like little bird
Beneath its mammy's wing . . ."

Maddy found herself studying Rich's face as he sang. He seemed to her in this moment to be so true and so good that she wanted to hug him. The whole family party in all its confusion and absurdity touched a deep emotion within her. It was something to do with the wordless old lady at the center of it all, and with the way everyone was so nice to her; and something to do with human frailty and the way life went on anyway. It felt like some kind of love. But what? This family was unremarkable, much like any other. Except they sang together.

"So lulla lulla lulla lulla bye bye
Does you want the moon to play with
Or the stars to run away with?
They'll come if you don't cry . . ."

# 24

## A father's love

When Maddy got home she found her father out on the shop forecourt painting a new coat of gold paint onto Cyril the camel.

"Have to keep him smart," he said. "Cyril's our best salesman."

Maddy thought of Joe and how he had asked after Cyril. That at least had been real. The memory hurt her.

"I've been at an eightieth birthday party," she said.

"Eighty, eh? Were there eighty candles on the cake?"

"Actually there were."

"There, now. Soon Cyril'll be almost as good as new."

Maddy's mother was sitting at the kitchen table with a mug of tea before her. The mug was full, the tea untouched.

"Mum?"

Mrs. Fisher looked up. Her cheeks were shiny.

"Have you been crying?"

"Just a bit."

She looked down again. Maddy felt a cold falling sensation in the pit of her stomach.

"Is it Dad?"

Her mother nodded her head. With the fingers of one hand she rubbed at the back of her other hand as if to erase some invisible stain.

"There's another woman." Her voice came out small and low. She didn't want it to be real. "In China. A Chinese woman."

*I don't want to grow up*, thought Maddy. *Everything just gets worse.*

"But he's outside. Painting Cyril."

*Stupid thing to say. As if that meant he wouldn't leave them.*

*That's what men do. They don't care. They only think of themselves. Men don't do love. Not even Dad.*

She found she was crying too.

Not even Dad. Dad who swung her up in the air and carried her on her shoulders. Dad who smiled and called her his little Madkin and made her feel as if all the world was bright. Oh, Dad.

"He says he wants to go back to China."

"Well, he can't. Tell him he can't."

She put her arms round her mother and hugged her like a child.

"What I mean is, he won't. He's only saying it. He won't leave us. You'll see."

"Oh, Maddy. Darling. Oh, darling, darling. I'm so tired."

"He's a monster. How can he do this? I hate him."

"No. Don't hate him. I don't want you to hate him. I shouldn't have told you. It's just all got on top of me, somehow."

"Has he done this before?"

"Not like this. Not saying he wants to go and live with someone else. I expect there've been others. I don't ask. He's away such a lot. You can't really blame him."

"I blame him. I blame him totally."

"All I do is nag him about money, and the business. It's such a long journey. When he gets home he just wants to rest and be fussed over, and I go on at him about the overdraft and bank charges and unsold stock. Of course he wants to be back with this woman."

"No," said Maddy. "No. He hasn't the right."

"I don't think there is any right anymore." Her mother tried to smile, wiping her eyes. "People just do what they want."

"Then you should do what you want too. It's time you had your turn."

"I just want not to be so tired all the time." She squeezed Maddy's hands and looked at her and finally managed a smile. "I don't want him to leave."

"He won't leave. I'll tell him he can't."

"The thing is, darling, he says he's happier with her than he is with me."

She said it so humbly, and was so hurt by it, that Maddy had no more reassurances to offer. *This is betrayal,* she thought. *This is desertion. This is the crime for which they shoot soldiers in wars.*

"I'll talk to him," she said.

He was no longer out on the forecourt. He was in the shop's big back room, which had been the function room in its days as a roadside inn. He was there among the wedding chests going through the stock, checking price tags against a list, just as if nothing had changed.

"Dad?"

He looked round.

"Ah. Maddy."

The shop was still open for business, but it was late. There were no customers browsing in the cavernous space. Maddy passed between chests and wardrobes to the back aisle where her father stood. He waited for her, pretending to study his list.

"Just what do you think you're doing?" said Maddy.

"Well, I—" He held up his clipboard.

Maddy swiped at the clipboard, knocking it out of his hand.

"I'm not stupid, Dad."

She swiped again, wanting to hit him, to hurt him. Her flailing hand brushed his arm.

"What do you think you're doing?" she said again.

"Not now, Maddy. Please."

"Yes, now."

She struck again, hitting him on the chest. She wanted to beat him down, but there was no force behind her blows. She used both hands, beating at him. He did nothing to resist.

"Go on. Say it. You don't care. You don't give a fuck about us."

"That's not true."

"Say it. Say you're happier with her than with us. Say you don't want us. Say you never loved us. Say it."

"No, Maddy. No, no."

"You can't have it all, Dad. You can't have everyone love you. So go back to fucking China and leave us alone. If you don't want us, we don't want you."

"I do love you. I do want you."

He said the right words, but he spoke them without energy, feebly, as if he knew he had already lost the battle. Maddy wanted him to fight back and he wouldn't. He let her hit him, accepting the punishment, passive, almost cowed.

Inside she was crying out to him: *You're my father, you're stronger than me, you're the one who keeps me safe, you're the man who'll always love me. How can you turn out to be so weak?*

"Why did you say such horrible things to Mum?"

"Jenny shouldn't have talked to you. It's all too soon. We're sorting things out. It'll all work out in the end. Maddy, darling, I promise."

"I don't want your promise. What happened to your promise to Mum? You made her a promise. What about that?"

"We'll sort it out somehow. We will."

A group of customers came into the room, a young couple with a baby, an older woman. The husband carried the baby in a sling at his chest. Maddy and her father fell silent, inhibited by the presence of strangers.

"We'll talk about it later," he said.

His eyes were pleading with her for a soft word in parting, but Maddy was unforgiving in her anger.

"Why should you be the only one who gets what he wants?"

She retreated to her room and locked the door.

Alone at last she curled up on the bed with Bunby in her arms and cried and cried. She was crying for her childhood. She was crying for a lost world where people loved each other. She was crying for her handsome carefree father who had always come home from his trips with something special for her in his bag. His presents were all lined up on her window sill, her treasures: the tiny jade elephant, the inlaid mother-of-pearl pillbox, the peacock feather, the drop of ruby glass as big as an egg. All her most precious jewels lay in the beaded jewel case he had given her, where she had hidden her pills. Even so, as she sobbed and told herself it had all been a lie, she couldn't believe it. He was too deep in her, the Dad who loved her. Maybe there was now another Dad who didn't love her anymore. But the old Dad, the real Dad, hadn't changed. She wouldn't let him change. She was his little girl. Of course he loved her. He always had and he always would.

*And I love you, Dad. Even though you're useless and a cheat and a liar. I just do love you because I can't help it. I can't do without you. So you can go if you want but you won't have left me. You'll just be somewhere else for a while. And I know you'll walk back in the door one day and swing me up in your arms and say, "How's my little Madkin?" And I'll say, "Have you got me a present?" And you'll look grave and shake your head and say, "A present? I must have forgotten." But you won't have forgotten because you never do, and you'll open your bag at last and say, "I wonder what this can be", because you always bring me a present. And I won't even care what it is, I'll just love it because it's your present, and all your presents are little pieces of your love for me. I've still got them, Dad. You can't take them back. I've got your love. It's on my windowsill.*

When she could cry no more Maddy went to the bathroom and washed her face. She could hear her parents talking

244

downstairs but she didn't feel ready yet. She went back to her room and thought maybe she would call Cath but then she didn't. If she talked to Cath on the phone she'd have to tell her about the crisis, it would all come out whether she wanted it to or not, and it felt too soon. To tell Cath would be to make it real. Maddy didn't want it to be real.

*I'd like to phone Rich.*

That was an odd thought to have. As soon as she'd had it she knew Rich was exactly the person to talk to about all this mess. He'd be interested and he'd understand but he wouldn't turn it into some kind of hysterical fuss. But Rich didn't have a phone.

How stupid and irritating of him. What use was a friend without a phone? Maddy resolved to tackle him on the subject, and if necessary force him to get a phone. She remembered how she had said to him, "What if someone wants you?" and he had replied, "They come and find me." Such an arrogant answer. As if people had all the time in the world to go hiking across town just to suit his prehistoric whims.

For a few brief moments she did actually consider going to find him. But then she imagined knocking on his door and him saying, "Yes, what is it?" Somehow she couldn't see herself answering, "I'm feeling sorry for myself because my dad turns out to be a bastard." And even if she did, what could Rich say?

And yet the thought of Rich gave her comfort. She

remembered the way he'd walked into the lamppost, and once again she laughed, just as she had then, and felt a following pang of pity, just as she had then. But Rich no longer seemed to her to be pitiful. "I expect nothing and everything," he said. She could laugh at him without it being unkind. He allowed it. She thought of that stupid book he got from Mr. Pico that said, "Love is a power that produces love," and that stupid letter from the pope, and that stupid petition, and singing that stupid lullaby to his old Gran. She found herself smiling.

*It can wait till Monday,* she thought. *I'll see him at school.*


Driven downstairs at last by hunger, she found her father alone in the kitchen.

"Where's Mum?"

"She went out."

"What do you mean, she went out?"

"I think she may have gone over to see Anne Forder."

Anne Forder was their old friend and neighbor. Maddy said no more. She took down the oats and the golden syrup and fetched butter from the fridge without offering to share with her father. Not that he would have wanted it.

He was drinking coffee, pressed up against the stove. *He's too thin,* she thought. *He should eat more.*

"You want some of this stuff?"

"No, thanks. I'm not all that hungry right now."

She banged the dish in the microwave and waited for the

releasing ping. She had decided she wasn't going to say anything more about the crisis. If he had anything to say let him say it.

"I'm so sorry about all this, Maddy," he said.

"Me too."

Ping. Out with the bowl. Stir with the spoon.

"I know I've made a mess of everything."

She put the bowl down on the table. Sat on one of the rickety chairs. All the pieces of furniture in the house were rejects from the shop.

"There's nothing you could say against me that I wouldn't agree with, really."

"Oh, for God's sake, Dad. If you're going to do it at least get something out of it. Otherwise what's the point?"

"That's not how it is."

"It looks pretty simple to me. You've got some other"—she couldn't bring herself to say *woman*—"some other life in China that you like better. Fine. Go and live it."

"But it's not simple at all. How can I leave you and Imo and Jen?"

"You tell me."

"I couldn't bear it."

"So what's all this you've been telling Mum, then? What's all this about another woman?"

Her golden syrup oats were going cold. She'd lost her appetite.

"Like I say, it's not simple."

"You want everything, and you don't care about hurting people. Seems pretty simple to me."

"Yes, I suppose it does."

"So. Tell me how I'm wrong."

She said it angrily. Why did it have to be forced out of him? Why couldn't he just say something that made it all be different? Like, I turn into a werewolf when there's a moon. Like, I'm a paranoid schizophrenic.

He sat down at the table facing her and put his head in his hands. She didn't speak. His fuck-up. Let him do the talking.

"I've always had this problem," he said. "It's not easy to describe. I've not been good at seeing things through. Even when I was a boy. Making those Airfix models, whatever. I never finished them. I got bored or something. That's what I used to think. But it wasn't that. If you want to get something done you have to believe you'll get it done. If deep down you don't believe that, then after a while it gets hard to carry on. Impossible, in fact."

Maddy listened but didn't understand. This wasn't the father she had always known.

"But Dad, you've done lots of things."

"I've managed this and that, maybe. But nothing very much. I'm sorry, Mad, I shouldn't be bothering you with all this. I just rather want you to understand."

"Maybe you haven't ended up a millionaire. But who needs that? You've got a good business. You've got a family that loves you."

"Jen's built up the business. I could never have done it. And Jen's made the family too."

"So why do you want to leave?"

"I don't want to leave. I want to—to—" He searched her face, looking for sympathy, wanting her to understand without the words having to be said. But Maddy didn't understand. She made him say it.

"I want not to hate myself," he said.

Not what she was expecting.

"Hate yourself?"

"Yes."

"Why would you hate yourself?"

"Because I don't really believe—not really—that I'm any good."

"Dad!" Tears sprang into her eyes.

"Nothing so very terrible. But at times it gets too much. Then I just want to be somewhere where no one expects anything of me. Where I can just drop into a chair, have a drink, switch off."

"Is that what it's like with her?"

He nodded.

"So it's somewhere to run away and hide."

"Yes. You could call it that."

"But you can't."

"Can't run away. Can't hide. Have to be a man. Face the music. Show some self-respect. Fight the good fight."

"Yes." But she was beginning to understand. It wasn't what he said so much as the tone of his voice, and his sad smile.

*This is all about despair,* she thought. *Dad's despaired.*

"You've despaired, haven't you?"

"Oh, long ago."

"Why?"

"I remember thinking when I was quite young, when all my friends were pushing and jostling to get to the front of the lunch queue and I was waiting at the back. Someone said, 'Look at Michael, he's the only one of you who's got some manners.' But I knew it wasn't manners. I knew there was something broken inside me."

"No, Dad. No!" Maddy shook her head, willing it away. "You're wrong. There's nothing broken. People are different."

"I can't go on letting you all down, Mad. I can't go on failing Jen. I can't go on hating myself."

She looked at him, feeling tears rise up to her eyes.

"Mum loves you. I love you. Imo loves you. Isn't that enough?"

"I know it should be. But you see, I have to deserve it."

"No. That's not how love works." Something clicked into

place in her mind. "You don't get loved as a reward for something. People need to love. They just do it. We just do it."

*Girls just do it,* she added silently. *Women just do it. Men are something else. Dad is something else.*

He looked at her wistfully.

"I'd like that to be true."

"I'll tell you how you deserve it, Dad. You accept it. That's all you do. So don't run away. Don't hide. We have to have someone to love."

Is that pathetic? Is that surrendering to men's selfishness and uselessness?

He was gazing at her with love. At least it looked like love.

"You've grown up, haven't you? You're so beautiful. I'm so proud of you, Maddy."

"Oh, Dad. What are we going to do about you?"

She was crying freely again, helplessly. Because he had said she was beautiful.

"Jen and me'll have a talk."

He moved his arms as if wanting to touch her across the table.

"You can bloody well get up," she said.

He got up and they hugged, just the same way they'd always hugged, except now she was as tall as him.

# 25

## The moreness of things

Rich didn't come to school on Monday. Neither did Grace.

"Maybe they've eloped together," said Cath.

"Please," said Maddy. "Enough surprises."

The rumor was that Grace had collapsed at a party on Saturday night, but no one knew for sure. There was no rumor about Rich.

"He's probably ill too," said Cath cheerfully.

"Typical male," said Maddy. "Never there when you need them."

She told Cath about her father and how she had pounded him with her fists. Cath was awestruck.

"You beat up your dad?"

"Yes."

"Mad, that's not like you."

"I'm not like me, Cath. My life is all going wrong. I cry all the time. I have terrible thoughts. I'm angry all the time."

"No more nice girl."

"I hate it."

"Even so. Might as well use it. I say go and beat up Grace."

"She's not here. And anyway, she's not the one I should beat up. Joe's the one who thinks he can have it all his own way."

This thought had been growing in Maddy ever since she had learned of her father's betrayal. It was as if some cord of loyalty had snapped. Why was it always men who got what they wanted? Joe needed some petty distraction because he was cheating on his girlfriend, so he flirted with Maddy and never even bothered to ask himself what effect it might have. It was all just a game that suited him for a moment. And what was he doing to Gemma? He was going on letting her think that he loved her so that she would kill her baby. How sick was that?

"Someone should tell Joe it's not on," said Maddy.

"Go Maddy!" cried Cath. "Beat up Joe!"

"It's not like I've got anything to lose."

"These boys think they can do what they like."

"And these men."

Seeing her mother in tears had hardened Maddy. Her mother was the innocent victim of male selfishness. Somehow by way of her mother's hurting she had stopped blaming herself for her own humiliating crush on Joe. And with the passing of self-blame the way lay open for anger.

"I told my dad. I can tell Joe."

She knew Joe's timetable well. That afternoon she was waiting outside the changing rooms as he loped back from the running track. He was in running shorts and a sleeveless shirt, his arms and face and neck shining with sweat.

"Maddy Fisher!" he cried as he saw her. As always he sounded blithely unaware that she might have any kind of a problem with him.

"Hi, Joe."

He gave her a smile and a wave as he jogged by.

"Can I have a word?"

"Sure," said Joe. "Just let me shower and stuff."

"No. Now."

He caught the seriousness in her voice. He stopped.

"Okay. What's up?"

"Can we go somewhere a bit more private?"

They went to the far side of the tennis courts, beyond the line of beech trees. This was where the smokers came to steal a quick cigarette before and after school. At this time, early in the afternoon, they had it to themselves.

"This isn't about me, Joe. You really have to believe that. I made a fool of myself, that's my problem. I can handle it. This is about Gemma."

Joe looked baffled.

"Okay," he said. "What about Gemma?"

"You just can't do this to her. I expect it's none of my

business but"—she drew a deep breath—"if you don't tell Gemma what's really going on, then I will."

"What's really going on?"

He looked so surprised that Maddy began to get angry. She had promised herself she would stay calm.

"I'm not a total idiot," she said. "Grace has told me everything."

"Grace? What's Grace got to do with this?"

So that was it. His strategy was going to be blanket denial. She hadn't been prepared for that.

"Grace has told me all about you and her."

"Me and her?"

"About you going out with her."

"Me going out with Grace? Grace told you that?"

"Yes."

He burst into laughter.

"And you believed her?"

"Yes. Of course."

"Maddy, I'm not going out with Grace. I've never done anything with Grace. My girlfriend's Gemma Page. Everyone knows that. Grace has been having you on."

The more he denied it the angrier Maddy became. He must think she was an imbecile.

"I'm the one you sent the emails to, Joe. Remember? I've still got them. You can't just pretend it all didn't happen."

"What emails?"

"The emails you sent me."

"I never sent you any emails."

"Stop this, Joe! You can't just make up your own reality. I've got them on my laptop. They exist. You and Grace used me as a cover to stop Gemma guessing about you. Grace has told me everything."

"Grace Carey told you I sent you emails?"

"I've got the emails! The emails are real!"

He looked so bewildered that for the first time she began to doubt her own version of events. But it was true: she hadn't dreamed the emails.

"I can show you them."

"I'd like you to do that, Maddy. Something's seriously not right here. What did you mean about stopping Gemma guessing?"

"About you and Grace."

"If I was having a thing with Grace, which I'm not, why wouldn't Gemma know anyway?"

"Because of her being pregnant."

"What!"

"You're trying to make her get rid of it."

"Gemma is not pregnant, Maddy."

"Grace told me. That's why you sent me the emails."

Joe put both his hands on her shoulders as if to steady her, and looked directly into her eyes.

"Okay. Let's take this one step at a time. One, Gemma isn't pregnant. Ask her. Two, I've never had any kind of a thing with Grace Carey. Three, I've never sent you any emails. I don't even know your email address. Four, I love Gemma."

Maddy closed her eyes. She felt giddy. Joe sounded horribly convincing. Was it possible there might be a whole other explanation?

"You're on Hotmail, right?"

"No. I'm on Googlemail."

"What's your address?"

"FlyingFinn@googlemail.com"

"Have you ever had a Hotmail address?"

"No. Hotmail's rubbish. They cut you off if you don't keep on using it. And you know what? Anyone can open a Hotmail account in any name they like."

"JoeFinn41."

"JoeFinn41?"

"That's who sent me the emails."

"And you thought it was me?"

"Yes. It was you. The emails talked about things you and I talked about in school."

"We've hardly talked about anything."

"Cyril the camel."

"The emails were about Cyril the camel?"

"Yes."

"Someone's playing a joke on you, Maddy. What else did the emails say?"

"Nothing much."

Now that Maddy had begun to doubt everything that had happened to her, her anger at Joe was turning to shame. But if the emails to her were fake, then he had never read the emails she had sent back. That meant he knew nothing about her crush on him.

Then she remembered the emails about Leo. Surely they could only have come from Joe.

"You said things about Leo, for me to tell my sister. About him being mean and unstable."

"That wasn't me, Maddy."

"Imo phoned Leo and he talked to you about it."

"No. Never."

"Joe, everyone can't be lying! Are you saying that Imo and Leo and Grace all made this stuff up together? Why would they do that?"

"I don't know. But I'm going to find out."

"I mean, who would do that?"

"It has to be Grace Carey," he said. "But why? What have I done to her to make her tell all these lies about me?"

"Grace," said Maddy. "You think it's Grace?"

"As far as I can tell, this whole story has been fed to you by Grace. But I've no idea why."

Already a new reality was beginning to take shape in

Maddy's mind. That story about turning Gemma's suspicions on to her: it didn't really make any sense. And now that she looked back she realized that Joe's behavior, which had seemed strange at the time, stopped looking strange if you took away the emails. The moment at the school gates when Joe hadn't seemed to understand her. The meeting outside the cinema. His untroubled cheeriness. It all made sense now. What didn't make sense was Grace.

"Let me get changed," Joe said, "and we'll go and find Gemma. I want her to tell you for herself that this is all total bullshit."

"No, it's okay. I'd rather just forget about it."

"So do you believe me now?"

"I suppose I have to."

"I'm really sorry about this, Maddy. Someone's played a shitty trick on both of us."

"Looks like it."

"I've got an idea or two. I'm going to sort this thing out. And when I do, I'll tell you."

"I think it must be Grace. I'll talk to her. Leave it to me."

They both stood there for a moment by the tennis courts, wanting to go, not able to go. It didn't feel like it was properly over, whatever it was that had taken place between them.

"Why didn't you tell me about this sooner?" said Joe. "I mean, like when these emails started coming."

"You said not to."

"I said not to?"

"You said that I was to go on the same as ever at school. Like, it was to be a secret."

"Somebody really thought this one out."

"Only it turns out it wasn't you."

"Why was it supposed to be a secret?"

"Because of Gemma."

"So I was supposed to be cheating on Gemma with Grace Carey and with you too?"

"Just forget about it. It was just Grace playing games with us. No harm done. I'm glad I sorted it out in the end."

"Even so, I'd like to know why. Do you think Grace was trying to break me and Gemma up or something?"

"I don't know, Joe. I'm a bit confused, to tell you the truth."

"Gemma and me have been together since we were sixteen. People think Gemma's dumb because she's pretty, but she's not dumb at all. She's just very sweet-natured. She sees the good in people, always. When I tell her about this I know what she'll say. She'll say, Grace can't have meant any harm, she must have thought it was all a game, she wouldn't want to hurt anyone. Gemma thinks that way because she'd never want to hurt anyone herself. She's a good person, she really is. I'll tell you what she is. She's innocent. I think that's what I love so much about her."

If Maddy had any remaining doubts this speech laid them

to rest. It did more than that. It restored to her a Joe she could like and respect.

"You'd better go and get changed," she said. "And you don't have to tell Gemma. It would only upset her."

"I can't not tell her," said Joe. "We tell each other everything."

"Okay."

He gave her his cheery wave and loped back past the tennis courts to the changing room.

Maddy followed more slowly, deep in thought.

Where was Grace? She would probably answer her phone if she called, but it wasn't the sort of conversation she wanted to have over the phone. She needed to see her face to face.

She could find Cath, and amaze her with the new revelations. She did want to share it all with Cath, to puzzle out with her what had been going on. But not quite yet.

Maddy found herself in a strange state. She was no longer miserable, the way she'd been after losing Joe's love—his imagined love. She wasn't angry, the way seeing her mother in tears had made her angry. She was what she'd said to Joe: confused. She felt as if she'd been stirred up inside with a big wooden spoon and now none of her thoughts and feelings were where they used to be. It was a little frightening, like being lost, or being in a country where you don't speak the language.

But here was a strange thing: she no longer felt her life had no meaning. It wasn't that she'd found a meaning, far from it. What she'd found was the *moreness* of things. There was so much *more* than she'd realized before. People were much more complicated. Joe had been desirable, then hateful, then admirable, all within a few days. Her father had been missed, hated, pitied, loved, all within a span of forty-eight hours.

*I know nothing,* Maddy said to herself. *I've been going about in a dream. Maybe even now I'm only half awake.*

It was like coming out of a curtained room into bright daylight. She was dazzled, overwhelmed. There was so much to see, so much to know. And not just about this startling new world. About herself.

*I don't know who I am. I'm not who I thought I was. I'm more. I'm complicated in ways I've never realized before. Not just happy or sad, but both, and all the shades in-between, all the time. I can be afraid of the melting glaciers and still turn up the radiator in my room. I can buy cheap jeans in Primark and still feel sorry for exploited garment workers. I can contradict myself. I'm not supposed to be simple. I'm complicated. I'm a mess. I can think a hundred different things at once. I'm one insignificant creature and I'm the center of the universe. My existence has no meaning and my existence is its own meaning. I am therefore I am.*

Where was Rich? He was the one she wanted to talk to about

all her new thoughts. Not Cath, not Grace. She cursed Rich all over again for not having a phone. Right now she wanted to be with Rich more than any other person in the world. Typical male. Never there when you need them.

So I suppose I'll just have to go and find him.

# 26

## All at once the feelings

Maddy made her way down the street where Rich lived, and found herself paying attention to her surroundings. In the strange new mood that possessed her she felt as if she was seeing everything for the first time. The houses she was passing were large detached Edwardian villas divided by hedges or walls. How odd it must be to live in a street. For Maddy as for everyone her own house was the original, the house of which all others were distorted copies. Her house was out of town and flanked by woods and fields. Here every house had others beside it, pretending to be just as important. Surely it made you feel less special living in a street, living in a house that had a bay window and a porch and high gables just like the house next door. The small front gardens were all different, and the front doors were painted in different colors; but these were homes that identified themselves by numbers. The Rosses lived at

Number 47. How could you feel individual if you lived in a house known only by a number?

And yet Rich was individual. He was the most individual person she knew. He had said to her, "A whole lot of unusual stuff goes on in my head." It was true. She thought of the Larkin poem, and the letter from the pope. Who thinks of things like that?

She opened the little iron gate and went up the path to Rich's front door. The big bay window of the kindergarten room was decorated with transparent colored butterflies. There were no visible signs of life within.

She rang the bell. It jangled clearly in the hall beyond the door. No one appeared. She rang again.

It then occurred to her that Rich might have had some kind of accident. Maddy's mother was such a proficient worrier that Maddy rarely worried for herself; but once begun she took to it with a dismaying facility. Perhaps Rich had electrocuted himself on the doll's house lights. Perhaps he had been mugged on the way to school for the phone he did not possess. Perhaps he had severed an artery on a kitchen knife while unloading the dishwasher. When you started to think about it there were so many ways to be injured. So many ways to die.

She went back down the path and out through the iron gate. She stood, uncertain what to do, looking up and down the street.

A car appeared. Maddy tracked it with her gaze: it was dark blue, a high, boxy people-carrier. It came nearer. She recognized Rich's father at the wheel. Too late to hide. She stood by the gate and watched the car pull up before her.

The entire family got out. Rich saw her with surprise; Kitty with curiosity. Maddy felt foolish.

"I was on my way home," she said. And meeting Rich's father's gaze, "Rich hasn't got a phone."

"Gran's dying," said Kitty.

Now Rich was by Maddy's side.

"We've been at the hospital all day," he said. "Gran had another stroke."

"Oh. I'm so sorry."

They all went into the house. Maddy was going to leave, but Rich seemed to expect her to go in with them.

"Gran's in a coma," he said.

"She's going to die," insisted Kitty.

"She might, darling," said Mrs. Ross. "We don't know. We have to be prepared."

Kitty's eyes fell on the stair-lift. She started to cry.

"Who'll ride in her stair-lift?"

Mrs. Ross took her in her arms.

"You don't want Gran to go on if she can't talk or move or recognize any of us anymore."

They gathered in the kitchen.

"I should go," said Maddy. "If I'd known I wouldn't have bothered you."

"Where do you live, Maddy?" asked Mrs. Ross.

"Out on the old North Road. The shop with the camel."

"Oh, yes. I know. It's a wonderful shop."

"I'll walk with you," said Rich. "I'd like to get out. I've been in the hospital all day."

"So have I," said Kitty. "But I don't want to come too."

So Maddy and Rich set off together.

At first Rich didn't seem to want to talk.

"I'm really sorry about your gran," said Maddy.

"It's sad," said Rich. "They kept doing all these tests on her and she couldn't talk or anything. She was just all floppy." Maddy could hear the edge of tears in his voice. "When she was young she was very beautiful. She had six proposals of marriage. Now this."

"Will she really die?"

"I hope so. She's almost not there already."

They came to the junction with the road out of town. The tree-covered slope rose up on the far side.

"This is the start of my secret walk," said Rich. "Up through the wood. That's the way I'd go if I was on my own."

"You do your secret walk. I'm okay going the rest of the way."

"Or you could come too."

"Wouldn't you rather be alone?"

"No," said Rich. "I'd rather be with you."

As simple as that. Neither of them questioned it. The nearness of death made them unselfconscious.

They crossed the road and turned off up the rutted farm track. The late afternoon sun was still high above, the air warm. The track led up the rising slope into the trees.

"I've never met anyone else here," said Rich. "I feel like it's my private wood."

"It's beautiful." Maddy looked through the galleries of tree trunks on either side. "I ought to know the names of all the trees but I don't."

"I think most of them are beeches. That's an oak."

They climbed higher and higher, stopping from time to time to look back through gaps in the trees at the town below.

"Everyone leading their busy little lives," said Rich. "Living and dreaming and dying."

"And we don't know any of it."

"I'm glad. It would be too much."

"Do you think there's a lot of unhappiness?"

"More than we can ever know," said Rich.

They reached the gate at the end of the wood.

"We could go up onto the top," said Rich. "Or we could have a rest in the tree barn."

"I'm all for a rest."

The tree barn delighted Maddy.

"It's got a tree growing inside it!"

"I love this place," said Rich. "I don't know why."

"It's amazing. It's like being inside and outside both at the same time."

They went in under the ash tree's spreading branches. Maddy felt the dead leaves that were heaped on the ground.

"Dry," she said, surprised.

"It only gets wet here after heavy rain. The wall shelters it."

Maddy sank down onto the soft leaves, grateful to take the weight off her weary legs.

"Oof!" she said. "You can tell I don't take enough exercise."

Rich sat down nearby. For a moment neither of them spoke.

"The doctors say Gran won't last more than a few days," Rich said. "She'll have another stroke and that'll be it."

"So all you can do is wait."

"I just can't imagine her gone. She's always been there."

"It must be so strange."

Maddy found she was thinking of her father. He'd always been there. Hard to imagine him gone.

"She has this Zimmer," said Rich. "It makes such a special sound when she goes by on the landing. I hear it outside my room." The beginnings of tears in his eyes once more. "Stupid the things you realize you'll miss."

"I came home yesterday," said Maddy, "and found Mum

crying in the kitchen. Dad says he wants to leave. He's got this other woman in China."

"Why in China?"

"That's where he goes to buy furniture."

Rich considered this in silence.

"Is he really going to leave?"

"I don't know. Maybe."

"That's awful, Maddy. That's worse than Gran dying."

"Yes. It's pretty bad."

"My God! If my dad left!" A new thought came to him. "Dad's the one who's going to miss Gran most." Then, absorbing the significance of this news for Maddy, "Are you totally traumatized?"

"Probably," said Maddy. "I talked to him. He's kind of sad. He says he feels useless. He's despaired."

Rich gazed at her in sympathetic dismay.

"But he's your dad. He can't despair. Not until you've grown up and left home."

It was funny really. Delay the despair, Dad. Fulfill your duty. But it was exactly what Maddy felt.

"I suppose I'd better buck up and grow up."

"If you have children you have to stick around and look after them. You don't have the option of walking away just because you feel like it."

"I'll tell him you said so."

"Tell him the pope says so too."

"What is it with you and the pope?"

"I just like his style. He says he's infallible. You have to be pretty sure of yourself to say you're infallible."

"Do you think you're infallible?"

"No way. Not by a million miles."

"But secretly you're quite arrogant, aren't you? You like to say you're not like other people, but what you mean is you're superior to other people."

Rich thought about that.

"Maybe I do mean that. I never quite thought of it that way."

"I'm not saying you're wrong. You probably are superior to most other people."

"And yet there are times when I'd give anything to be someone else."

"Who would you rather be?"

"Oh, someone who sails through life with a smile on his face. Joe Finnigan, maybe. The one you fancied."

That brought back all the confusions of the day for Maddy. Rich saw her frown and look down.

"Sorry," he said. "None of my business."

"No, it's okay. It's just that I had a long talk with Joe today. He's not really the way I thought at all. He's nicer, but he's more ordinary somehow." She couldn't bring herself to tell Rich the whole story. It was too shaming. "I like him more and fancy him less. Also he was so sweet about his girlfriend. He said she was innocent."

"In a way that meant he approved?"

"Yes. Definitely."

"Then he must be a good person."

"I think maybe he is."

They remained for a few moments in a companionable silence. Maddy was struck by Rich's sure touch. He had understood at once the new perception she had of Joe, and had found better words for it. She had called him more ordinary. Rich called him good.

She stretched out, lying down on the bed of leaves. Above her and to one side Rich was partly in silhouette against the sky, framed by the old roof beams. His gaze was fixed on some distant point, his expression meditative. She found herself studying his features. He had an interesting face: a high brow, wide-set eyes, a nose that seemed a little too small for his face, a beautiful mouth. A perfect mouth, really, the lips delicately curved and clearly outlined. He looked young for his age, younger than her; but at other times she felt he was much older. She wondered whether to tell him about Grace. Except she hardly knew what to tell him.

"So are you still dreaming of Grace Carey?"

He threw her a reproachful look.

"I shouldn't have told you."

"I told you about Joe."

"I suppose I do think about her sometimes."

"She's not right for you, Rich."

"You mean she's out of my league."

"No. She's a game player. She manipulates people. You don't."

"I'm like Gemma. I'm innocent."

She could tell from the way he said this that he didn't like it.

"Not innocent. Apart. You don't seem to me to be down in the mess with the rest of us."

"Maybe I should be down in the mess with the rest of you. Maybe it would be more fun."

"It's not fun at all. You're better off where you are." Then, although it didn't really follow, she said, "There's no one else I can talk to like this."

"Same," he replied.

"I wonder why."

"It could be because I'm so wise and perceptive and mature for my age. Then again it could be because I'm a loser."

He gave her a funny smile.

Here I am, Maddy thought, alone in the woods with Rich. Why have I come here?

"Why would I want to talk to a loser?"

"Because I'm no competition. No threat. You don't have to mind what I think about you."

"Honestly, Rich. The things you come up with."

"I don't care, actually. I've decided not to mind what people think about me too. I've decided to just get on and do things."

"What sort of things?"

"Life being short and so on."

"Like what?"

"Like having a girlfriend. I mean, a real one. Not an imaginary one like Grace."

"So what have you decided to do?"

"Nothing, so far. It's not so easy. I'm out of practice. Or rather, I've never been in practice."

"Then you'd better start."

"Sure. But how? It's not like there's a class you can go to."

"I wish there was."

"Really?"

"Why should you be the only one?"

"Everyone can't be useless at it. I mean, the human race would die out."

"Let it."

But she didn't mean it. Lying there on the bed of leaves looking up at the fading sky she felt at peace in a way she hadn't known for days. For weeks, really.

Rich slipped down to sit leaning against the flint wall, his knees folded up by his chest.

"Mr. Pico should start up a class," Maddy said. "The art of loving."

"I don't want it to be all theory."

"No. Not just theory."

"You know what?" he said, hugging his knees. "I've never really kissed a girl. Not a real kiss."

Maddy said nothing. Strange thoughts were stirring within her.

"That's how much of a loser I am."

"That's not being a loser."

"I bet you have. Kissed a boy, I mean."

"Yes." She thought of the times she'd kissed boys at parties, on darkened dance floors, wriggling in each other's arms. "Not real kisses, though."

"What wasn't real about it?"

"A real kiss is one you really want."

"I'll settle for actual lip contact with an actual girl."

"Oh, Rich. You wouldn't. You'd have to want to kiss her."

"Yes, I suppose you're right." He sighed a long sigh. "Why does it have to be so hard?"

She felt the leaves under her hands. She grasped a small handful and threw them up in the air, so they came floating down again all over her body. Then she threw a handful at Rich.

"What's that for?"

"Nothing."

He reached his hand out between them.

"See that?"

His hand was shaking.

"Why's it doing that?"

"I don't know. Sometimes something happens inside me. I just start shaking."

She took hold of his hand to stop it shaking. She held it in both her hands, and felt how he was shivering all down his body. She knew without him having to say it that he was shivering because of what they were talking about, and because she was there, close to him. It gave her an odd, warm, protective feeling.

After a few moments the shivering stopped.

"There. You're not shaking now."

She let go of his hand and rolled over onto her side, facing him. He stretched out his bent legs and wriggled about until he too was lying full length on the ground. He turned to her and smiled his funny smile.

She reached out one hand and touched his cheek.

"Your face didn't do any shaking."

"No. It's all inside my chest, and my tummy."

She touched his chest. She could feel his heart beating.

"That just means you're not dead."

He reached out his hand and touched her cheek.

"You neither."

His touch was so light she hardly felt it.

Next she touched his brow with one finger, traced it down

276

over his nose to his lips. Then he did the same. She felt the soft pressure of his finger on her lips.

She looked at him. He was so intent, so grave. He's beautiful, she thought. Why didn't I see it before?

She leaned her face towards him and touched his cheek with her lips. Barely a kiss at all.

"Practice," she said.

He kissed her cheek in his turn.

"Is that what you meant?" she said.

"Yes," he said.

She moved her body so she was right beside him.

"We need to be closer."

She moved her lips to his and, barely brushing them, they kissed. She felt his body start to shiver again.

"You're shaking again."

"Yes. Sorry."

"I don't mind."

She kissed him again, once, twice, three times, short and light kisses, both restrained and intimate. She felt his lips move against hers. Such a delicate touch, like whispering to each other. Moment by moment she could feel an emotion welling up from deep within her, but she didn't know what it was.

He put his arms round her, burrowing one arm through the dry leaves.

"Do you mind?"

"No. That's good."

He held her cradled in his arms, not tightly, but it made them both more comfortable. She put her upper arm over him.

This time he drew her close and their kiss lasted much longer. They were so close that Maddy could feel his heart beating, and the shivering all down his body. Their lips searched and nuzzled each other, still gentle, still respectful, but growing bolder with each passing moment. They both had their eyes closed.

Then his lips moved to kiss her neck, her cheek, her temple. She lay still and let him explore her, while the feeling inside her grew and grew. He lifted his lips away.

She opened her eyes. He was looking at her, and silent tears were rolling down his cheeks.

"I'm so happy," he said.

All at once the feelings broke within her, and she began to sob. She clung to him, pressing her face against his chest, and cried and cried. All the grief and the hurt came streaming out of her in a flood she couldn't control, the loss of Joe, the loss of her father, the loss of all the love she'd wanted so much and now would never have. She cried because she knew she would always love more than she was loved. She cried for all the hurt to come. She held Rich tight and she cried in his arms.

He said nothing and made no move to stop her.

Slowly the wave of emotion passed. She brushed the tears

from her eyes with the back of her hand. She found a tissue in her pocket and blew her nose.

"You cried too," she said in self-defense. "I don't know why I did that."

But she did know. Too many bad things had happened to her recently. She needed something good. And kissing Rich was good.

"Maddy," he said. He kissed her softly.

"Yes," she said. "Me too."

They got up and brushed the dead leaves off each other's backs. They walked down through the steep wood, hand in hand, in silence. When they reached the gate that led from the farm track onto the road they came to a stop.

"Will you be going to the hospital tomorrow?"

"I don't know. Could be."

She took his hand and pushed up his sleeve and wrote her phone number on his arm.

"Call me."

"Of course."

"And get a bloody phone, you loser."

# 27

# Imo in tears

Maddy found her parents side by side at the kitchen table going through the shop accounts.

"Jenny's quite right," said her father raising worried eyes from the columns of the spreadsheet. "Things are looking a bit grim."

"Don't say that, Dad. You know how Mum worries."

"You mustn't stop him," said her mother. "It's so much better than telling me it's never going to happen. That just makes me worry more."

"What do you want us to do, Mum? All start panicking together?"

"No. Just so long as I know someone else is doing some worrying."

"Something's got to be done," said Maddy's father. "That's for sure."

"Well, I'm worried too," said Maddy. "And not just about the shop."

This was the closest she could bring herself to speaking about the family crisis.

Her mother said, "Mike's agreed to put that on hold for the time being."

"On hold?"

"You know, like a phone call."

"Yes, I know, Mum. Where they play you Vivaldi's 'Four Seasons' and tell you how important your call is that they're not answering."

"We don't want to do anything in a rush," said her father.

Maddy wanted to shout at them both. What was this *anything*? What was happening? How could they both be so quiet? But then came the sound of a car pulling up in the yard outside the house, and the slam of a car door.

"That must be Imo," said Maddy's mother.

Imo had been away for four days. She came in looking exhausted, but as soon as she saw their father she threw herself into his arms.

"Dad! You're back! Oh, I'm so happy!"

She kissed him again and again. He was taken aback by the intensity of her greeting.

"There's a welcome. How's my best girl?"

"Still your best girl. Oh, Dad. I'm so glad you're home."

She burst into tears. She clung to her father and wept uncontrollably, while he held her tight and bent his head over hers. He made no attempt to console her other than to rock her gently in his arms.

"What is it, Imo?" said her mother, glancing at Maddy. Her eyes asked: *Did you tell her?* Maddy shook her head.

Imo stopped crying at last.

"What is it, Im?" said her father. He spoke very quietly as if he might startle her.

"Nothing, Dad. I've just missed you. I didn't realize how much."

"I've never had tears before."

"I know. I'm sorry. I just couldn't stop myself. But I'm okay now. I've had a few bad nights, that's all."

"Home now. Home now. Sleep as long as you like."

"And you're home, Dad. So everything's going to be all right."

Imo went up to her room, saying she needed to have a shower.

"She's upset about something," Maddy's mother said. "You haven't told her, have you, Maddy?"

"No. Nothing."

They both looked at Maddy's father. He shrugged his shoulders.

"For once it seems I'm not to blame."

But something was wrong.

"Go and talk to her, Maddy. She'll tell you."

Maddy went up and knocked on Imo's door.

"It's me. Can I come in?"

"Just a minute."

Maddy waited. She heard Imo draw back the bolt on the inside of the door.

Imo was in her kimono bathrobe, with her hair scraped back. She'd been cleaning the makeup off her face and looked pale and fragile. Maddy sat on her bed while Imo sat before her dressing-table mirror and finished scouring her face bare.

Imo's room was so different from Maddy's, mostly because she was away so much. It looked both messy and unused. Long ago they had shared a bedroom, whispering secrets across the space between their beds, planning in great detail the birthday parties of their cuddly animals. Imo's equivalent of Bunby was a panda called Princess Pandy. Like Bunby, Pandy had always been tucked up beneath the bedclothes, head on the pillow, ready for bedtime. But now Pandy sat on a cushion in the corner with a pretty necklace round her neck, a princess in exile.

Maddy waited in silence until Imo was finished. It was always best with Imo to let her start the talking. That way you knew what sort of mood she was in. Imo could be prickly.

At last she turned round from her mirror and spoke.

"Men are shits," she said. "They're all shits, every last one of them. Except Dad."

Maddy said nothing.

"I was wrong telling you to get a boyfriend, Mad. Don't bother. Boy and friend, that cancels itself out. It's a—what is it?"

"Oxymoron."

"Oxymoron. Clever Maddy."

Imo always became spiteful when reminded that Maddy was cleverer than her. But she forgot almost at once.

"I should go to the police. Except they'd be no use."

"The police!"

"You wouldn't believe what that fucking shit did to me."

"Is this Leo?"

"What Joe said about Leo, that was spot on. One up for you, Maddy."

What Joe said: *Leo's unstable. Leo hurts girls.*

But the emails hadn't come from Joe at all. They'd come from Grace. And here was Imo telling her they'd been right.

"Thanks for not saying I told you so."

"Please tell me, Im. Something bad's happened."

"You could say that."

"Can you tell me?"

Imo stood gazing at Maddy in silence. Tears rose to her beautiful big blue eyes.

"I'll show you."

She untied her kimono and opened it to show her naked upper body. Faint bruises discolored her chest and breasts. She turned round, pulling the kimono clear. There were bruises on her buttocks.

"Oh my God!"

Imo wrapped the kimono back round herself and sat beside Maddy on the bed. She began to cry again, but noiselessly. Maddy put one arm round her, timidly at first, expecting her to shake it off. But Imo pressed herself into her sister's embrace.

"He did it last night," she said. She whispered through her tears. "It was so horrible. So frightening. I couldn't stop him."

"You have to tell someone, Imo. That's a crime."

"He just changed, in one minute. It was like he turned into a different person."

"You have to go to the police."

"No, you don't understand. I can't."

"I mean it, Imo. He should be locked up."

"I can't tell anyone. I can't. I don't want anyone to know. It started as a game. Then he wouldn't stop."

"It's not a game, Imo. Beating someone up isn't a game."

"It is for Leo. It's what turns him on."

"What's sexy about beating you up? I just don't get it."

"He went crazy. He hit me and hit me. I wanted to shout but I didn't. I didn't make any noise at all. I should have screamed for help or something. But I just let him hit me. I suppose I didn't want anyone to know. Even while he was doing it I was ashamed. As if it was my fault."

She cried softly in Maddy's arms.

"Imo, Imo, Imo. I can't bear it."

"But you mustn't tell anyone, Maddy. Promise you won't tell anyone."

"He has to be stopped."

"But don't you see? He'll say I was in bed with him of my own free will. He'll say if I didn't like it, why did I stay?"

"Like it!"

"He says lots of girls like it."

"Being hurt?"

"Yes. He says girls like it."

"He's sick." Maddy felt angry now. "He's perverted."

"But don't tell anyone. Promise."

"All right. I promise. But you've got to tell someone, Im."

"Who?"

"Mum and Dad?"

"What can they do? I don't see Dad going round to Leo's place and knocking him down."

"Actually I think that's exactly what he would do."

"Do you?"

Maddy hesitated. It wasn't a good moment, but there was never going to be a good moment.

"Dad's been having some problems. He's come home feeling he's not much use to us all."

"Not much use? Why's he not much use?"

"He says Mum does everything and we've grown up now. I didn't realize it, but apparently he feels he's no good at anything. He wants to run away and hide."

"Run away where?"

"He's got some woman in China."

"What!"

Imo's eyes blazed with sudden fury. She jumped up off the bed, tying her kimono tight round her bruised body.

"He's not running anywhere!"

"No! Wait! Imo!"

But it was too late. She had already stormed down the stairs to the kitchen.

"Dad! What's this about you leaving us?"

"Imo, darling—"

"If you do I'll track you down and kill you! You got that? There's not going to be any running away from us! We need you, so you're staying! Got that?"

"Darling, please. Leave this to me and Jenny. Please."

"No, I won't! I'm involved too. Maddy's involved too."

"Yes, I know that—"

"And we say you can't go. So that's it. You're outvoted."

"We have to talk later, darling. All of us. When we're calmer."

"What's there to talk about, Dad? So you're having a bad time. Deal with it. Life's not roses all the way."

Maddy thought Imo was magnificent. With her stripped gaunt face and her hand raised as if to strike she was an avenging fury. Her father quailed before her.

"I really could do with a drink," he said.

"Me too," said Imo.

She got a bottle of wine out of the fridge and poured everyone a glass.

"So you're not leaving, right? That's agreed."

"Yes," he said.

They all drank to that, as if they were sealing an oath.

Rich rang Maddy that evening. She didn't recognize the phone number and didn't know it was him until he spoke.

"It's me," he said. His voice sounded nervous. "Rich."

"Where are you calling from?"

"The phone in the schoolroom."

"Are you alone?"

"Just about."

"How's your gran?"

"No change."

"Will you be in school tomorrow?"

"Yes. Dad says there's no point in hanging around the hospital."

"Right. So I'll see you in school."

"I was thinking. Maybe we don't want too many people to know. At school, I mean."

"Why not? Are you ashamed of me?"

"I thought you might be ashamed of me."

"Oh, Rich. You are a dope."

"So you're not?"

"No. I'm proud of you."

"Well, I'm proud of you. Why wouldn't I be? You're so beautiful."

"So are you."

"Me?" He sounded genuinely surprised.

"Yes. But maybe you're right. I don't want to make it be a school thing. Let's go on at school the same as ever."

Like Joe wanted with me. Only it wasn't Joe.

"And meet up after school?" he said.

"It's a deal," she said.

"I'd better go. Kitty's got sharp ears. Just one last thing I wanted to ask you."

"What?"

"Did it really happen?"

"Yes. It really happened."

"Just checking."

"You thought you might have dreamed it?"

"Yes. It was too good. I thought it had to be a dream."

"No. It was real."

"Real's better, isn't it?"

"Real is better."

# 28

# Rich in love

Kitty saw the change in Rich.

"You've gone all funny," she said.

"No, I haven't."

"Yes, you have. You're not listening half the time."

"So? Maybe I'm not interested half the time."

"I think it's because of Maddy Fisher."

"What's she got to do with anything?"

But he blushed. Kitty gave a cry of triumph.

"I knew it! You've got the hots for Maddy Fisher!"

"I have not! And anyway it's nothing to do with you."

"You have! You have! If you don't admit it I'll tell everyone."

"That doesn't make any sense."

"I will. You'll see."

"Why can't you keep your big nose out of my business?"

"Have I got a big nose?"

She felt her nose, suddenly critical.

"Your little nose, then."

"But I'm right, Rich, aren't I? I think she's great. And I know for a fact she's got the hots for you."

"What is this *hots*, Kitty? Where do you get this stuff from?"

"She has, though. I saw the way she was looking at you at Gran's party. Do you love her, Rich? Do you kiss and everything?"

"You keep out. You're too young."

"But I have to learn! How else am I to learn? You have to tell me things. Mum and Dad are ancient, they're not going to be any use. You're all I've got. And anyway"—she clung to him, wheedling—"I want you to be happy. Just tell me you're happy."

"Okay. I'm happy."

She flung her arms round him and held him tight.

"You're in love! You're in love! You're in love!"


It was true. Rich was in love. This was way beyond any dreams he had had of Grace Carey. He passed the hours in a blissful daze, thinking only of the time when he would be alone with Maddy Fisher once more.

"You know what?" said his friend Max. "You've become ultra boring."

"Sorry."

"What are you writing?"

He took the sheet of paper from Rich and read out: "'The deepest need of man is to overcome his separateness.'"

"What the fuck's that?"

"It's from the book Pablo lent me."

"It's bollocks. The deepest need of man is to get his end away."

They were lying on the grass by the edge of the sports field, supposedly revising for a forthcoming test. A spell of autumn sunshine had brought half the sixth form out into the open.

"Why do you always go on about sex, Max?"

"I don't know. I expect it's something to do with hormones."

"Don't you ever think about anything else?"

"No."

"Suppose you were able to get as much sex as you wanted. Suppose there were girls just there for you, all the time. Ten times a day if you wanted. Wouldn't there come a time when you'd start wanting something else?"

A dreamy look came over Max's round pink face.

"Girls I could fuck whenever I felt like it. That would be something."

"You'd get bored with it. You know you would."

"I'll tell you what I'd do. I'd have a fuck after breakfast. Then a little doze. Then I'd have a fuck for elevenses. Then another little doze. Then lunch. Then another fuck. Then another doze—"

"Yes, okay. I get the picture."

Maddy Fisher passed by with a group of friends. She waved a greeting.

"That Maddy Fisher's all right," said Max. "Shame she's got no tits."


They met in the tree barn in the woods that early evening. Maddy was carrying a folded-up Indian rug.

"Now we don't have to get leaves all over us."

She spread it out under the ash tree.

Rich was astonished by the rug. Why hadn't he thought of it? The part that astonished him was that Maddy had been making plans for their meeting. His own obsession he took for granted. He had not yet come to believe that Maddy could truly be thinking about him when he wasn't there. It seemed to Rich that Maddy had joined him out of the sheer goodness of her heart, because she knew he wanted her so much. He could not conceive that she wanted him.

"Any news about your gran?" Maddy said.

"No. Mum and Dad were with her this morning. She still hasn't woken up."

"I'm really sorry, Rich."

They lay down together on the rug. Maddy was wearing jeans, a T-shirt, a blue top.

"Where did you tell your parents you were going?" he said.

"To meet Cath."

"Does Cath know?"

"Not yet. I'll tell her tomorrow."

"It's funny about telling, isn't it? I feel shy about it. I don't really know why."

"Me too."

"It's because I don't really believe it yet, I think."

"What don't you believe?"

"That you want to be with me."

"You shouldn't put yourself down all the time, Rich. You're a very special person."

"Well, that's the thing. Sometimes I feel I'm so far ahead of everyone else that I must have landed from some other planet. And sometimes I feel like I'm just nobody."

"That's how I feel too."

"You can't ever feel you're nobody, Maddy. You're so gorgeous."

"I don't feel gorgeous."

"But you are. You just are. It's just a fact."

"I don't have much of a figure."

"What do you mean, not much of a figure? You've got an amazing figure."

"Not exactly a sexy figure, though."

"Who told you that? You're so sexy it kills me. Maddy, you're sexy to die for."

"Well, I'm glad you think so."

They kissed as they had kissed before, very softly.

"Remember," she said, "we're just practicing."

They held each other very close and their kissing became more eager. Rich felt her body against his. He started to shiver.

"There you go with the shaking," Maddy said.

"I wish it wouldn't do that," he said.

"Why? I like it. It makes me feel like everything's for the first time."

"It is."

"Me too."

"But you've kissed boys before, Maddy."

"Not like this. And not anything more than kissing. So it really is the first time for me."

"Don't you wish I was experienced and knew all the right moves?"

"No. I love it that it's new for you. I love it that no one else has ever done this with you before. I feel like you're giving me something no one else has had and no one else can ever have."

"Even if I do it all wrong?"

"You won't do it all wrong. That's why we're practicing."

They kissed again. He kissed her neck, her throat. He felt her hands moving over his back, pulling him close against her. He felt her hips pressing against his.

"You could take off your shirt," she said. "Then I could feel the real you."

He pulled off his shirt. To his own eyes his bare torso looked white and skinny in the fading evening light. But Maddy seemed happy enough.

"Look, you've got tiny chest hairs."

She stroked his chest. She tickled his nipples.

"Is that sensitive?"

"A bit."

She kissed his chest, rubbed her face against his bare skin.

"Aren't bodies wonderful?"

"You don't think I'm too skinny?"

"No. You're lean and lovely."

Her hair fell down on either side of her face and tickled his skin. "I could just eat you up," she said.

He couldn't ask aloud the way she did. He was still too shy. So instead he slipped his hands under her T-shirt and felt the bare skin beneath. He stroked his fingers over her back, pushing her shirt up, feeling the bumps of her spine.

"Why don't I take it off?" she said.

She sat up and pulled her T-shirt over her head. She wasn't wearing a bra. She sat there for a moment watching him looking at her.

"You like?"

"You're beautiful. More than I ever knew."

"Talk about skinny."

"Not skinny. Perfect."

Very gently he ran his fingers over her breasts. She saw the wonder in his eyes.

"Not like the glamour pictures."

"A million times more gorgeous. Feel. My hands are shaking."

And his blood was racing. And his legs were tingling. And his cock was pushing at his jeans.

"Oh, Rich. You're so sweet."

He kissed her breasts, first one, then the other, with tender care. Then he put his arms round her and drew her down so that they were lying pressed against each other on the rug. He kissed her lips. He felt her hand slip down to his crotch.

"Do you mind if I feel?" she whispered.

"No."

It wasn't the sort of thing you could keep secret. He felt awkward about it and almost unbearably excited, both at the same time. His cock was hard now, he had to tug on his jeans to let it stand straight. Maddy felt the ridge that it made beneath the denim. She stroked her hand up and down it.

Her touch overwhelmed him. No one else had ever touched him there. The solitary pleasures he had given himself had never brought with them this sensation of thrilling otherness. Someone else, someone outside the control of his own will, was giving him pleasure. He had entered a region of unknown delights. And to add to the sheer tingling shock of her touch there was the unthinkably wonderful fact that she *wanted* to please him. This bewildered him. It seemed impossible. The pleasures of sex had until now been so private, so wrapped around with secrecy and guilt, that it seemed only in dreams could they ever be shared with another.

"I think I should undo your jeans," she said. "You look so uncomfortable."

She undid the top button. She drew down the zip. She pushed aside the waistband of his pants. His cock stood free.

Rich found himself unable to speak a single word.

Maddy touched his cock. Then she stroked it softly, as much feeling it as stroking it.

"I don't really know what I'm doing."

She was wrapping her hand round his cock now, moving her hand up and down. He gave a gasp.

"Sorry. Did I hurt you?"

"No. It's not that."

"Oh. You think you might come?"

"It has been known."

"As quick as that?"

"Well, I am rather excited."

"Am I exciting you?"

"Yes, Maddy. Very much."

She stroked his cock with light touches.

"Cath and me watched some porn not so long ago," she said. "I thought it looked so boring. But with you it isn't boring. It's exciting."

"I bet his cock was bigger than mine."

"Yes, it was. Much."

"Sorry about that."

"What do you mean, sorry? Who says bigger's better? Do you wish I had bigger boobs?"

"No. Not at all."

"There you are, then. I love your cock just the way it is."

She bent down and kissed it. It twitched.

"Oh, it twitched!"

"What do you expect?"

"How long will it stay hard?"

"Pretty much until it gets what it wants."

Maddy returned to stroking his cock lightly with one hand.

"Do you mind if we don't go all the way?" she said. "Not today, I mean."

"No. I don't mind."

"It's just that I don't want it to happen too fast."

"Me neither."

"Does it hurt if you don't come?"

"No. Not hurt. It's just like anything else you want a lot and don't get."

"Poor cock. It seems so unfair."

She kissed it again.

"It's a bit the same for me, you know," she said. "I'm getting quite interested."

"Maybe you should undo your jeans too."

"Okay."

Once again, Rich was amazed. The stuff of fantasy was

turning out to be simplicity itself. All you had to do was ask.

Maddy wriggled her jeans down to her knees. Underneath she was wearing pretty white panties. Through the cotton of the panties Rich could see the dark triangle of her pubic hair.

She took his hand and placed it between her thighs. He stroked her, feeling the soft mound under the white cotton. He felt a throbbing in his cock.

"This could be too much for me."

She put her hand over his hand and pressed it against her crotch, moving it up and down.

"That feels nice."

Then she pushed her panties down and made his hand feel the tangle of hair, and the folds within. She guided his forefinger. She eased his fingertip up a little, in a little.

"Can you feel that?"

"Not yet. What am I supposed to be feeling?"

"There's a little bump there. There! You're on it now."

"Oh, yes."

"That's what gives me good feelings."

He pressed the little unseen bump, and moved his fingertip back and forth over it. She took control again, holding his finger in hers, making it go round in small circles.

"That's what you like?"

"Yes. Just there."

He told her what he liked. She told him what she liked. It was so simple, so obvious, and to Rich a revelation beyond wonder.

His body was convulsed with longing. His mind was dazzled by the nearness of her almost-naked body. But more than everything else he felt flooded with gratitude.

*She wants to please me. She gives me her body to please me. She strokes my cock to please me. For this I give her my love now and forever. All for you, my Maddy. My darling Maddy.*

A distant crashing of footsteps in the wood. They both froze. Someone was coming up the path.

Rapidly, in total silence, they pulled their clothes back on and separated, sitting a little apart on the rug. A dog appeared, a black Labrador, and looked at them. A woman's voice called, "Susie! Susie!" The dog ran off. A half-seen figure passed by between the trees, heading up the path and out onto the top of the hill.

"Maybe we should go back," Maddy whispered.

They stood up and Maddy shook out the rug and folded it up.

"We'd better find somewhere else for next time," said Rich.

"I've got somewhere. If you don't mind coming to my place."

"What about your parents?"

"Not in the house. In the shop. After it's closed, of course. There's even a bed."

He put his arms round her and pulled her close. They kissed.

"I love you, Maddy."

"I love you, Rich."

They returned through the dark wood, descending from their own private retreat to the world of other people. In the shadowy spaces between the last of the trees they kissed again before coming out onto the open road.

"Tomorrow evening, then."

"Tomorrow."

# 29

## Joe brings news

Maddy had a lot to tell Cath. She started with the easy part.

"I finally got to talk with Joe and guess what? Grace made it all up."

"Made what up?"

"Everything. Her and Joe. Gemma being pregnant. The emails. Everything."

"She isn't going out with Joe?"

"And Joe didn't send the emails."

"So who did?"

"Has to be Grace herself."

"But why?"

"You tell me, Cath. I say she has to be insane."

"And the rest! She should be put down. That is so sick."

"Well, she is supposed to be sick, isn't she? That's why she's not in school."

"I'll give her sick. Sick's too good for that bitch. I vote for dead. Don't you want to kill her?"

"I want to know why she did it. But no, I don't want to kill her."

"You're too good for this world, Mad. It's not healthy."

"I don't really care that much about Grace anymore," said Maddy.

She had more to tell. What she had said so far came under the category of surprise. The next part was more like betrayal. For so long she and Cath had been boyfriend-less together, mutually supportive in a world of couples. When she had embarked on her great crush on Joe she had invited Cath to be part of it from the beginning. This time it was different. Cath was on the outside.

"I've got something else going on," she said. "All very new. I've started seeing more of Rich Ross."

"Rich?" Cath stared in disbelief. "You and Rich?"

"Yes."

"How? When? You never said a word." Her eyes started to blink rapidly. "You never even signed his petition."

Maddy knew then that it was even worse than she had feared. Cath had had secret hopes of Rich for herself.

"Oh, God," she said. "I'm sorry, Cath."

"It was only a tiny glimmer. Only a baby dream. I thought maybe if he had no one else . . ."

Her voice trailed away.

Maddy said, "I wouldn't have done anything if I'd known."

"So you've done things already?"

"Not much. It's all really new."

"I didn't think he was your type."

"Nor did I."

"Oh, well," said Cath. "I'm not surprised he'd go for you. But you going for him—that's a new one on me. I mean, he's not exactly Joe Finnigan, is he?"

"Maybe that's what I like about him."

"So you really do like him?"

"Yes."

"Out of ten?"

"Nine."

"Joe got nine. Nine means ten but you don't want to say ten because ten means it's perfect and then God gets jealous and spoils it."

"All right. Eight."

"Anything over seven's in love."

"I don't know, Cath. It's not like it was with Joe. I don't feel all churned up with excitement. I just want to be with him, and when I'm with him I feel good."

"Oh, God. Oh, God. Oh, God."

"Okay. I won't say any more."

"No, you're my best friend. I want to know all about it. I just wish I had someone to love me too. Oh, I do, I do, I do." She did a little dance of frustration. "I suppose I'll have to have a go at Mini-Max. Do you think if I don't mind him being a dwarf he'll not mind me being a hag?"

So how far should they go? The question no longer existed for Maddy, because they had already begun. There was no stopping now. They would go where the road led them. Their time together this evening, already planned, was only one part of that journey. Whatever they did tonight, it could never be "all the way." The way had to be longer than that. But it might be, most likely would be, that semi-mythical milestone in a girl's life, her "first time."

Maddy sat alone in a library cubicle, her workbooks open before her, and thought about sex. The prospect was unreal to her. It had so many associations, it was so grown-up and glamorous, but there was also something ridiculous about it. How could such a presumed transformation be achieved by a few minutes of clumsy fumbling in the cushion room, just a few hours from now?

*Maybe I'm not ready. I don't have to do it.*

This thought stopped her in her tracks. Why was she assuming her blossoming love affair with Rich had to turn sexual so soon? In the past couples kissed and cuddled for months, even years, before ending up in bed together. Rich certainly wasn't forcing the pace. Neither of them were. They were letting happen what they wanted to happen.

Who's doing the wanting here?

Maddy did her best to be honest with herself. Would she be more at ease if they put the brakes on the rush towards sex? She imagined being in Rich's arms again as they had been in the tree barn. There was her answer. Every touch was leading them there. It was what was coming next. It was tomorrow. It was this evening. Soon it would be now.

And she wanted it to happen. She wanted it because it would then be the bond between her and Rich, the shared secret that made them more than friends; just as Gemma had said about Joe, "I'm the only one he does it with." Maddy didn't expect a wild explosion of passion. She'd questioned her friends who'd done it, and picked up that there was more discomfort than pleasure the first time. But on the plus side it didn't take long, the boy was grateful, and ever after you could say you'd done it. It gets easier, they said, like smoking. Hang on in and you start really liking it.

When she imagined it Maddy saw it as an extended form of kissing and hugging. *We'll kiss and hug, and get closer and closer, until we're as close as two people can ever be. And that will be sex.*

"Here you are! I've been looking all over for you."

It was Joe Finnigan. He dropped down into a chair facing her.

"Listen," he said. "I think I've found out what's been going on with Grace. I had a sort of idea and I checked it out last night. Grace Carey has been seeing my brother Leo."

"Leo!"

"Whenever something bad happens in my family it's always down to Leo."

"Grace has been going out with Leo!"

"Apparently he picked her up in a club over a year ago."

"Grace has been going out with Leo for a year?"

"So Leo says."

"But it's over now."

"It's not over at all. She's with him now."

"But Leo's going out with my sister."

"That doesn't mean he's not seeing Grace."

Maddy struggled to put all this new information together. Why would Grace not have told her?

"What do you mean, she's with Leo now?"

"She's in Leo's flat. Leo says she's ill."

"What sort of ill?"

"I don't know. Leo doesn't give much away. I told him Grace's story about you and me and he laughed and said yes, he knew. That's when it came out. He said she was jailbait when she first came onto him. He said, 'You know me, Joe. I can resist anything except temptation.'"

"And Grace is with him now?"

"Apparently."

"Joe, Leo's got a mean streak." Maddy was trying not to give away what Imo had told her in confidence, but she couldn't stop herself. Something had to be done. "Almost like he's sadistic."

"Leo's very mixed up," said Joe. "You can thank our dear papa for that. Not exactly the best role model. Very charming and very unpredictable. He left years ago but he still shows up from time to time. Mummy says he's a total bastard but she's never loved anyone else."

"Was he violent?"

"I think he might have been."

"But your mother still loved him?"

"Yes. Still does."

"Joe, Leo's violent. He hit Imo. He hurt her."

Joe's face darkened.

"I'm sorry," he said. "Really I am. She just has to keep away from him."

"She's keeping away now."

"I wouldn't wish Leo on any girl, even though he's my brother. Not even Grace Carey."

"Shouldn't he be reported or something? I saw what he did to Imo."

"I suppose so. It's hard. He thinks it's just fooling around."

"Do lots of boys like to hurt girls? Do you?"

He looked up quickly, shock in his eyes.

"No! Never! I wouldn't hurt a fly. Ask Gemma."

"Somebody has to talk to him, Joe. Can't you talk to him? Make him see it."

"Maddy, I'm his little brother. He'd just laugh at me."

"Someone has to do something."

Joe brushed his hair out of his eyes and gave an awkward shrug of his shoulders. He stood up.

"Well, anyway. That's what I came to say. Whatever Grace has been up to, it's something to do with Leo."

What had Grace been up to?

Maddy went over it and over it but could make no sense of anything. If she'd been going out with Leo all the time, why the concealment? Why the lies? Why the elaborate made-up stories?

If Grace was still not in school tomorrow Maddy determined to go to Leo's flat and find her and make her tell her the truth. And if Leo was there too there were things she had to say to him.

Tomorrow.

Before then came tonight.

# 30

## Grace's story

Maddy prepared herself that evening with care. She had a shower. She put on her prettiest underwear. She chose a short blue denim skirt, not tarty short, but easier to manage than jeans; a tight fitting white cotton T-shirt; and a long loose cotton-knit top the color of strawberry ice cream. She brushed her hair and pulled it back into a ponytail. She spent half an hour making herself up, but so subtly that Rich would most likely think she was wearing no makeup at all. She sprayed on three very short bursts of perfume. She took her evening pill, which was the sixth since she had started. No side effects so far.

Alone in the kitchen she added vodka to a carton of orange juice and shook it vigorously. She wasn't going to get drunk, just a little bit relaxed.

She unlocked the shop and climbed the stairs to the cushion room. She drew the curtains closed round the big Indian bed, even though no customers would appear at this hour. She lay down among the cushions in the softly tinted evening light and took a swig of the vodka and orange and waited for Rich to call.

As she waited she thought about him. She imagined him there with her, lying on the bed by her side. She imagined him kissing her, the way they had kissed in the tree barn, very lightly. She imagined putting her arms round his naked body. She whispered, "I love you, Rich." She felt his body all down her body. "Shall we?" she whispered. "Shall we do it?" She felt him shivering in her arms the way he'd done before, and she knew he wanted to do it more than anything in the world. "Do you love me, Rich?" she whispered. "Do you love me?" And he did, he loved her with his heart and his mind and his body, and this was how she knew it, he was giving himself to her without reserve. She held him naked in her arms and he was as close as anyone ever could be, and that was love.

Her phone rang.

Rich was calling from the hospital. He couldn't come.

"I'm really sorry, Mad." His voice quiet down the phone, the sounds of the hospital tannoy in the background. "You know I want to more than anything. But we're all here."

"Is it bad?"

"They say so."

"Don't worry about me. Call me when you can."

"I should be thinking about Gran," he said. "But I'm thinking about you."

"Me too."

After the call was over Maddy lay for a moment longer pondering what to do. Then she did what she always did at such times. She phoned Cath.

Cath came round at once. They drank the vodka and orange together and Maddy told Cath all she now knew about Grace.

"Leo?" said Cath. "It's Leo? I can't keep up. Am I just stupid? What's going on?"

"Ask Grace."

"Where is Grace? She hasn't been in school for days."

"Joe says she's at Leo's place," said Maddy. "He's got a flat on the High Street. Above Caffè Nero."

They looked at each other. Maddy took another swig at the carton, and handed it to Cath.

"Are you thinking what I'm thinking?"

"You bet I am."

Cath took a long swig.

"She'll be there right now."

"Sniggering with that weirdo Leo."

"We could talk to her."

"We could smack her stupid face."

"No, I don't want to get into a fight," said Maddy. "I just want some answers."

It was past nine in the evening when Maddy and Cath found themselves standing on the empty pavement outside the dark café. The night air was chilly. In the vodka-induced excitement of their departure Maddy had not thought to put on a warmer top and now she was shivering with cold.

"Anything left in that carton?"

"Mad, we dumped it way back. We're running on righteous anger now."

"Righteous anger. Right."

She rang the bell for the first-floor flat. It made no sound.

"I don't think the bell works."

She knocked. There was no response.

They stood back on the curb and looked up at the first-floor windows. The curtains were drawn, but there were lights on inside.

"Someone's home."

Then the street door opened and Leo Finnigan came out.

"Hello," he said.

He was wearing a leather aviator jacket and a scarf, apparently on his way out somewhere.

"Is Grace in there?" said Maddy.

"Yes, she is."

"We want to see her."

"She's not feeling too good," said Leo. "Is it important?"

"Yes, it is."

Maddy realized Leo had not recognized her. She saw no need to enlighten him.

"Come on in, then."

They followed him up the stairs.

"I was just going out to the pub to catch the last half of the game," he said. "It's not very cool to admit it these days but I'm a secret Man United fan."

The flat's living room was furnished with familiar items from Maddy's family shop, some of them very pricey. Leo's mother had spared no expense. The chest on which the TV stood was top of the range, inlaid with many different woods to create pictures of lakeside palaces. The remains of a takeaway meal lay on the floor among a litter of DVDs. Discarded clothing hung from chair backs. Discarded shoes, both male and female, were heaped under the table. Cigarette butts in plates on the windowsills.

Grace lay on the sofa, covered by a duvet. Her skin was pale and waxy, her hair unkempt, her eyes wide and staring. She was watching *Breakfast at Tiffany's*.

"What are you doing here? Who told you I was here?"

She sounded frightened.

"Joe," said Maddy.

"None of his fucking business," said Grace.

"My brother my keeper," said Leo with a smile. He turned

off the television. "What can I get you? I've got whisky. I've got water. I've got whisky and water."

Maddy was staring at Grace. Her appearance shocked her.

"We don't want anything," said Cath. "We've come to talk to Grace."

"She may not be up to it," said Leo. He put one hand on Grace's forehead. "She had a temperature of one hundred and two this morning. I've been feeding her paracetamol all day."

Leo the caring nurse.

"I'm okay," said Grace.

Leo looked from Grace to Maddy and Cath.

"So if it's girl talk why don't I leave you to it?"

He turned to go. Suddenly Maddy couldn't bear it.

"Why don't you give my sister a call?" she said. "Imo Fisher."

"Ah." Leo stopped in the doorway. "You're Imo's sister."

"She could do with some paracetamol too."

Maddy meant to wither him with scorn but Leo took her words at face value.

"Why? What's up with her?"

"Bruises. All over her body."

Leo frowned. He sounded concerned.

"How did that happen?"

"You should know. You did it. You beat her up."

"Me? Is that what she told you?"

"Yes."

"I'm sorry, sweetheart, but your sister must have me confused with someone else. I don't beat people up."

"I've seen the bruises."

"Not me. Not my style at all. Is it, petal?"

This was addressed to Grace.

"Of course not," said Grace.

Leo checked his watch.

"Twenty minutes to go," he said. "I'm going to leave you girls to entertain each other. I'll be in the Rainbow if you need me."

He gave a cheery wave that was scarily similar to Joe's, and went off down the stairs.

There was a silence. Leo's blank denial had left Maddy confused and uncertain.

"If you're not going to say anything," said Grace, "let's have the film back on."

"You're the one that has to say something," said Cath.

"I've got nothing to say."

Maddy began to breathe rapidly.

"That's not good enough," she said. "You've lied and lied and lied."

"Well, there you are, then," said Grace. "No use in listening to anything I say."

Her pale face and listless voice only fanned Maddy's anger.

"Just tell me, Grace."

"Think what you like," said Grace. "I don't care anymore."

"Since when did you care?" said Cath.

"Whatever," said Grace.

"Listen, bitch," said Cath. "I don't care how sick you are. I hope you die. But before you die you better tell Maddy why you screwed her around like that."

"Or what?" said Grace.

"Or you'll be fucking sorry."

"Oh, that. I'm fucking sorry already. I don't need you to make me fucking sorry."

Maddy lost it.

She took hold of the duvet and ripped it away. Grace's thin body lay exposed, shivering on the sofa in pajamas. She shrank back from Maddy, afraid.

"That's just for starters," said Maddy.

She was shaking. She realized she wanted to hurt Grace. She wanted to rouse her from this state of passive resistance.

She leaned over the sofa and pushed Grace's shoulders, jerking her back.

Grace opened her eyes very wide.

"You want to hit me?"

"I'm drunk," said Maddy, "and I've been wanting to do this forever."

She pushed her again, harder this time.

Grace turned her frightened eyes on Cath.

"Cath," she said. "Tell her I'm sick."

"I don't care if you're sick," said Cath.

Maddy started to hit Grace with little jabbing stabs of her hand.

"So are you going to talk or not?" she said.

Grace was shrinking away from her attack. Maddy took hold of her by her thin shoulders and shook her hard.

"Please! Don't!" Grace was staring at Maddy with big fearful eyes. Her voice had become small and pleading. "Come and sit here by me."

"I don't want to sit by you."

"Please. I'll tell you everything."

She drew her legs up to her chest to make room, behaving like a little girl.

"Please."

Maddy stared at her for a long moment. She could feel the blood racing in her veins. Her own anger thrilled her. She felt powerful in a way she had never known before.

She had frightened Grace. She had made Grace submit to her. But now, seeing Grace clutching her knees like a child, so frail and timid, she could not sustain the glorious surge of rage.

"Please sit by me."

So Maddy sat down beside Grace. Grace curled up against her, laying her head in Maddy's lap.

"Go on, then," said Maddy. "Tell."

"I will. I'll say whatever you want. But it won't do any good. You'll never understand."

"Why not?"

"Because you're not like me."

"Guess what, Grace?" said Maddy. "You don't know anything about me. You don't know what I'm like or what I'm not like."

Grace clung to Maddy, gazing up at her with her big beautiful eyes.

"I don't want you to hate me, Maddy. We're friends."

"Wrong. We're not friends, Grace. That was all over long ago."

Tears welled in Grace's eyes.

"Do you hate me too, Cath?"

"Yes," said Cath.

"You wouldn't if you knew."

"Knew what?" said Maddy. "All I know is you faked a load of emails and told lies about you and Joe and Gemma, and all for nothing at all as far as I can see, except to hurt me."

"Not to hurt you," said Grace. "To show you."

"Show me what?"

"What it's really like."

"What what's really like?"

"Love. Boys. Sex."

"Why?"

"So you'd know. You were such a smiley little virgin."

"Me!"

"She's jealous of you," said Cath. "Can you believe it?" She rounded on Grace. "You just wanted Mad to be as miserable as you."

"I wanted my friend back."

Maddy stared at her.

"How would making a fool of myself over Joe do that?"

"Then you'd know. Then we'd talk about boys and how they're all no good and how we've got each other." Tears rolled down her cheeks. "It was only a game. I was going to tell you right away, but you just bought the whole thing. So I let it go on a bit."

"So that you could have a good laugh at me."

"I didn't know how deep in you'd got, Maddy. Truly. I thought it was only a bit of fun."

"Why did you tell me you were going out with Joe?"

"It all went too far. I didn't want you finding out and hating me. I had to stop you talking to Joe."

"So what was the point of all those emails about Leo?"

"To stop Imo seeing Leo." She wiped her eyes. "Leo's mine."

"Was that all made up too? About Leo hurting girls?"

Grace hesitated. But by now they had come too far.

"No," she said.

"Even though Leo just told me it wasn't true and you backed him up."

"What he means is he doesn't do anything they don't want. If Imo got hurt by Leo it's because she wanted it."

"That's crap, Grace. No one wants to be hurt."

"Yes, they do. Lots of people want to be hurt."

"Why?"

Grace stared back in silence for a long moment.

"It's how you know someone loves you," she said.

Maddy was dumbstruck.

"Look," said Grace.

She sat up and opened her pajama top. Her skinny body was dark with bruises, just like Imo's.

"It's how he shows he loves me. I want him to do it to me. That's what you don't understand, Maddy. You've not had sex with a boy. This is what sex does."

Maddy stared.

"That's not love, Grace."

"I knew you wouldn't understand."

"That's just sick," said Cath in a low voice.

"It's not sick," said Grace. "It's just how it is. Boys want sex so much it gives us power over them. So then they want to hurt us. If you want them to love you, you have to let them hurt you. It stops hurting after the first few times. After that, it feels like love."

Maddy gazed at Grace's bruised body and for the first time she felt a kind of pity. Not for the bruises: for the loneliness, and the deprivation of love.

"Oh, Grace," she said softly. "I'm so sorry."

"It's the same for you too," said Grace. "It's the same for everyone."

"No, it isn't. There are other kinds of love."

"Not with sex. You'll find out. I'm right, Cath. Aren't I?"

"No," said Cath. Like Maddy, the harshness was gone from her voice. "You've had bad luck. Leo's sick, Grace. You have to get away from him."

"I love him. I've never loved anyone the way I love him. If he left me I'd die."

"I'm going to report him to the police."

"No, Maddy! You can't!"

"Maddy's right," said Cath.

"I'll deny it," said Grace. "I'll say you're making it all up. You can't prove it. Don't make him send me away. Don't you understand? I love him. He could kill me and I'd die loving him."

Cath met Maddy's eyes.

"I don't want to do this anymore," she said.

Maddy rose from the sofa.

"Put on some clothes," she said to Grace. "We're taking you home."

"No!"

Grace turned her face into the sofa and once more drew her skinny knees up to her chest.

"Get out! Go away!"

"We can't leave you like this. I'm going to tell your parents."

"No! It's got fuck all to do with them. You think they care?" Grace was screaming now. "Just fuck off! Get out of my life! You said we're not friends anymore. Just leave me alone!"

Maddy stood gazing at the frail trembling body curled up on the sofa. Then she picked up the duvet off the floor and covered her once more. She turned on the TV and started the film again.

"I'm really sorry, Grace," she said softly. "If you change your mind, just call. Come on, Cath. Let's go."

Out in the street Maddy looked at Cath and Cath looked at Maddy. They were both in shock.

"It's been going on for a year, Cath."

"Did you hear what she said? She said she told all those lies to show you. She wants you to be as unhappy as her, Mad."

"God knows what she wants. She's in a bad way. We have to tell her mum and dad. They have to get her out of there."

Maddy looked towards the brightly lit windows of the Rainbow.

"But first I have to talk to Leo," she said.

In the pub the television was blaring. The match had just finished. Leo was there, sitting at a table with a group of friends, all men, drowning their sorrows.

"Hi, sweetheart," he said, seeing Maddy approach. "Have

you come to cheer us up? We could do with some cheering up."

"I've come to ask you a question," said Maddy.

"What's that?"

"Why do you hurt girls?"

The pub went quiet.

"Why do you get off on hurting girls?"

Leo gave an easy lift of his shoulders and threw a smile at his companions.

"Women, eh?" he said.

The men round the table chuckled.

There were three beer mugs on the table: two half drunk, one empty.

"What's the matter with you all?" she said. "Do you all like hurting girls?"

"Don't knock it till you've tried it, sweetheart," Leo said.

Maddy picked up the nearest mug and threw the contents in Leo's face. She did the same with the second. He gasped and raised one hand. He was still smiling.

Then Maddy picked up the last, empty beer mug, leaned across the table, and swung it hard down on Leo's head. It struck him with a loud thud. He cried out and clutched his head in his hands.

"Whoa!" said one of the men. "Easy now."

Leo lowered his hands from his head. There was blood on his fingers. He looked at his friends and managed a crooked grin.

"I think she loves me," he said.

They all laughed: a great breeze of tension-releasing laughter.

"Come on, Mad," said Cath.

Maddy let the beer mug fall. She heard the smash of glass as it hit the brick floor. She felt Cath pulling her out of the pub into the cold night air. She was still shaking with anger.

"They laughed, Cath. They just laughed."

"What do they know? They're just men."

"No," said Maddy fiercely. "No. That's what Grace wants us to think. That isn't how all men are. It can't be."

"You really whacked him, Mad. It was amazing."

"He doesn't care."

"He bled."

"I'm glad."

They walked up the street.

"I was so angry I didn't know what I was doing. Do you think I hurt him a lot?"

"I hope so."

"Oh, Cath. Hold me."

They came to a stop halfway up the High Street and hugged each other tight.

"I've never, ever done anything like that before," said Maddy.

"You're a killer."

"I don't want to be a killer. I don't want to feel so angry. I just want everyone to love each other."

"Me too. Let's whack everyone until they get the message. Love each other or die."

# 31

# The big question

Time passed slowly at the hospital.

For a while it seemed Gran would die at any moment. Several times they thought she had already died. But then there would come a soft snuffle and they knew she was still alive. She lay in a side room with Rich's father sitting by her. Rich's mother and Rich and Kitty went in and out. When it got too tiring being sad about Gran, Rich and Kitty went off to fetch cups of tea from the WRVS stall.

"Maybe she'll get better," said Kitty. "Maybe she'll come home."

"I don't think so," said Rich.

Gran had been asleep for two days.

"What if she just goes on sleeping? I mean, like, for years?"

"I don't know, Kitty. We'll just have to wait and see."

The WRVS stall was closed. There was a machine that

dispensed tea and coffee. Rich felt around in his mother's purse. There were only enough coins to get one cup of tea.

"They'll have to share it."

"What about us?"

"We'll be okay."

"I won't be okay."

Kitty started to cry.

"I'll tell you what, Kitty," said Rich. "I think Mum's going to take us home soon, since Gran's going on sleeping. When we get home we could make ourselves hot chocolate icebergs."

"Do you think we could?"

"Definitely."

They carried the single cup of tea back to Gran's bedside and gave it to their father.

"I think you children had better go home," he said. "Give Gran a kiss in case she goes in the night."

"Are you going to stay, Harry?" said their mother.

"Yes. I'll be fine."

They all kissed Gran. She showed no signs of knowing they were there. Her skin was soft and dry and smelled of roses, like it always had.

"I love you, Gran," whispered Rich.

In the car Kitty said, "Will she just go on and on sleeping?"

"The doctors say it won't be long now," said their mother. "She's very lucky, really. It's how I'd like to go."

"I wouldn't," said Kitty. "I'd like to say good-bye and have everyone round me crying and telling me how much they love me."

"Gran knows that anyway, darling."

At home Rich made the hot chocolate icebergs as promised. This was a family invention, only allowed on special occasions. You made hot chocolate in the normal way and then put into each mug a scoop of vanilla ice cream. You had to drink the hot chocolate before the ice cream all melted so that you got hot-ness and coldness in each mouthful.

Kitty was happy again. You couldn't not be happy with a hot chocolate iceberg.

Rich went up to his room and wrote in his diary.

> I am evil. Gran is dying but all I think about is Maddy. I want to be with Maddy more than I want to be with Gran even if it means missing her dying. I want to be with Maddy so I can tell her how evil I am. She's the only one who'll understand.

He played the Beach Boys because it was what he had played when she was here. He lay full length on his bed and gazed up at the ceiling and thought of Maddy. His thoughts weren't about sex. He wasn't reliving the magical hour of kissing and touching.

He was slowly absorbing the incredible fact that she loved him.

Rich was only now discovering that he had never expected to be loved. His family loved him, of course. But Maddy was someone else, a stranger, a person with no reason or duty to love him. Rich's understanding of love was that it could only be prompted by out-of-the-ordinary merit. You could be loved for being strikingly beautiful, or famous, or heroic, or wealthy. He was none of these things. Why therefore would anyone be interested in him? He himself, of course, had a powerful urge to love. He did not seek as objects of his love only the beautiful, or the famous, or the rich. But somehow he had never thought that it might be the same for others: that girls too might have an impulse to love, just as he had, and were waiting not for the perfect boy, but for a little returning kindness.

He got up off his bed and wrote in his diary.

> Don't fuck this up. This is your only chance. There's only one Maddy Fisher in the known universe. If she dumps you, you're on your own for the rest of your days.

After that he lay back down on his bed and thought about sex.

Among the many thousand ways he could mess up, sex

came number one. Rich both longed for it and dreaded it. If there was any chance of it ruining his relationship with Maddy he truly would rather give it a miss. He wanted her love far more than he wanted sex.

There was so much to go wrong. There was the actual doing of it, which still baffled him, for all the pornographic images lodged in his brain. It wasn't simple, like putting a key in a lock. You couldn't quite tell where the lock was, for a start. And even if you found it there were certain specialized ways of proceeding which made it good for the girl, and other ways of proceeding, far more other ways, that left the girl entirely unmoved.

Then there was the matter of stamina. Judging from the intense few moments when they had lain together on the rug, once engaged in actual sex he would last about fifteen seconds. This was not enough. Rich was not sure how long *was* enough, but fifteen seconds wasn't it. In the porn videos he'd watched, the banging went on for what seemed like hours.

Then there was the matter of contraception. He had got himself a pack of three condoms. He knew how to roll a condom on. What entirely defeated him was the question of timing. In a perfect world you would put it on in private, before ever meeting your date, as part of your preparations. Then come the moment all would be in place and nothing need be said. But this was not possible with a condom. Your cock had to be hard first. In theory you could make your cock hard and put the condom on and then go out on your date. But unless the date proceeded directly and rapidly to sex your cock would go soft again and the condom would drop off, and you'd never be able to get it on again. So really there was no way out. You had to wait until the critical moment and then call for a pause. But the act of putting on a condom was not erotic. There was something calculated about it that ran counter to the rising tide of passion. Rich was rather relying on the rising tide of passion to carry him along. He did not want to stop for an intermission, least of all an intermission prompted by thoughts of pregnancy, childbirth, and babies.

Then there was the matter of virginity. His own virginity gave him more than enough to worry about, but he must also consider Maddy's virginity. She had made it clear to him that she had not had sex before. So what should he expect? Would there be resistance? Would there be blood? As soon as the word "blood" entered his mind he shut down the whole chain of thought. Don't ask. Don't look. Somewhere round that corner was a realm of biological detail that made him feel queasy. Maybe, it struck him for the first time, what he really needed to carry him through this formidable ordeal was alcohol. Once well and truly drunk nothing would seem all that alarming.

Add to all these real and practical concerns the fact that he would be negotiating them while in a state of almost frenzied arousal, and it seemed to him that he was certain to peak too soon. He would boil over like a pan of milk. Then what would they do? So much anticipation, so much preparation, all undressed, and nowhere to go. It really didn't seem fair. Why was the one part of your body that was needed at this most sensitive and potentially embarrassing time so totally out of your control? Whose idea was that? What evolutionary purpose did it serve? It felt like a trick. Maybe it was God's way of limiting the population. The incompetence method.

Rich didn't believe in God. He believed in karma. Karma meant you got what you deserved.

Did he really deserve Maddy?

Not in a million years.

Then came the rush of gratitude. Rich felt this now a hundred times a day, it came over him in waves, the sensation of grateful wonder. *She loves me. Unbelievable but true. She loves me.*

Then he remembered that Gran was dying and he'd given her not a single thought. His father was sitting in faithful silence by her bedside all night and Rich was obsessing about sex.

*I am evil. I am selfish. I am in love.*


The next morning his father phoned to say Gran was still alive, and still asleep. Rich and Kitty were to go to school.

Rich found Maddy before the start of classes.

"Gran's still clinging on," he said. "I can't make any plans."

"No, of course not," said Maddy. "I'm sorry. It must be hard."

"It's strange. At first it seemed like a big deal. But if something goes on long enough with nothing happening, it stops being such a big deal."

"Until it happens."

At the end of the school day Maddy and Cath and Rich walked into town together.

"I'm not being a gooseberry," said Cath to Rich. "I'm being camouflage."

Maddy told Rich about Grace: about how she was ill on a sofa, and about her bruises. Rich was deeply shocked.

"So you were right, Rich," Maddy said. "You guessed there was something wrong with her. You saw what none of us saw."

"I never guessed it was that bad."

Cath left them at the turning to her street. Maddy walked on with Rich to his house. She waited outside while Rich checked for news of Gran.

"Mum says come in. She's squeezing oranges."

"Any news?"

"Nothing. Dad's at the hospital."

They took their glasses of juice up to Rich's room for privacy. Rich sat on the bed and Maddy sat beside him. Then she lay down and put her head in his lap.

"I want Gran to die," said Rich. "That proves I'm not a good person, doesn't it?"

"I think it's just natural."

"I should be thinking about Gran. But actually I'm thinking about you."

"Oh, well," said Maddy. "That is quite bad."

She gave him such a sweet upside-down smile when she said "quite bad" that he put down his glass of juice and pressed one hand to his chest.

"What's wrong?"

"Nothing," he said. "Just a gratitude rush. I get them from time to time."

She put her hand to his chest and felt his heart beating.

"I am selfish, you know," he said. "All I want is you."

"That's not selfish. If you're thinking about me you're thinking about another person, so it's not selfish."

"Really I'm thinking about you thinking about me."

"Oh, okay. That's definitely selfish."

A knock on the door. Kitty's voice from the other side.

"Rich? Are you in there?"

"We're talking," said Rich.

"Fine," said Kitty. "Go on *talking*."

They heard her footsteps going away down the stairs.

"Maybe she needs you," said Maddy. "She's so fond of you."

"She'll be all right."

"Anyway, we are just talking. You don't mind, do you?"

"No. I love talking to you."

"I mean, having to wait."

"No, I don't mind."

"It's just that sometimes I think I don't understand boys at all. They're so different."

"Don't judge all boys by Leo Finnigan."

"You don't want to hurt girls, do you, Rich? Not even secretly?"

"Not in any way at all. I don't get that one."

"Grace says it's because of sex. Boys want sex from girls, so girls have power over them, so they want to hurt them."

"But that's not how it feels to me. Not at all."

"Boys do want sex."

"Yes, of course. But boys want girls to *want* to have sex. If you think the girl doesn't want you, that's a turn-off right there."

"What about rape? Men do that."

"I don't get that. It must be all about hatred. You'd have to really hate women to do that. If you love someone you don't want to hurt them. You want everything to be good for them."

"The thing is, I think you may be nicer than most boys."

"I don't see why. Most people just want to be loved."

"But sex isn't the same thing as love."

"It feels the same to me."

There it was, the big question.

"Listening to Grace was so horrible," said Maddy. "And so

sad. Sometimes I get the feeling that the world is full of pain. I watch the news and it's all about people hating each other and being greedy and destroying the planet and nobody caring. And then I think, what am I doing that's so great? What makes me any different? My life isn't such a big deal either."

"It is to me. Your life's a big deal to me."

"Maybe that's why we all want to be loved so much. Because we'd feel so useless otherwise."

"I've never thought of it that way," said Rich. "I always thought I wanted someone to love because without it I wasn't finished. Like, I wasn't complete. But maybe you're right. Maybe we want someone to need us."

"No, I like your idea better."

"I'll tell you what it is." Rich was thinking it out as he went along. "There's two kinds of love. There's the love you get from someone else, and there's the love you give to someone else. People think the best part of loving is to have someone love you. But I think the best part is having someone to love. Someone who lets you love them."

"You got that from Pablo's book."

"It could still be true."

"But lots of people might let you love them. It doesn't mean you can. Cath would let you love her if you wanted to."

"That's different."

"You don't want to love Cath?"

"I want to love you."

"What if I died?"

"Don't say that."

"You'd forget me and love someone else."

"Maddy, you just have no idea."

"I'm not that special, Rich. Really."

"You're the most special person in the universe."

"Only to you."

"You can't believe that."

"I do. Truly. I can't see what difference my life makes to all the important things. I can't stop wars, or cure diseases, or slow down global warming. I can't even make my mum and dad happy. So what's the point of me? And don't say to make you feel good, because that's not enough."

"It feels enough to me," said Rich.

"You're just one person. One's just not enough."

"How about four? Suppose four people needed you. Me, your sister, your parents. Is that enough?"

"Well, no. Not really. I mean, they're my family."

"Okay. Suppose we add in another six. Friends and neighbors. If ten people needed you, would your life have a point?"

"I don't know. Which ten people?"

"Just anybody."

"I don't see where you're going with this."

"Okay," said Rich. "Let's start at the other end. At the big end you've got the world. Seven billion people. If you did some-thing that made a difference to the whole world you'd say your life had a point, right?"

"Right."

"But it doesn't have to be all seven billion people, does it? Suppose you found a cure for AIDS and saved a billion lives. That would do it."

"Sure."

"How about a million?"

"A million's good."

"How about fifty thousand? A whole stadium full of people whose lives have been saved by Maddy Fisher."

"I'll take that."

"Ten thousand?"

"Okay, okay." Maddy raised her hands in protest. "I see where this is going now."

"I'm just trying to find out how many people's lives you need to affect for you to feel your own existence has a point."

"That makes me sound so crass."

"Don't you see? One's enough. None's enough. Your life has value, full stop. Every breath you take changes the atmosphere of the planet. Every word you speak goes on forever. Sound waves never die, did you know that? Every single thing you do makes a difference."

"Same for you. Same for everyone."

"Is that a problem? Do you want to be more important than everyone else?"

"I'm not sure." Maddy thought about that. "I'd like there to be at least some people who are less important than me."

"Okay. I nominate Grace."

He was smiling down at her, stroking her hair.

"Rich," said Maddy. "You are an amazing person. You get more amazing all the time. I've never talked to anyone the way I talk to you."

Somewhere in the house they heard the phone ring. Then came the sound of Kitty's footsteps running up the stairs. She pushed open the door, eyes wide with the importance of her role as the bringer of news.

"Gran died," she announced. "Dad just called. Gran died five minutes ago, while I was watching *Neighbors*. Mum says we're to go."

Rich and Maddy got up from the bed. Rich's mother appeared in the doorway behind Kitty.

"Over at last," she said. "Dear Gran."

Rich hugged them both, and Kitty started to cry. Rich didn't cry. He found he didn't really feel anything very much.

"She never woke up," said his mother. "It's a good way to go."

Rich saw Gran before they moved her from the hospital bed. She was lying there as she'd lain for the last three days. She looked the same and different. There was no change to her appearance, but it was quite obvious that she was no longer there. Whatever made her be the Gran he knew was no longer in the room.

His father hugged him and Kitty.

"She just slipped away," he said. "I was here but I didn't even notice. You know how Gran never made a fuss."

Only when he was back home and climbing the stairs to his room did Rich suddenly catch the true feeling that Gran was dead. It was the sight of her stair-lift standing faithfully at the foot of the stairs, and her Zimmer waiting at the top. She wouldn't be coming back, ever again. That familiar *shuffle-clunk* as she pushed her Zimmer across the landing would never sound again. He'd never hear her funny scrambled speech again.

The absoluteness of death struck Rich then with a deep cold horror.

He opened his diary and wrote:

> Gran has died. I don't understand. I want her to come back again. Other things come back. Leaves on trees. Sunrise. Christmas. I want Gran to come back when the clocks change, or with the spring. This death thing is a bummer. I'm against it. Come home, Gran. We love you.

Then he lay on his bed and cried.

# 32

# Reconciliations

Imo was waiting for Maddy when she got home.

"You. Up in my room."

The door closed behind them.

"What the fuck do you think you've been doing?"

Maddy was caught by surprise.

"I say tell no one," said Imo, her voice cracking with fury, "which to me means *no one*, and you tell the whole fucking world! Are you totally insane, or do you just hate me so much you want to shame me in public? Is that it, Maddy? Have you always hated me?"

"No—of course not—"

Maddy tried to stop herself, but tears were pushing at her eyes. It was so unfair. She'd done it for Imo.

"You want the whole town to laugh at me? Well, you've done it. Well done Maddy. I'm the town joke."

"I don't want that. I swear, Imo. I was just so angry."

"You think you're angry? Have a go at being me."

"I had to do something. He just didn't care. He just laughed at me."

"Why did you have to do something? Why? It's got fuck all to do with you."

"That's not true, Imo."

"Just because you're my sister. You're not my guardian. You're not my protector. I don't need protecting, okay? I need leaving alone."

"He did it to Grace too."

"What?"

"Leo did what he did to you to my friend Grace. He beat her up."

"Grace who?"

"She's in my year at school. Grace Carey." Maddy hesitated, and then went on. "He's been seeing her for over a year."

"Over a year?"

"She's with him in his flat now."

Imo fell silent.

"She showed me her bruises. She told me not to tell anyone, just like you. I couldn't stand it, Imo."

"What a shit he is." She was talking to herself. "Over a year."

"I had to do something," said Maddy. "I wanted to hurt him back, so I did. I made him bleed."

Imo stared. Evidently this part of the story hadn't reached her.

"How did you make him bleed?"

"I hit him on the head with a beer mug."

Imo's mouth twitched.

"And there was blood?"

"Lots."

"What did he say?"

"He laughed. All the men in the pub laughed. Like being hit over the head by a girl was fun."

"Oh, the fucking bastard! They're all fucking bastards!"

"I'm sorry about telling your secret, Imo. I wasn't thinking straight. I'd come from seeing Grace. I wanted to kill him."

"I wish you had. God, I wish you had. Kill them all while you're about it. Christ, I need a drink. Do you want a drink?"

They went downstairs together, reconciled. Their father was in the kitchen, wine bottle in hand, pouring himself a glass.

"Me too, Dad," said Imo. "A big one."

"Me too," said Maddy.

"What's up, girls?"

"Just the usual fear and loathing of the male sex," said Imo.

"Excluding Dad, of course," said Maddy.

"No. Not excluding Dad. The last I heard you were about to do a runner."

Their father took a long pull at his glass of wine.

"Actually I'm not running away," he said.

"Does that mean you're staying?" said Maddy.

"Yes. For now. Jen and I have had a talk."

Maddy went to him and hugged him.

"I'm really glad, Dad."

He kissed her.

"Me too," said Imo. "But I'm not going to cry about it. I've had it with crying."

She hugged him too.

"You just better watch yourself, Dad. Step out of line and Maddy'll hit you on the head with a beer mug."

Maddy went looking for her mother. She was in the shop storeroom unpacking and pricing the latest delivery of glasswork from Rajasthan.

"You shouldn't be doing this, Mum. Ellen can do this."

"I like to keep busy. You know me."

"Dad says he's not leaving."

"No. Not for now, at least."

She went on cutting her way through layers of brown parcel tape.

"Is that what you want?"

"Yes," she said. "I think so."

"So does it make you a little bit happier?"

"Yes. A little bit."

Mrs. Fisher put down her scissors.

"Come here, darling."

Maddy went gladly into her mother's arms.

"It's all because of you. The things you said to Mike made all the difference."

"What did I say?"

"He says you told him we all have to have someone to love. He says he never thought of it like that before."

"I hope I'm right."

"It's a start, at least. You can't love someone who won't be loved. It wears you out."

"I'm so sorry, Mum. You deserve better."

"I've got what I've got. I'd rather have him than not have him. We've been together for twenty-five years. That's almost half my life. Mind you, he's been away a lot. Has he been any good as a father?"

"He's just been Dad. I've never really thought." Maddy thought about it now. "I've always loved him. And I've always felt he loves me."

"He does. Very much. Funny old Mike."

"I couldn't bear to have him leave us."

"You know," said her mother reflectively, "I truly don't think he had any idea how much we all loved him. He still seems slightly stunned by it all. I think he imagined we'd just say good riddance."

"Aren't men strange?" said Maddy. "Like children. If they

don't get everything they want they go into a sulk and say they want nothing."

Her mother smiled tenderly.

"What do you know about men, my darling?"

"Nothing, really."

"I do so want it to be better for you than it was for me."

Maddy knew how much her mother wanted her to be happy. She never cross-questioned her about her boyfriends or the lack of them the way so many mothers did. Now that there was something to tell her at last it seemed mean to keep it to herself.

"I have got a sort of a boyfriend," she said.

"That's nice, darling."

Just the right tone to her response. Pleased, but not too eager for details. Taking it in her stride.

"He's a boy in my year. He's called Rich."

"And you like him, this sort of a boyfriend?"

"More than I expected. A lot more."

"Well, I'd like to meet him. If you want me to."

Maddy couldn't bring herself to say she was in love. She was shy of making such a grand claim. Time enough to talk of love later. It was all so new.

Rich phoned after supper.

"We've got this tent," he said. "I was thinking we could pitch it in the tree barn."

"Rich," said Maddy, "hasn't your gran just died?"

"Yes."

"Shouldn't you be thinking about her?"

"I've thought about her. Now I'm back to thinking about you."

"So what's this tent?"

"I was thinking it would give us some privacy."

"Oh. Right."

"Do you think it's a good idea?"

"What about the cushion room in our shop? That's private."

"Yes, but it's yours. The tent would be ours."

Maddy understood at once. He wanted to create a new space for their new life that was about to start. She would never have thought of that.

"You have been thinking about it."

"All the time."

"Isn't this all a bit, well, planned?"

"You think everything should happen on the spur of the moment?"

"Well, a bit."

"The thing is, I think of nothing else."

"Me too."

"So we might as well give up on the spontaneity thing and go with the planning thing."

"You don't think that might be a passion killer?"

"Only if it is for you."

"All right. Let's go with the tent."

"I think we should wait until after Gran's funeral," said Rich. "I don't know why. I just feel we should."

"A last act of respect."

"The funeral's Thursday morning."

"So Friday, then."

"I was thinking in terms of Thursday evening."

"Won't your house be full of relatives?"

"All the more reason to have somewhere else to go."

"Thursday evening, then. You bring the tent. I'll bring some brownies or something."

"And I'll come prepared."

Maddy understood. She had been wondering if he would raise the matter.

"Actually, that's not a problem. I'm fixed up."

"Oh. Great." Relief in his voice. "Brownies sound great too."

By the next day Maddy found the tale of her attack on Leo was the talk of the school. It had grown in the telling. The word was that she had clubbed Leo down with a chair and kicked him in the head as he lay on the floor. What no one knew was why.

Maddy refused to explain.

"He had it coming," was all she said.

The natural assumption was that she had been having an affair with Leo and that they had had a falling out. This raised Maddy hugely in the general estimation.

Max Heilbron said to Rich, "Did you hear about Maddy Fisher beating up Leo Finnigan in the Rainbow? Oh, man! I wish she'd beat me up."

"I expect she had her reasons," said Rich.

"Fucking Ada, Rich! Why do you have to be so sensible? A girl who fights is a girl who fucks."

"How do you know?"

"Everyone knows. It's all about getting physical."

"I don't think Maddy Fisher's been doing anything with Leo Finnigan, if that's what you mean."

"Oh, grow up, Rich. Of course she has."

He called over to Cath Freeman, who was near by.

"Hey, Cath. Maddy's been getting it on with Leo Finnigan, right?"

"Wrong."

"Oh, yeah. Sure I'm wrong. Like, I'm not stupid, you know."

"No. You're a tit."

"Who're you calling a tit, dog face?"

Cath flew at Max, fists pummeling. Max went down, arms over his head, trying to defend himself from the rain of blows.

"Rich! Get her off me!"

"A girl who fights, Max."

"Help! Ow! Stop!"

"Apologize!"

"Yes! I apologize. I won't say it again."

Cath stopped punching.

"Oh, boy!" She shook her arms. "That felt good."

Max stood up. His eyes were fixed on Cath with an entirely new look in them.

"You hit hard," he said.


Joe found an opportunity to talk to Maddy alone.

"Me and Mum sat Leo down last night and told him he had to get help. He's going to see a shrink."

"You think it'll make any difference?"

"We told him he was going to end up in prison if he didn't sort himself out."

"Joe, he doesn't even think he's doing anything wrong."

"Yes, he does. His problem is it's the only way he can get there."

"The only way he can get aroused?"

"Yes."

"Oh, God. Sometimes I just want to give up. People are so messed up."

"You hitting him. It really shocked him."

"He looked like it was all one big joke."

"No. It shocked him. And he has a huge bump on his head."

"I didn't mean to. It just happened. I was so upset about Grace and Imo. And there he was, laughing."

"You've done him a favor, Maddy." He gave her his easy smile. "You're quite a girl."

# 33

# The first time

They met at the gate by the track up the wooded hillside. Rich was already there when Maddy arrived. At his feet stood a bulging rucksack.

"How long are we going away for?" said Maddy. "A month?"

"That's the tent," said Rich. "And the sleeping bags. And the pillows."

"Pillows!"

"I thought it would make us more comfortable."

"Oh, Rich."

"Do you think I'm a bit odd?"

"I think you do a lot of thinking ahead. I'm very glad you do. But it is a bit odd." She laughed and then gave him a kiss. "A good kind of odd."

Rich heaved his pack onto his back and they set off up the track. The sky was overcast, threatening rain, and between the trees there were deep shadows. They walked one behind the other in silence, hearing their footfalls, aware of no other sounds.

At the tree barn Rich lowered his pack and took out the bundle that would become their tent. He paced out the ground beneath the spreading branches of the ash tree.

"Just big enough," he declared.

They put up the tent together in the fading light. It was harder than Rich had expected.

"Funny," he said, trying to puzzle out which way round the lining went. "It was easy when I did it in the garden."

"Did you practice in the garden?"

"Yes. It was easy."

"What on earth did your family think you were doing?"

"The Tiny Footsteps thought it was for them. They played houses in it."

He got the groundsheet the right way round at last, and quite suddenly a tent-shape rose between them. It was a rectangular ridge tent of the old-fashioned kind, made of dark green fabric. Its two tent poles refused to stay upright on their own. Maddy held one up while Rich ran out the guy ropes. This revealed an unforeseen problem. The guy ropes needed a far greater area than the tent itself. In two of the four directions they ran up against the stone wall of the ruined barn.

Rich gazed at the obstacles in dismay.

"You could tie one rope to the tree," said Maddy.

"Yes. Good idea."

Then he found a heavy iron staple embedded in the wall. Another rope could be tied to that. By the time they were done the two poles were tilted in opposite directions, but the tent was up.

Rich now unrolled the two sleeping bags he had brought. He and Maddy zipped them together to form one double bag. It filled the entire floor of the tent. The pillows followed.

"Now you go in," said Rich.

Maddy stooped and crept into the tent.

"There's not much room," she said. "It's dark."

Rich followed, bringing with him a small electric lantern. He put it down at one end and switched it on. At once the fabric of the tent became solid and substantial.

They sat on the sleeping bags, their arms round their knees, and looked round them.

"It is a bit small," said Rich.

"I expect it'll seem bigger when we're lying down."

"We should have gone to your cushion room. This is a stupid idea."

"No," said Maddy. "I love it. It's like living in the woods."

Through the half-open door flap they could see the lower branches of the ash tree, and beyond it the trunks of the beech trees in the twilight.

"Let's hope it's waterproof," said Rich. "The forecast is for rain."

"Why didn't you tell me?"

"I didn't want you to change your mind."

"But what if it rains?"

"Too late now."

"Honestly, Rich."

He put one arm round her. She leaned close against him. They kissed.

"Is the idea that we get inside the sleeping bag?" she said.

"Yes. That's the plan."

"In our clothes?"

"Well, maybe some of them. Or none."

"None would be best."

They kissed again, but they made no move to take off their clothes.

"No hurry," said Maddy.

Despite their intentions for the evening they were both shy of undressing. So they stretched out in the light of the lantern and talked.

"Does it all seem to you to have happened really quickly?" said Maddy. "It does to me."

"How long has it been?"

"How long since when?"

"Since you started thinking of me this way?"

"I suppose it started at your gran's party. I watched you singing with your family and it made me feel happy. I wanted to join in."

"Not at Pablo's house?"

"Oh, yes. I forgot about that. Yes, that was special. But you were still going on about Grace."

"Only as a cover."

"Really?"

"It started for me when we sat by the river and ate yum-yums."

"Oh, God! That was so gross."

"I just liked being with you."

"But I bet you never thought you'd end up here."

"No. Never."

"Then I came back to your place and you did the lights for Kitty's doll's house. It was so pretty when the lights went on. I was almost as excited as Kitty."

It gave them both exquisite pleasure to retrace the steps they had taken towards each other. And here they were at the end of the journey, in this little green tent.

"Actually, you know what," said Maddy. "I think it started for me when you walked into the lamppost."

"It did not! You were mooning over Joe Finnigan."

"Yes, I was. But that's when I first really noticed you."

"After all these years."

"Well, I'm sorry. Anyway, you can't talk. You walked into the lamppost because you were staring at Grace."

"I must have been off my head."

"She is very beautiful."

"Not half as beautiful as you."

"Oh, Rich. That's silly."

"No, I mean it."

He raised himself up on one elbow so that he could look into her close smiling face. The low light of the lantern cast deep shadows.

"Cross my heart and hope to die," he said.

"Don't die," she said. "We're only just starting. Even if we are going a bit slow."

"I don't mind."

"Don't you, Rich? Really?"

"I can't believe I've got this far. Any moment now you're going to say, 'Off you go, it was all just a joke.'"

"No, I won't. I've had enough jokes." She stroked his face, tracing lines over his nose and lips. "This time it's serious."

"You have no idea how serious."

"Don't I?"

She felt down his body to his crotch. There she found a hard ridge.

"How long has that been going on?"

"Ages. It's not nearly as shy as me."

"Maybe we should do something about it."

She reached down and unzipped his jeans. He pushed his underpants out of the way so that his cock could stand free.

Maddy stroked it softly.

"I love you, Maddy," he said. "I love you."

"That's just sex."

He rolled into her arms, his body pressing against hers. They kissed eagerly.

"My turn," said Maddy. She started to pull her top over her head.

"I'll tell you what," said Rich. "I'll switch out the light."

He reached over to the lantern and clicked its switch. The tent was plunged into darkness.

"Now I can't see a thing."

Both of them knew that they were happier getting undressed in the darkness. It was an odd sort of shyness, and not one they wanted to talk about.

Rich was still tugging off his jeans when Maddy started to wriggle her way into the sleeping bag.

"Oh, there's the pillow. That's lovely." Then, a moment later, "Ow. There's lumps underneath."

"Oh, God," said Rich. "They'll be under the ground sheet. I should have thought of that."

Naked, he joined her in the sleeping bag. They lay side by side gazing up at the dark roof of the tent. Their eyes adjusted to the gloom, and they could make out the strip of gray light where the tent flap was not fully closed.

Maddy felt with her hand for Rich's body. Rich started to shiver.

"There you go," said Maddy.

"I can't help it."

"Have you got sharp lumps under where you're lying?"

"Yes."

"Next time bring a mattress too."

They stroked each other, lying side by side on their backs. A slow time of exploration.

"Which part do you like me touching best?" she said. "Apart from the obvious."

"Here." He placed her hand on his inner thighs.

"Like, the nearer your cock the better."

"Pretty much."

"Do you want me to worship your cock? Would you like it if I wore bunny ears?"

"No," he said. "I like the ears you've got."

"How about sucking?"

"Do you want to?"

"I'm not sure. I've never tried. I'm a bit nervous about it."

"Then don't. I like what we're doing now. To be honest I'm about as worked up as I could be, just having you by me with no clothes on."

"Really?"

"Here. Feel my heart."

"Wow."

"That's what you do to me."

"But wouldn't any girl do the same? So long as she was naked."

"Maybe," said Rich. "But with you I feel excited and safe, both at the same time."

"That's how I feel," said Maddy.

He wriggled his body, all the way down to his toes.

"I love having a body," he said. "You make me love having a body."

"I love having your body too," she said.

They rolled onto their sides and intertwined their legs, pressing their bodies close together again. Rich found he was moving his hips against her.

"Eager, eager," said Maddy.

"It's not me. It's it."

"It knows what it wants. "

"But I don't think it's got much of a clue how to get there."

"That's the whole point of practicing."

"Are we still practicing?" said Rich. "I thought maybe this was it."

Maddy pushed herself against Rich's cock, loving the sensation of his body's longing for her. She felt a warm tingling inside.

"Stroke me," she said, drawing his hand to her breasts.

Rich stroked her breasts, feeling gently round the nipples. Then he bent his head down and kissed her nipples, one after the other.

"I like that," she whispered.

"I'm getting a bit excited myself," he said.

"Is it hard to hold out?"

"It might be. I can't tell. I've never done this before."

"Maybe we'd better get on with it, then."

She felt for the head of his cock and guided it between her legs. He moved to lie over her.

"Will it be okay for you?" he whispered.

"I don't know. I've never done it before either."

"So it might hurt."

"No. I don't think so."

She wriggled her hips and guided him until the head of his cock was nuzzled up against her soft slit. Then she found her clitoris and pressed it with the tip of one finger.

"I'm going to stroke myself a bit."

"That's good," he said.

She felt little shivers of pleasure start to flow through her body. Rich eased his cock forward, and then back. With each push she opened up a little more. But progress was slow.

"Sorry," she said. "Can you last a little bit longer?"

"I think so."

She drew her hand away from her crotch so that he could

lie fully against her. He gave another push and she felt his cock enter her.

"Lie still," she said. "I have to get used to it."

"Oh, Maddy," he murmured. "Oh, Maddy."

"Don't come yet."

"No. Oh, it's so warm."

"Of course it's warm. What did you expect?"

Rich hardly dared to move lest he unleash the flood. His entire body was in a state of electric arousal.

"Oh, Maddy."

They heard a sound outside. A long black nose appeared in their tent doorway. They froze, feeling each other's hearts beat.

A call from the woodland track.

"Susie! Here, Susie!"

The flash of a torch. The dog padded away.

Rich started to move again. His cock pushed in a little further.

"Lie still," said Maddy again.

He lay still, gazing down at her face in the darkness. But he could see her.

"No one could ever be as beautiful as you are now," he said. "You're perfect."

"Do you love me, Rich?"

"Yes, I love you, Maddy."

"Will you still love me afterwards?"

"And after that. And after that."

"Me too. I'll love you after that, and after that."

He laid his head on the pillow beside her head and felt the tickle of her hair against his cheek.

"You can move again now," she said.

He moved, and suddenly he was all the way in.

"Warm!" he exclaimed again.

"There," she said. "You're there now."

"I can't hold out much longer," he whispered.

"That's okay." She found his cheek with her lips and kissed him. "Only practicing."

He gave a long sigh. She felt him ease his cock back and then ease it forward again. He gave a shudder. His cock twitched inside her. Then he lay still.

She stroked his back with slow movements of her hands. Her whole body glowed with a sensation of sweet heat. *So close,* she thought. *Closer than close.*

Then came an unexpected rush of tenderness. She found she was crying.

"Was it okay?" she whispered, kissing his face so he wouldn't see her tears.

"Yes," he said. "Yes. I couldn't stop it."

"You didn't have to."

"But you. I didn't give you time."

"I don't mind. Really I don't. Next time. Or the time after. We're only beginners."

"Maddy, it was so wonderful. I can't tell you how wonderful it was. Still is."

"I loved it too."

"I'll get better. I'll make it wonderful for you."

"It is wonderful for me."

And she meant it. She felt proud and happy in a way that took her by surprise. Part of it was the pleasure she got from seeing Rich so overwhelmed, and knowing that it was her doing, her body, her gift. His joy in her gave her joy in herself too. And part of it was the discovery that sex and love could be the same after all. At least for her and Rich. At least on this day.

"I do love you, Rich," she said.

She could feel his cock dwindling. And now it was out.

"Feel in my bag," she said. "I brought some tissues."

He sat up and fumbled about until he found them for her.

"Really it's your mess." She dabbed at the trickle between her legs. "But it's always the girls who are left to clean up."

He lay down once more by her side.

"I'm so happy, Mad."

"It's over now. You've had what you want. I expect you'll fall asleep in a minute."

"No. I want to go on feeling this way."

A patter of raindrops fell on the canopy of the tent above

them. Within moments the patter had become a heavy shower. The rain drummed on the green canvas.

"Do you want a brownie?" said Maddy.

"Did you really bring brownies?"

"Of course. I said I would."

She got them out and they had one each. Rich ate his slowly, looking out through the crack in the tent door at the falling rain.

"It's really good."

"Only from a packet mix."

"It's the best brownie I've ever had in my life."

"You're easy to please."

Then for a while they lay quietly in each other's arms, waiting for the rain to pass.

"Sorry about the rain," said Rich.

"I don't mind," said Maddy. "Do you?"

"Oh, I don't care about rain now," said Rich. "Let it rain."

"Let it rain," said Maddy.

**WILLIAM NICHOLSON** says: "I've long wanted to write a love story for teenagers: something that reflects the reality of love—the self-doubt, the insecurity, the intense longings, the mistakes, the misunderstandings, the hurt, the pain, and of course the passion and the joy. I wanted to tell the story from both sides, so that girls would get some idea what it's like to be a boy, and vice versa. I wanted it to show the process of two young people discovering love for the first time. And I wanted to make it as true as possible."

Mr. Nicholson is an award-winning fantasy author and playwright, as well as an acclaimed Hollywood screenwriter, whose work includes *Nell*, *Shadowlands*, and the Oscar-winning *Gladiator*. He lives in England with his wife and their three children.